I Am the Moon

By
Carlo Morrissey

PublishAmerica
Baltimore

© 2007 by Carlo Morrissey.
All rights reserved. No part of this book may be reproduced, stored in a retrieval system or transmitted in any form or by any means without the prior written permission of the publishers, except by a reviewer who may quote brief passages in a review to be printed in a newspaper, magazine or journal.

First printing

All characters in this book are fictitious, and any resemblance to real persons, living or dead, is coincidental.

PublishAmerica has allowed this work to remain exactly as the author intended, verbatim, without editorial input.

ISBN: 1-60441-454-5
PUBLISHED BY PUBLISHAMERICA, LLLP
www.publishamerica.com
Baltimore

Printed in the United States of America

Acknowledgements

Thank you to Paul Pizzarella for his time and interest in this and other stories. Thank you to Bob McMackin for his considerable feedback on this, and editing help on other stories. Thank you Carol Morrissey and Catherine Whalen for their encouragement and insights. Special thanks to my brother Bill, who patiently tackled this and other stories, line by line, giving me both support and grammar lessons. To my wife and daughter, without peace and love at home not a word would have been written, thank you.

Chapter One

There is something about happiness I know to be true, because it happens to me all the time, good things, or should I say good feelings just evaporate, poof, gone, blown out like candles on a birthday cake, before you have time to realize this was something really good. Unlike the birthday party, nobody snaps a picture of that word, or those sensations that hit you just right, making you feel like Superman and Santa Claus all rolled into one. But, the needle nosed critics of you and your life, forever hanging around at your elbow, like bedposts ready to get smacked in the night, need no pictures to be remembered. No. You wake up and go to bed with their miserable chorus of gripes, should haves, and of course, the mother of so many crushed spirits, 'what were you thinking?' Before you get the wrong idea and think I'm some morbid depressive, or deep intellectual, who has analyzed life to the point of not being able to decide on paper or plastic at the supermarket, relax; I'm just a high school senior who hopes to play baseball and basketball well enough to get a free ride through college, anywhere, preferably someplace warm. I've also been in love with Linda McCurry since ninth grade, even though we've been friends since my first memories. I would also love to see my father grow up and my mother smile, just once. The last two items are beyond my control as Tony 'Tarzan' DeMarco, my boss and the most together guy I know, has told me, while letting me know that if you want to enjoy this life you have to take the good with the bad, and what might be a bed of roses for you might be a horror show for the next guy. So those last two items right now are debatable. Although, I'm still leaning towards, hey Dad, get with the program. You're forty-five. Pull your head out of the clouds, and Mom, all news is not necessarily bad.

I love sports, all sports. When not playing, I'm usually thinking about playing. When I run across a street, and I do run, as I can't stomach those slow strutting pups that look like they're asking you to mow them over, I imagine breaking off tackle with clear sailing for the end zone. If I'm standing around, I usually find something to grab, a stick, book, pillow, or whatever and swing, rehearsing for my next at bat. And the way I've been growing, Coach Inhorn thinks colleges will offer me something, since, besides having a great three-point shot, a cannon for an arm, and play a slick shortstop, I've kept my GPA hovering near 3.00.

But there is, as Linda likes to call it, this 'great disconnect' between my family and me. Last spring we, the Central High Eagles, were playing our cross-town, rich punk rivals, the Kennedy High Panthers, who we refer to as the panties. Kennedy and Central represent contrasts in everything. For starters Kennedy was built in 1984, Central in 1904. A new wing was added to Kennedy in 2002, the same year Central's heating system crashed and we had to wear coats and gloves in class for all of January. Kennedy boasts of 96% of its graduates going on to college while Central is annually among the state's leaders in dropouts, with threats coming out of the State Board of Education every few years to close us down. Kennedy teams tend to kick our butts as they compete for spots in the end of season regional tournaments, while we aim at simply not embarrassing ourselves too badly. You get the picture. Kennedy is where you'd like your kids to go. Central is where some of us have to go.

Our last game of the season was against Kennedy, who would be going to the area playoffs if they got by us. We were completing our seventh straight losing season, with one of those early lopsided loses coming at the hands of Kennedy. A twelve to three drubbing, that was made worse by the Kennedy subs tacking on three runs late in the game. My father had seen me play a total of six innings spread over three years. I would usually remind him the day before a game, and he would agree to try and make it. He often steamrolled flat my dreams with, 'You know you can't make a living playing ball', which I would like to counter with, tell that to Alex Rodriguez. I, however, always take it in silent resignation, realizing my father thinks I'm wasting my time, having heard this and similar balloon busters since I was young enough to think he was actually giving me good advice. Somewhere between learning to tell time and how to bunt, I realized my dad was wrapped up so tightly in his own bundle of crap that he had trouble giving me even a verbal pat on the back. He means well, it's just he has always had this high culture, snobbish outlook, as if what he thought was the prized acorn and we were all a bunch of eager squirrels wanting to know. Dad, this time, followed up with, "You should really think more about using your brains."

I then made a critical mistake and asked, "Doing what?"

"Exploring big ideas, something important," he said, with impatience and eyes flaring, making me wonder if I had insulted him, or perhaps he could hear me thinking, what a waste of time this conversation was. I recovered and told him I was thinking of majoring in physical education if I went to college. I don't know what was more troubling to him the 'if' or the 'physical education' part. "Oh," he said, eyes disappointed as if I had said, I want to see America and signed up to be the broom and bucket man for the elephants at Ringling Brothers. He headed out the door, looking as if he wanted to say more. I'm sure he felt better once in his yellow taxi, listening to Bach and contemplating the value of Michelangelo, while pretending that he was working hard on his great project that would one day become, as he says, 'a pivotal work in our understanding of Western Art and Civilization'. I say pretending because of his lack of production. This project has been with my family it seems like forever.

Don't get me wrong my father probably knows more about art than the guys running the Boston Museum of Fine Arts. The problem is I've been listening to him weighing the greatness of Dante over Chaucer, Picasso over Matisse, and Beethoven over Mozart all of my life. I've seen him over the last few years turn our five room apartment into an art historian's paradise, cluttering up every available space with books, notebooks, and journals on topics ranging from astronomy to archeology. My father helps pay the bills by driving a cab. He knows his calling in life is to write, what he refers to as, the classic study on the ten greatest artists of Western Civilization. 'It is a book that will change how we view art.' My father believes this, I know, however I think of his progress and shudder. The problem that dear old Dad runs into is that his top ten keeps changing and about the only thing he writes are what he considers insightful tidbits about an artist, who is either on his or her way on or off the list. Dad, a 1981 graduate from the Concordia School of Art, was at one time working on his doctorate in Art History. He taught part-time, courses on the American Impressionists and the French Romantics, at B.U., while making a few extra bucks driving a cab. Somewhere along the way he blew off the Ph.D. and got lost in the world of cabbie/art historian.

CARLO MORRISSEY

Well, in that final game of the season I was moved to short instead of my regular centerfield. Donny Del Greco our regular shortstop twisted his ankle the day before, goofing around after showers in the locker room. So there I was playing a position I hadn't played in a couple years because Coach Inhorn, who coaches both baseball and basketball at Central, decided, "Danny you'll play short, I need my best athlete there." Coach that day announced to my world that I was his best athlete. Hell Coach, any walls you want me to run through.

It was the bottom of the fourth when I noticed my father's yellow cab parked on the hill that ran parallel to the field. There were two outs and we were leading six to four. I had driven in two runs with a double at the top of the inning. I began wondering if my father had seen my clutch hitting, or the earlier diving stab of a liner that saved a run. I scanned the bleachers until I spotted him, high in the last row, along the first base side. By himself, hunched forward on his arms, wearing a white t-shirt and I assumed his hundred-year old, coffee and sweat stained Red Sox cap that he kept in the cab. The fifth and sixth innings were quiet affairs for me, no at bats, and one routine grounder neatly handled and delivered to first for the out. Kennedy had gotten to within a run on a solo bomb by their star, Pete Kozlowski, a horse who looked like he was twenty-five. Top of the seventh and I led off. Dad was still in the stands. My mind was waving to him as I took a pitch inside and low. The next pitch was belt high and caught the inside corner for strike one. I thought I'll do something special. Show the old man that I truly excel at this game I love. "Strike," the umpire barked, and I woke up. God, I'm in the hole, one and two. I swung at the next pitch, which was a bit high and outside. I caught a piece of it with the end of my bat. The ball spun off, rising like a lazy lollipop, heading for the first base bleachers. The first basemen and right fielder charged and converged. I was sure it would fall harmlessly in the stands, but it hung at the mercy of a gentle breeze like a paper airplane. "Out," the umpire called, as the right fielder snatched it a foot before the first row of bleachers. I didn't look up to see my father. I moved quickly to the bench, dropped my bat and helmet, and laid my head in my hands. We went meekly one-two-three.

Kennedy was down to their last two outs, with the tying run on second. The base runner took an expanding cocky lead. Our pitcher concentrated only on the batter, Kozlowski, who had hit the ball hard three times. The count moved in his favor two balls, no strikes. The runner widened his lead. I made head gestures as if anticipating a throw to stall his advance to third. The pitch was grooved down the middle and Kozlowski lets fly a rocket over the pitcher's head. I sprung, reaching for the clouds. The runner hesitated for a moment between second and third. The second baseman was frozen, staring up at me, as I flew forward and speared down the ball. The ball snagged deep into the glove's pocket. I landed inches from the bag, stepping on it a millisecond before the runner's slide toppled me. I dropped like a bag of cement on the runner's chest, as the umpire gave an emphatic out sign. Our bench emptied and everyone jumped on top of me as if we had won the World Series. I looked up at the bleachers and the few remaining fans, no sign of Dad. I looked to the street where he parked; the space was vacant.

*****

I've been working for Tarzan, and everybody calls him Tarz, since I was fifteen. Tarzan owns a neighborhood market that is a deli, Italian specialties store, and neighborhood rumor mill. The store is a city landmark, attracting customers from as far away as Quincy and Burlington. These long distance shoppers are mostly people who grew up here and moved out. They come back, some weekly, some at Christmas or Easter, for items they can't find anywhere but in Boston's North End, or they get hit with pangs of nostalgia for the old neighborhood and find themselves loading up on Tarzan's imported cheeses, cold cuts, and homemade sausage.

The story that began circulating, by impressionable lost boys on the corner years ago, as to how Tarzan got his nickname was pure fiction, but knowing Tarzan you believed it even after you knew it wasn't true. According to the story, while in Vietnam, Tarzan had to swim across a river swarming with crocodiles in order to blow up a VC command post. When passed on, by our local creative knuckleheads, the account of our Tarzan made Rambo look like a wimp. Tarzan explained the name one afternoon during an August hurricane wind and rainstorm, while I was sorting, by color (green, pink, red) box after box of tomatoes in the store's backroom. Tarzan's near-deaf, second cousin Old Mike, a long pencil of a man who wore thick horn rim glasses and greeted everyone with, "What'ya know?" was working the front. Old Mike, owing to his often missing half of what was said, had trained customers to slowly shout their orders at him. Old Mike, always eager for conversation, would persist with questions until the customer shared something. Often that something was said loud enough so everyone in the store knew whatever Old Mike was told. The source of countless neighborhood rumors can be traced to someone wanting a pound of provolone.

That day the torrents of rain and gusts of wind were making the store's plate glass front windows shimmy. Business slowed to an occasional customer who needed one item for that night's dinner. Old Mike, elbow on the cash register supporting his head, watched Waverly Avenue flood.

Tarzan was playing chess with Jose, a tri-lingual maintenance worker at city hall, who looked like a short, burly Jesse Jackson. Jose, always smiling unless he was playing chess, had a way of saying hello that made you feel like you were the most important person in his life. He had served in 'Nam at the same time as Tarzan. When he came into the market ten years ago, after just moving into the neighborhood, wearing an old faded Army field hat, a conversation started that hasn't ended. Tarzan and Jose had the Army, Red Sox, and chess in common, enough to bond them like butter to mashed potatoes. Jose generally would show up near closing time and see if Tarzan was up for a game. The two would sit in the backroom on wooden cantaloupe crates around a broken 1950's style red Coca-Cola cooler staring for hours at the chessmen. They were equally matched, yet each believed the other was superior. Tarzan always positioned himself so he could see or hear if Old Mike or I needed help out front. Once the store closed the two would either go home or stay sometimes into the wee hours of morning. Occasionally my father, Sam Alberti, joined Tarzan's after-hours club. Dad discovered by accident, about five years ago, that Tarzan and Jose liked listening to his ramblings about art.

That afternoon, as I was deciding the fate of a yellowish green tomato, Tarzan looked over to me, as he pressured Jose's queen with a knight. "Danny, do you know your Uncle Charlie gave me the name Tarzan?"

The question startled me. It was unimaginable to see Uncle Charlie in the jungle with Tarzan. Uncle Charlie, five years my father's senior, lives in what my mother calls 'the blue-blood hills of Wellesley'. He owns and operates the Charles Alberti, Consulting Firm. Uncle Charlie has that soft, pasty look that takes over people who spend too much time in air-conditioned places looking over what they think are extremely important papers. I don't know whom he consults with, but who ever it is they are paying him big bucks, for two years ago we were invited to his son John's high school graduation and the affair, from palace garden to fancy catering, complete with college kids in sick suits, made me feel like my zipper was open the whole time.

I looked at Jose for some sign that Uncle Charlie had a life buried somewhere under his hundred dollar silk ties worthy of mention in connection with Tarzan. Jose's nose almost touched the miniature plastic men before him. He had a look of defeat as he contemplated how to evade his lady's capture. I was straining to imagine Uncle Charlie as Tarzan's buddy. Tarzan, the neighborhood legend, with biceps as big as my head, war hero, high school all-city football, linebacker and fullback, the greatest hitter Central High ever produced, and Uncle Charlie a geek in a suit.

"Uncle Charlie?"

"That's right." Tarzan looked at Jose and his queen's dilemma, and realized it would be a while before his troubled opponent made a move.

"Uncle Charlie was in Vietnam?"

"No, he had brains enough to go to college. Vietnam?" Tarzan said, smiling.

"Yah, I heard you had to swim through alligators in order to blow up a Viet Cong stronghold."

"Alligators?"

"Crocodiles," I corrected myself, knowing as I spoke that wasn't the main thing being questioned.

"Jose did you hear that." Jose looked up and sighed, a leave me alone until I get my queen out of trouble kind of sigh. "I know that crazy story, but Danny, I was known as Tarzan long before I had to eat mud in rice paddies."

"Oh."

"Yeah, and it was your Uncle Charlie who named me." Tarzan smiled broadly. His voice quickened as he told the story. "You see, me and your Uncle Charlie and Ralphie Ponti were going fishing. We were about ten years old and you know the nearest water around here. Water where there's fish, is the Atlantic Ocean, which is too far to walk, and then there's Atkins Pond. Well, we were kids with a rough idea where Atkins Pond was and so armed with your grandfather's and my father's deep-sea fishing poles we headed south to find Atkins Pond." Tarzan started laughing as he continued, "I had a hook on my line." He spread out his finger and thumb about three inches. "We thought big, maybe sharks."

"Go ahead take her," Jose said as he moved a pawn in position to take a bishop.

"We walked for hours until our legs were going to fall off. The great adventure was tuning into sore feet and hungry guts. Well, we got to this park and asked this old geezer if Atkins Pond was nearby. He looks up from the paperback he's reading and says, 'Atkins Pond is about five or six miles through these woods.' Five or six more miles sounded as far away as California. So I drop my pole and run for this giant oak tree that was waving one great limb towards us at the entrance to these deep woods. I started climbing and called for your Uncle Charlie and Ralphie to follow. They do, but they're staying close to earth, hugging the tree limbs like they were long lost lovers. I kept going up and up. They start getting scared and head back down, calling to me then pleading with me to come down. Finally, after awhile they say they're going home so I start heading south, bounding from limb to limb, like a monkey. About twelve feet from the ground I lose my grip and my feet slide out from under me. Your Uncle Charlie looks like he's seeing a train wreck. I let out a scream like Tarzan did in the old movies." Tarzan laughed. "I thought Charlie shit himself, I still see his look. Well, my legs broke through the skinny lower branches okay, and I landed on my feet a few scratches but nothing worse than you'd get tripping on cement. So your uncle says, 'Like freaking Tarzan'. And the name stuck."

Tarzan opened the market a few years after he got home from Vietnam. "The Army was the best thing in the world for me. You meet a lot of different kinds of guys, a lot of good ones, some real numb-nuts, but you got to depend on them when your ass has a bulls-eye on it. But it taught me, there's no place like Delmont and no place better than Fairview. I don't care if you go from here to China this is the best place." And then with all the power that makes Tarzan seem bigger than life, he stretched out one of his beefy hands as if presenting the wonderful world of Fairview, and in a deep magnetic voice asked, "Do you know why?" And I, with dumb faced youth spread from ear to ear, shook my head. "Because of the people," he bellowed.

Fairview is the name given to the section of Delmont that has turned in recent years, or at least since I can remember, into a dying 'Little Italy'. The way my father, explains Fairview and Delmont to me is like this; Delmont once was farm country. The first settlers were farmers who helped feed Boston. That was before the industrial revolution. Fairview was the last section of town to turn from plowing the land to making boots and widgets. That was before the Civil War. Since Lincoln freed the slaves, Fairview has been home to first Irish, then French-Canadians, then Italians, and today it is like thousands of urban neighborhoods across America changing once again. Waverly Avenue divides Fairview. My mother, Elaine, refers to our side as 'the good' side of Waverly. It's the side that has changed the least. Most of the three-family houses are still owned by the now senior citizen children of Italian immigrants. Like the apartment we rent has been own by Mrs. Leonetti's family since her father was able to save up five hundred dollars during the boom years before the Great Depression and put up a big enough down payment, allowing him to hang on to it during the Hoover bust years. Mrs. Leonetti still talks about those times. How her older brothers had to steal coal from railroad cars in order for them to heat the house. How they would hire themselves out for fifty cents a day. A twelve-hour day down at the old Considerable Glue factory, or wait around all day at Delmont Steel in hopes there was work. 'What we didn't have in money we had in fun, in each other,' is how Mrs. Leonetti almost always ends her 1930's history lesson.

She lives alone on the first floor and we rent the second. My father and I shovel the snow for her in the winter, and Dad does whatever painting and small jobs that are needed. My mother writes out the checks to pay Mrs. Leonetti's bills and reads her mail to her. Mrs. Leonetti gets confused with the billing formats and fine print. However, my mother says she's still real sharp, makes the best marinara sauce on the block, knits sweaters that last forever, and takes her guidance from the daily newspaper horoscope. My mother's dealings with Mrs. Leonetti need to be kept from Joey, her son. Joey Leonetti, a short, triple-chinned guy, who runs, according to Mrs. Leonetti, the biggest insurance company in Cambridge. Joey lives like most of the children of the old landlords in the suburbs. Joey's main ambition in life, according to my mother, is to put his mother in an assisted living community, and start renting out the third floor apartment, which has been empty since the Montes moved out twelve years ago. Mom also frets over how Joey will probably triple our rent. We get, I guess, a terrific deal.

The old Italians who first settled in Fairview were attracted to laborer jobs at the Delmont Steel Company, whose decaying five acre corpse is now an eyesore to the adults of the community, while for the kids its cracked weedy parking lot serves as a great place to play stickball from April to September, and an asphalt football field the remainder of the year. The rusting buildings continue to be used by young kids experimenting with cigarettes and alcohol, and by teens of both sexes who are interested in cheap street drugs. Many a Fairview youth has lost his or her virginity on the Delmont Steel Company grounds. My father, since I was old enough to roam the neighborhood with friends, always told me, "I don't ever want to hear that you're in those buildings." The warning was something most parents gave, but few, including me, took seriously after reaching an age when you knew you could get away with stuff, as long as you didn't say much when asked those obligatory 'what did you do today?' questions.

The good side of Waverly still has mostly small businesses like Tarzan's Market. In the space that separates our three-decker on Whitman from the three-decker that Linda McCurry and her mother live in on Oakmont, two streets over, stands Peewee's Cleaners, Silvo's barbershop, the Capri Restaurant, Sophia's Bakery, Gino's Bar, and Tarzan's place. Across Waverly in the same amount of space there's a new CVS pharmacy, Blockbuster Video, Dunkin' Donuts, Burger King, and a Cumberland Farms mini-market and gas station. Less than a sneeze away from the Dunkin' Donuts is the entrance to the abandoned former Delmont Steel Company. Sometimes this world seems claustrophobic, other times it seems enormous, either way I've been dreaming a lot with my eyes open, dreams of a gigantic year both on the basketball court and the baseball diamond. The kind of year recruiters from schools, with great programs, like BC, UMASS, or UCONN will notice and take me out of here.

Chapter Two

About noontime on Labor Day, I showed up at Linda's door, as planned the night before. We both had the day off. Tarzan was closed for the holiday, and Linda, having worked both Saturday and Sunday at Blockbuster, was free. Linda wanted to spend the morning cleaning and helping her mother. Mrs. McCurry had an assortment of physical troubles that prevented her from lifting, vacuuming, scrubbing, and general cleaning. Mrs. McCurry was a thin woman with a grating voice, stolen from someone's dying grandmother. She had the look of permanent helplessness. When she offered or announced she was going to do something, Linda or I would immediately volunteer. I did this initially to earn brownie points with the two McCurry ladies, but as I spent more time with them a growing fear mounted that Mrs. McCurry might drop dead from the strain of the most ordinary of household tasks. Linda assessed her mother's troubles as being ninety percent mental. Looking Mrs. McCurry over, I was certain the other ten percent was plenty to kill her. Last year Linda and I had been very excited about taking Mrs. Kelsey's Psychology class, hoping it would shed light on our hopelessly screwed-up families. However, all it did was raise new concerns.

Mrs. McCurry had worked as a secretary in a downtown law office. She left the job when Linda was born. Not knowing, that two years later Mr. Gregory McCurry would leave them for good. Mrs. McCurry for many years struggled to raise Linda on welfare and periodic handouts from her mother who died when Linda was nine. The past few years they've eked out a living on Mrs. McCurry's cashier's pay at the Stop & Shop and Linda's earnings babysitting and cashiering at the neighborhood Blockbuster Video. Mr. McCurry has not been heard of in years. He started a new life in Florida, working as a tile setter last time Linda heard from him. "Those guys make good money," Linda commented, overwhelmed by the bitterness that comes from an injustice that spanks your bottom regularly. Here she was bite-size and scrawny, like her mother, only beautiful with full straight golden brown hair, which fell to the middle of her back. Her face all sweetness sparkles no matter what she is doing. Her gray-blue eyes speak of charity, while her days become filled with managing more and more things at home. Her mom when not at the Stop & Shop fades into her favorite upholstered wing back chair in front of the twenty-one inch, twenty-year old RCA. Linda imagines her father young, as he appeared in photographs of happier times, but now in sunny Florida with a pocket full of cash, spending it on who knows what, as she and her mom try not to suffocate during the summer in their five room third floor apartment.

    I arrived to Mrs. McCurry at the kitchen table, cutting out supermarket coupons and composing a shopping list. Linda had pulled out the washing machine about two feet from its corner of the kitchen and was on hands and knees scrubbing the floor behind the washer. "Spring-cleaning," Mrs. McCurry said in her 'oh woe is me' voice.

    "I thought maybe we could have an indoor cookout here," Linda said, popping up from her hiding place like an enthusiastic jack-in-the-box. "I invited Eric over. Give him a break, not leave Mom alone. I picked up two movies. I know you'll like them, murder mysteries. Sean Penn is in one, Nicholas Cage is in the other. Kind of movies I can't watch alone."

    "I made a list," Mrs. McCurry said, motioning to a five by seven pad with two columns of red ink, and supermarket coupons attached with a paper clip.

    Linda had reshaped our day. I thought last night when I talked to her on the phone we were going over to Eric's house for the LeBlanc's Labor Day cookout. The LeBlanc's own the three-family they live in. It's one of the few that has a small backyard with grass. In a flash I'm feeling uncomfortable needing to reassess the day and major portions of my life. I feel indigestion from Mrs. McCurry and her helpful coupon clipping. I imagine fumbling with the coupons at the checkout, while Linda gets lost in the cosmetics aisle, or keeps a safe distance from me ogling a *Star* magazine. And that is not any big deal, but there will be a cashier and bagger team composed, I imagine, of some foxy junior or senior I know and one of my teammates. I will have been reduced by Mrs. McCurry, from one of Central High's top athletes and all around cool guys, to a frugal shopper who spends his Labor Day hunting supermarket shelves for bargains.

My heartburn passed, as I realized it would not be so bad. For being with Linda, matching the right jar of pickles to the fifty-cent off coupon would be fine because I was with her, and any un-coolness attached to coupon shopping would be squashed by her presence, for when a cool couple does the occasional un-cool thing their collective coolness wins out.

We were a couple that was beginning to resemble a mismatch of the long and short of humanity. I had shot up six inches over the last nine months, so when I stretched my spine and squared my shoulders I was six foot three and rising. This meant that I would probably shift from a shooting guard position to forward and maybe center on the undersized Central High Eagles basketball team. For Linda and I it meant more creative positions for necking, more of my bending down and her reaching up, more of my literally sweeping her off her feet. I loved it.

Linda had considered, unlike selfish me, how her mother would spend the day. Mrs. McCurry also had the day off from the supermarket. It made sense for us to do something at the McCurrys. Linda's thoughtfulness was in ugly contrast to my leaving home without even a foggy notion regarding what my mother was doing today. My father had left in his taxi early and said something about maybe going to Boston. "I might swing by the BU library, see if it's open." The remark until now meant little, but now I saw the real possibility of Dad spending hours lost in research. The last few months he talked more and more about the importance of Renoir. Explaining how his work is really a tribute of one's love for others and for life. "No one shows compassion for his subjects, and therefore for all of humanity like Renoir." He asked me the other morning over cornflakes and bananas, "Is that not an extension of Christianity?"

"I don't know."

"Think about it Danny," he said, with urgency, his eyes excited.

"I will," I said, fearing, maybe for the first time what was one of the biggest weights on my mother's head, the Alberti insanity strain. My father was the youngest of six children born to Lorenzo, who worked at Delmont Steel for thirty years before dropping dead at age fifty-eight, and Louise, who like most of her generation stayed home to care for her family. Grandma is still going strong living with their only daughter, Aunt Theresa-Marie, in the trendy Delmont Heights section of the city. My father assures me that grandpa's sudden demise had nothing to do with heart disease, even though he had a massive coronary, but rather his heart had been broken too many times by life. My father would say things like that on the verge of tears, which made me wonder about Dad's mental toughness, but not until the Renoir bulletin had I thought he might be starting to crack up.

Dad's oldest brother Larry, known as Junior, died in a car accident at age sixteen. He and three buddies were joy riding, along Route 20 in Sudbury. It was March and the evening drizzle began to turn to sleet and ice, inexperience and speed sent Larry's '56 Pontiac Star Chief rocketing off the road and crashing into a three foot round maple. The steering column crushed Larry's chest. The three others, dazed and limping, survived.

Then there's Uncle Bobby, a year younger than Larry, my father explains him as never recovering from Larry's death. "They were close, did everything together, even slept in the same bed." Bobby dropped out of high school in his senior year and drifted around the country, discovering marijuana and flower power in the mid-sixties. Bobby came back to Delmont in the late seventies, and for as long as I can remember has been the black sheep of the clan. My mother describes him as someone who thinks the world owes him a living. I guess Bobby cheated my parents out of some money back when I was in diapers. Mom and Dad were just making ends meet when Bobby hit Dad up for what was suppose to be a loan. Eight hundred dollars so Bobby could finish his course in refrigerator repairs or something. Bobby ended up disappearing with his girlfriend, Annette, who Mom describes as 'that druggie loser.' Bobby and Annette rented a trailer in Bourne, enjoying the beauty of Cape Cod at my parents' expense. That is my mother's interpretation. Bobby returned to Delmont about three years ago, with Annette and a little Bobby. They opened up the A&B Tattoo and Piercing Parlor, down at the end of Main Street that no one we know travels. Bobby is a taboo subject in my home.

After Bobby came Charlie, who from the distance looks like he's living the American Dream. My mother has put every word spoken and gesture made by Uncle Charlie and Aunt Janet, his wife, at their son John's graduation party through her cynical translator. She concluded that Aunt Janet has an eating disorder, basing this on her being a size six, control freak, known to gobble up food at family functions like the government issued famine warnings, yet never gains an ounce. As for Uncle Charlie, Mom's appraisal with furrowed brow is, "He thinks because he lives in Wellesley, his shit doesn't stink."

Next in line is Uncle Danny, my namesake. Dad describes him as the brightest and most creative of the bunch. Unfortunately, Uncle Danny was diagnosed at age twenty-three with schizophrenia. He had a complete meltdown, spending six months roaming around the city, living on the street and in shelters. Dad says Danny's illness on top of Larry Junior's dying is what killed grandpa so young. Danny, since before I can remember, has lived with Aunt Theresa-Marie and her husband, Jimmy Robustelli, their two kids and grandma. Jimmy owns a plumbing company and must weigh at least three hundred pounds. According to Aunt Theresa-Marie, who doesn't give up much in the heft department to Jimmy, Uncle Danny is doing better. He spends his days volunteering at the Delmont Animal Shelter. On his meds, Uncle Danny is able to answer phones, send out mailings, and generally meet, with kindness, people, who are looking to get or dump a dog.

So that brings us to my father, the baby of the litter, who my mother has over the past year begun to voice to me her fears that Dad may also have inherited the Alberti loose screw genes. My father has always been the kind of guy that personal grooming was low on his to do list. He generally shaves every third day unless Mom squawked. I know he sometimes wears the same t-shirt and pants for a few days at a time. The hairs in his ears and nose get attention when the mood strikes him. I remember Mrs. Kelsey talking about schizophrenia and how the person turns inward, relationships suffer, and they stop caring about personal hygiene. When I heard this, I saw Dad and Uncle Danny, thought my uncle was doing okay with his treatment and my father was more a preoccupied slob than a schizo. Maybe that's just what I wanted to believe.

I now began to have twinges of guilt. Mom would be sitting home alone worrying about Dad and my younger brother Tommy, worrying and probably overeating. She announced every few days her disgust with not being able to lose the thirty pounds she put on during the year, and how nothing fits her. The cause of her weight gain and lack of control around the food pantry and refrigerator is her fear over just about everything. There's our neighborhood going down the toilet, younger brother Tommy's certain appearance one day in juvenile court, our landlord's son's attempt to take over the three-decker we call home and raise the rent, the Puerto Rican families moving in around us, and lastly on really bad days Dad's future journey to Bonkersville. "I'm her rock," she tells me at the conclusion of her venting about our precarious existence. She assumes because the school, police, or our neighbors haven't called complaining about me that my life is great and I will, as she likes to say, 'Always do what's best.'

Tommy, two years my junior, has always been a disappointment academically, and now his behavior and attitude are parading in front of Mom like an angry picketer. Unlike me for which school has come easy, Tommy has struggled since day one, refusing to leave Mom's side on the first day of kindergarten, screaming like a cat sent to the showers. He never adjusted socially. Those first years Mom heard from the teachers often. Tommy had trouble waiting his turn, showing good sitting, using his indoor voice, and keeping his hands to himself. Fighting was a capital offense in grade K. Miss Oberfelt thought it best that he repeat kindergarten, hoping some maturing would intervene during the summer. Tommy's bad first year was followed by a string of mediocre ones until he hit junior high. With puberty came an appreciation for just how tedious it all was and how poor his academic skills were after years of neglect. Tommy at some point decided on a course of action that can be best summed up by a 'to hell with it' approach.

Tommy's poor attitude towards school spread like untended weeds into all aspects of his life during the last year or two. Recently the sight of him gets under my skin. I imagine hanging him by the ankles out of a window. The spike up my ass is his new association with Ricky Tarello and a group of gang wannabes who are doing pot, maybe cocaine, maybe ecstasy, maybe paint thinner, probably any God damn thing they think might get them high or down depending on their current condition. I try to keep Tarello and his gang of drug dealing, petty criminal clowns away from Mom. She has enough imaginary problems to fret over without me giving her a genuine disaster in the making. Ricky lives across the street from us in the most dilapidated three-decker in Fairview. There is no Mr. Tarello, and rumor has it Ricky and his four siblings have no fathers in common. Just turned seventeen, Ricky, the oldest of the Tarello lot, use to tell a story when we were young of his father dying in the Army. But, these new brothers and sisters kept showing up and all of them had his mother's maiden name. There never was a man around for more than a few months. My mother would complain that Lydia Tarello, Ricky's mom, was a magnet attracting all of the two-legged rats from Gino's Bar.

Tommy's character took a rapid descent. After years of being an underachieving pain in the ass little brother he added a new sleazy wrinkle about a year ago. I relate Tommy's fall with his coming under the spell of Ricky. The first major swipe at decency by Tommy that I'm aware of involved Mrs. Leonetti.

Before being our landlady, Mrs. Leonetti was first a babysitter on those odd times when I was small and Mom and Dad were both working, a giver of homemade Italian cookies and kind words, who made Tommy and I believe we were the two cutest and smartest boys in the world. She was calm when my mother was worried into a knot, making you know you were loved in everything she did or said. She was more of a grandmother than my grandmothers.

Mrs. Leonetti forever has been sticking money in envelopes to pay small bills, or to remember upcoming birthdays. The envelopes tucked under small statues of Saint Francis of Assisi or Saint Anthony on a kitchen shelf hanging over the table. One day Mrs. Leonetti sent Tommy to Tarzan's for some milk and bread. Tommy after running the errand disappeared into the lost world of the old steel mill. About an hour after Tommy had delivered the groceries Mrs. Leonetti discovered twenty dollars missing from her grandson's birthday card. Mrs. Leonetti and Mom conferred. Fighting back tears, Mrs. Leonetti explained how she had been napping in front of the television when Tommy returned. That Tommy was walking around her kitchen when she awoke. She was surprised to see him so far into her home without him calling to wake her. The old woman hadn't thought much of it until she discovered the empty birthday card.

Mom searched through Tommy's clothes and drawers and found half a pack of Marlboros but no twenty dollars. Mom and Dad, despite Tommy's raving denial of having lifted the twenty bucks, believed him to be guilty. They repaid Mrs. Leonetti the money, afraid if she mentioned this to her son, Joey, it would only serve to give him ammunition in his case that she was too old to be living by herself and should go into an assisted living apartment. Tommy ended up being grounded for a week because of the cigarettes, and Mom, Dad, and I grilled him repeatedly about stealing the money. I jumped in with both feet that week, getting uglier as the chip on his shoulder grew into a plank, which I was determined to knock off. That I didn't drive his head through a wall was due to my parents' interventions, including my mother's repeated petitions that I cool my jets. Tommy hung in there, maintaining his innocence, which no one believed. In the end the twenty-dollar theft turned what was a gully between us into the Mississippi. Tommy got into the habit of mocking me whenever I complained about anything. My response was to threaten him with my game face, to which he would walk off laughing. More and more, we acted like warring neighbors, letting our hedges grow higher and higher.

If I am a rock for my mother, she is a boulder for all of us, albeit an anxiety-ridden one. Mom teaches math at St. Christopher's High School. St. Christopher's, known as a jewel in the gutter by many of the locals, is a forty-minute walk from our home. St. Christopher's church, school and grounds form an impressive two city-block sanctuary that would seem more fitting in Victor Hugo's Paris than saddled between Delmont's decaying Main Street businesses such as Uncle Bobby's tattoo emporium and the low rent, can't believe people live in them, apartment buildings that form's the heart of Delmont's growing Haitian population. Mom's getting the teaching job at St. Christopher's was a Godsend she believes. Although, she earns about half of what she would have been making if she stayed at Central. I agree with her that it was a Godsend, but for very different reasons. I can't imagine walking the same high school halls where one of my parents teaches. Do you whack every bozo that makes a crack about their math teacher? Do you not acknowledge the relationship? Do you ride in together? I'm sure there would be a thousand other awkward moments in the course of four years of living and going to school together.

Mom was at a point six years ago when she had no other options but to leave her job at Central. Elaine Alberti, a square shouldered, imposing five-foot nine inch, woman from whom I inherited my height, became afraid to drive. As she was about to pull out of the drive way at Central, she was certain she had hit a student, who had actually smacked the side of her car with his hand as he passed by with friends. The kids were giving an end of the day, free at last hoot and holler for which Mom mistook as a shriek of pain. One of the happy pranksters pushed his buddy who dropped to the ground beside Mom's '92 Lumina. Mom who was vigilantly scanning her rearview mirror missed the push but clearly saw the disappearing body. Horrified, thinking she seriously injured the boy Mom slammed the car into park and buried her crying head onto the steering wheel. The kids, unknown to my now hysterical mother, had horse-played their dumb, little asses down the street. Mom startled back to action by the sound of a horn.

Still shaking when she got home, realizing her overreaction was symptomatic of bigger problems Mom and Dad had a serious heart to heart. They agreed Mom was stressed out and Dad would step it up at home. It sounded good. Dad did the supper dishes that night and talked about working Friday and Saturday nights. "What I can pull in from eight at night to two in the morning is more than I make all week."

Mom looking like she was about to jump out of her skin, deflated Dad's enthusiasm. "And get yourself robbed or killed."

"You take precautions," Dad said.

"What did you promise," Mom groaned.

"Things change," Dad's whispered.

"The city is only getting worse, a double homicide last month." True there was a shoot out not far from St. Christopher's. Police investigated rival street gangs and the mayor announced shortly afterwards that arrests were imminent. Years later we are still waiting for the arrests. Word on the street was the shooters were probably in New York or Colombia living it up. I had trouble seeing Mom's leap of logic that linked this battle over gang turf with Dad's being a likely target if he drives a couple home from a nightclub on a Friday.

"We'll see how it goes," Dad pleaded.

"Do you think me not sleeping, worrying if you're out there getting robbed or shot by one of these little punks is going to lower my stress?" The conversation just ended like many of my parents' talks without any change. Six years later and my father still hasn't driven past nine o'clock on any night, let alone the party hearty weekends.

The next morning everything seemed normal. Mom had made sandwiches from left over chicken for our school lunches. I was in junior high and my biggest concerns were would I ever start shaving and if my biceps were bigger than my best buddy Eric LeBlanc's. Tommy was in fourth grade and the teacher had requested a parent conference the week before because little brother had killed Mr. Winky, the class mascot. The way Tommy and my dad explained this grade school tragedy I figured all of little brother's stars must have been out of line.

Mr. Winky was an overweight, black and white guinea pig, who received his name because of a facial twitch that made him appear to be winking. Tommy's teacher, Mrs. Kerrigan, had a weekly routine in which a pair of different students would clean Mr. Winky's cage. It was Tommy and Jill Vallenti's turn to make Winky's home ready to receive another week of piss and poop. Jill, a shy nine-year old, found the critter to be a repulsive stink bomb. She wished she was home pretending to be sick instead of standing behind Tommy holding a large plastic trash bag into which Mr. Winky's smelly shavings would be dumped. Tommy placed a shoebox that had once held Mrs. Kerrigan's work boots on the window ledge next to the cage. Excited by the idea of helping his teacher, Tommy quickly released the snaps that held the cage's wired upper half onto the lower blue plastic base. Tommy leaned the wired top section against the radiator pipes and reached down for Mr. Winky. With one hand under the rodent's neck and belly he snatched the little guy up. Before lowering the creature into the shoebox, Tommy turned towards Jill and pushed the furry blob in her face. Jill yelled, "Tommy," as she jumped backwards bumping into Jake Lipkin, who was copying the ten weekly spelling words from his workbook to a piece of lined paper. Jake immediately overreacted to the indignity of a girl bumping into him, yelled, "Quit it," and pushed Jill back into Tommy. Tommy swung Mr. Winky to his left in order to avoid Jill's toppling body. Mr. Winky in what was purely a defensive move squealed and dug his claws into Tommy's thumb. Tommy thinking he was bitten shot-putted the flabby rodent up and forward with the force of an aspiring Olympian. Mr. Winky sailed towards the front of the room where Mrs. Kerrigan was explaining how to make wolf, wife, and knife plural. To the right of the teacher's desk a large American flag stood on an eight-foot high iron pole, which was crowned with a sharp three-inch blade. Mr. Winky soared towards the ceiling, then arched and began spiraling downward, spinning his chubby little body like a wounded kamikaze pilot into the flag's shaft. Students screamed, gasped, and laughed. Tommy stood smiling. Mrs. Kerrigan looked up with mouth open as the helpless animal twittered about for a few seconds before expiring. Mrs. Kerrigan sent one student for the custodian and Tommy to the principal's office.

Because of the flexibility Dad had with his schedule, he kept the next day's obligatory parent-teacher meeting with Mrs. Kerrigan. She recounted every detail of Mr. Winky's demise, repeating, "Why would your son hurl a poor defenseless creature? Hurl so hard that it became impaled. Do you know how terrible this was for the others?" Dad assured her that Tommy was sorry about Mr. Winky. That he wasn't a mean or malicious boy. It was just a tragic accident. Dad was able to patch things up with Mrs. Kerrigan, who seemed much relieved that the principal hadn't blamed her for Winky's horrific end, and that she had as yet received no irate calls from parents of traumatized kids. The slaying of a pet guinea pig was just one more piece of distressing information that my parents were amassing on little Tommy.

Dad sat in the den dunking slices of cinnamon toast slathered with butter into his extra light coffee. He was excited about having received from the Delmont Public Library that week a translation of a German article on the influence of Franz Schubert on later composers.

Mom as usual left before us. She needed to get to the high school for quarter past seven, a half hour earlier than my start time at Drake Junior High. Tommy had until eight before he could start terrorizing Mrs. Kerrigan. Dad would drive us in the cab. It was a big deal the first few times I got let out amongst the noncommercial small trucks, minivans, compacts, and station wagons, but was now beginning to become embarrassing.

Like every morning, Mom trucked out her expanding briefcase, crammed with papers, assignment book, grade book, and lunch. She told Dad to pick up some hamburger at the supermarket. It was a one-day sale. She told me it was okay to go to the Boys' Club with Eric and some other neighborhood kids after school, as long as I was home by five. She gave Tommy a pat on the back and told him she knew he was going to have a good day. Mom was doing a lot of praying and employment of reverse psychology on Tommy's behalf.

As soon as Mom walked out the door Tommy and I started making smores in the microwave. Dad, deep in thought and his cinnamon toast, was oblivious to our sweet second breakfast. This was, in Mom's book, a definite no-no, as she considered anything that used chocolate and marshmallows as junk food, to be eaten only as an after school snack. Before the microwave had finished ticking off its last few seconds, Mom pale and dazed came busting through the back entry. "Sam," she called, sounding in trouble. I backed up to the microwave in hopes that my body would hide our sneaking treats. 'What did she forget?' I thought, hoping she wouldn't look my way. Mom headed into the den as my father started out to meet her. Then as if some impostor had taken her place she started crying in my father's arms. Dad just held her, his eyes darted between kitchen and den as if he were looking for something to help explain my mother's tears. Her legs were trembling as she clutched Dad.

"What is it?" Dad asked.

"I started shaking, shaking all over the place. Worse than yesterday," Mom said, burying her face in my father's chest. My father eased her into the den and I could hear her sniffling and him moving papers and books off the couch. The microwave beeped and I set the plate on the kitchen table for Tommy, directing him with my eyes away from the den's entrance and to the gooey mess of piping hot smores. I sat at the end of the table nearest the den, allowing me to hear everything. Tommy started eating, gingerly holding a smore on fingertips, blowing on the area to be consumed then quickly snapping off a piece with his front teeth.

"This is crazy," Mom said, sounding better.

"It's stress. You need a break."

"It's a month until Thanksgiving."

"Well, call in today and see how you feel tomorrow," Dad said, gently.

"It's too late, they want call-ins before six."

"You were fine at six, tell them you lost your breakfast and feel like crap." There was a moment of silence and Tommy started on his second smore. He looked at me like I was growing a second nose because I was just sitting not trying to eat more than him. Dad got up and called Central High, "This is Sam Alberti. My wife, Elaine won't be in today. No, she's got a stomach bug and feels like hell. She just got sick. Thanks."

"Thanks," Mom said.

"Maybe you should see someone."

"I'll be alright. Just need to relax a little."

"You worry about everything. Things will be fine."

Mom sighed and then in fiery little spurts she fired, "Fine. You know most weeks we're down to our last dollar before you or I get paid. You know it only gets worse with the winter heating bills, and Mrs. Leonetti's little snake Joey has been leaving brochures for her to look at assisted living places. It gets her thinking maybe, and those kids hanging around all the time. The neighborhood isn't safe."

"She'd never leave this place."

"Never, look Sam she's seventy-six and healthy today. Who knows about tomorrow?"

"Tomorrow will take care of itself."

"That's why I'm cracking up," Mom screamed.

"What?"

"That outlook is a big part of why I don't sleep nights. Someone around here has got to be thinking about tomorrow."

"That outlook keeps me sane in this miserable world." You could hear the anger strangling my father's optimism. He came into the kitchen, looking at me as if he needed a life jacket. "Let's go boys. Danny, clean that up. Lainie I'll be back, we'll talk."

I grabbed my book-bag and before heading out stuck my head into the den. Mom was sitting quiet, eyes straight ahead. "You all right, Mom?"

"Oh sure, just got upset about nothing, really Danny I'm fine," She said without looking at me, without any joy, or hint that she was fine.

Mom ended up taking the rest of the week off from work. Dad kind of walked around here like a scared turtle, telling Tommy and me that everything was okay. Mom just needed some time away from work. Over the next few weeks Mom missed a lot of work, stopped driving and poured more and more of her time into surveillance of Dad, Tommy, and me. Dad convinced her to go see a psychologist who said she had a phobia about driving and an anxiety disorder. Mom agreed with the diagnosis and then stopped seeing the guy. Over baked macaroni and fried pork chops Mom announced, "I got a driving phobia. I can live without driving."

My father between documenting the vital link between Mozart, Schubert, Beethoven, Schumann and Brahms with the birth of the alienated modern man, did some investigating into phobias and anxiety disorders, and rattled off a bunch of treatments. When he finished I felt like we were getting to the bottom of Mom's driving freak-out and there was hope. Mom, who can dash a rising spirit with a side-glance, surprised the hell out of me. She must have screened out all of Dad's sugarcoated psychological babble, as she said matter-of-factly, "I saw Dr. Giusti he gave me Prozac." Dr. Giusti, who went to grade school with Mrs. Leonetti, was our family doctor. He was a man of few words, who seemed to know almost immediately what was wrong with anyone in our family, from my tonsils to young Tommy's constant ear infections, to Dad's kidney stones last year. Great! Better than hope, Mom was cured.

Dad tried to convince her that more than a few pills were needed, but Mom dismissed all of his arguments with an, 'I know best', look. You could tell she wasn't listening, Dad was wasting his breath, but he went on and on. Finally she said, leaving no room for discussion, "We'll sell the Lumina. I'm not driving anymore."

"Your school is three or four miles away," Dad said in shock.

"You'll have to take me until I find something closer."

Dad started cutting up his pork chop and no more was said. About a month after this major decision Mom got the job at St. Christopher's. She replaced a teacher, who was out on maternity leave. The new mother, however, could not bear to leave her baby and Mom has been there ever since.

The other important part of my revised Labor Day agenda was that Linda had invited Eric over to her house rather than us joining the LeBlanc clan at their place. This could set in motion a chain reaction as volatile as any television drama, for Mr. & Mrs. LeBlanc were always on the verge of killing each other and their four kids. Eric had confided in Linda and me yesterday that out of fear of his father he hadn't told his parents that he got fired from his job at Burger King. Eric had forgotten he was to work last Thursday from four to closing. Eric arrived twenty-four hours late, moaning his fate that he had nothing better to do on an end of summer Friday than to sweat over a BK fryer. When the manager confronted him, Eric snapped, "Sorry, I fucking forgot." This was done in front of four other young, impressionable employees and two elderly customers who were debating whether to get the grilled chicken or the fish sandwich. Eric got fired and a lesson that a moment of feeling really good is not worth the possibility of weeks or months of being broke. On top of empty pockets he had to explain things to his father.

The LeBlanc's owned the three-decker they lived in. Mr. LeBlanc was built like a boxcar with arms. He had an accident four years ago when he slipped with a wheelbarrow loaded with gravel. The wheelbarrow came crashing into his chest, permanently messing up his back. He got the house dirt-cheap twenty years ago because it needed a top to bottom rehab. Mr. LeBlanc was able to do most of the work himself, or through his connections with plumber and electrician friends. The renovations cost much in time, but little in dollars. In the winter, when construction work limped along, Mr. LeBlanc knocked himself out doing the indoor work. Weekends in the summer he concentrated on the outside of the place, planting hedges, painting, re-cementing walkways, a patio in the closet size backyard, slowly turning his fixer-upper into the best house on the street. With his back injury and loads of time on his hands, Mr. LeBlanc went from drinking after work to drinking sometimes all day and night. There were always cases of empty beer cans and bottles on the back porch. Eric explained, matter-of-factly one time when we were small, "My father drinks beer like some guys smoke cigarettes, one after another."

Although he hadn't worked in years, Labor Day was still a holiday that Mr. LeBlanc got psyched about. It was a LeBlanc tradition. They had this big family cookout each Labor Day. Eric always invited me over, and the last couple of years Linda came as well. Mr. LeBlanc's brother, Wilfred, who everyone called Uncle Willy, would be there with his wife and their three kids. Uncle Willy was a plumbing supply salesman, who Eric said was doing well for himself serving accounts from New Haven to Portland. Once Eric's father had finished grilling all the meat, the two LeBlanc men would sit on aluminum lawn chairs, a beer cooler between them, calling to their wives or daughters to fetch them some thing to eat while they guzzled beers. I marveled how those aluminum chairs managed all that weight.

Mr. LeBlanc naturally made you feel inferior. It was more in the sound of what he said than in the actual words. Other than his occasionally referring to Eric and I as girls, to which Eric would mumble under his breath, 'asshole', I can't recall him ever showing the verbal attacks that Eric said were worse than a beating. There was the one time when we were about ten or eleven, which was more Eric getting all weird than his father actually doing much of anything. But that was when we stopped hanging over Eric's. It's an automatic now, if we're just watching movies or whatever, we go to Linda's or my place.

I grew up with Eric. We've been best friends since always. We would play together as little kids either at his house or mine. This changed about seven years ago. Eric used to say little about his father, who I seldom saw. Between his working construction days and on the three-decker nights and weekends he was more shadow than reality to me. I was always impressed by the idea of how wide he was without appearing like a big fat guy, and of the great quantities of beer bottles that stacked up on their back porch. It was mid-August and a bunch of kids in the neighborhood had spent the morning playing stickball in the abandoned Delmont Steel Company's parking lot. As noon approached the air thickened and the sky filled with dark thunder that was dying to chase us home. The game ended with the first splats of rain the size of plums. Eric and I headed to his house for a game of Monopoly.

We raced, laughing down Waverly, wearing our baseball gloves on our heads as the wind and rain picked up. We turned onto Whitman and a great sizzling crack of lightning opened the sky's main water line drenching us. Dripping and laughing we crashed into Mrs. LeBlanc sitting in the kitchen watching her soap operas. She scowled, tossed us a dishtowel that was lying on the table and said, "Take your shoes off, dry up, and don't fight with your sisters. I'm warning you, I got a headache." There was no debating to be done with Mrs. LeBlanc. She was a squat manly woman, who I pictured holding her own with Mr. LeBlanc.

Eric was the oldest of four. His brother Kenny was two years younger and badly wanted to be included in whatever we were doing. Kenny's, need to be with us allowed on a regular basis for us to treat him like crap. Kenny, a little hurt, might distance himself for a while but sure enough within the hour he would eagerly come back for more. Then there were the twin sisters, Kimberly and Kelly, almost four years younger than Eric. They were in this just staring up at us and giggling stage at the time. Eric would yell at them and they would scatter, only to slowly sneak back and either ask Eric to do something, which naturally pissed him off, or would giggle and he would scream them back into another room.

Maybe it was Mrs. LeBlanc's warning, but that day we were playing as well as three kids our age can do anything. We had allowed Kenny to join us, and other than the odd flare up of Eric calling his brother stupid, relations were Kodak perfect. Kimberly and Kelly were in their room taking care of their dolls and once we got started playing their constant chitchat was lost. It was agreed that I would be the banker, since Kenny didn't trust Eric, and Eric assessed Kenny as a finger-counting numbskull. Each of us wanted the racecar so we ended up throwing dice to see who would get their lucky piece. Eric won and I resigned myself to the little dog as Kenny snatched up the man on horseback. The game was a cutthroat event. Eric and I took chances and Kenny kept landing on our property. Before Kenny was about to go bankrupt, I floated him a loan, which was allowed over Eric's objections. I misread Kenny's ability or perhaps it was more that his bad luck had to eventually change. Change it did, the little whiner began tiptoeing around the board missing enemy properties time after time. Whenever he landed on Community Chest or Chance it was good news. As Kenny's fortunes improved mine went sour. Each throw of the dice found me paying out my dwindling assets to one brother or the other. I quickly found myself begging Master Kenneth for my money back. It was with selling off my last hotel, in order to stay in the game, and the LeBlanc boys eyeing each other's wealth with envy, that the game came to an abrupt end.

"Don't tell me those two have been in all day," Mr. LeBlanc demanded from his wife.

"It was raining," she fired back with equal force. Eric and Kenny looked at each other and then at me. Fear ran across their faces and dropped their shoulders.

"It's not raining now," Mr. LeBlanc roared.

In robotic synchronized harmony the brothers said to each other, "You win," and then looked at me with urgent eyes.

I shrugged.

"It's summer. They should be out playing," Mr. LeBlanc said.

Eric looked at me pleading and said, "We got to go." Kenny scooped the houses and hotels off the board before I could agree. Eric began to organize the funny money for another time.

"Aren't you going to see who won?" I asked feeling somehow cheated, even though I was certainly the loser.

"He won," Eric said, putting an elastic band around a stack of bills. "Let's go out," Eric said, in a small voice.

Mr. LeBlanc was going to take a shower and I followed Eric and Kenny's lead as we slinked out past Mrs. LeBlanc, who was watching *Oprah* as she peeled potatoes. The torrential downpour that had sent us running indoors had left few signs of its occurring. We headed over to the empty Delmont Steel Company to see if anybody was out playing. As we walked, Eric confided that his father only yells at them. "Whatever I do, I know it's wrong, or I'll screw it up," he said, shaking his head and looking at the ground. "I hate seeing him," Eric said almost crying.

"And he hates seeing us," Kenny said, with a 'he can go to hell' tone.

I AM THE MOON

"Bet I can beat you," Kenny said, and we started running towards the dilapidated steel company.

From that day on, I knew Eric and Kenny were in their own hell.

Eric seemed to stop growing when he hit fourteen. He wore his dark brown hair straight and long. He slowly gravitated to black t-shirts and dungarees. He ran cross-country at school and put out some decent mile times. He never won, but was always in the hunt. He escaped into Science Fiction, always reading some new paperback about a futuristic society. He and Linda would get into longwinded jams about what the next century would be like. Linda was certain the world was moving in the right direction, using the United Nations, the collapse of the Soviet Union, medical advances unknown to our parents that we take for granted, the civil rights movement, and the basic good nature of most of mankind as her reasons. Eric would cringe and spout off a laundry list of major blunders that governments around the world, including our own, had committed. They would often look to me to break their deadlock. Depending on my interest, the hour of the day, and my appetite I would either throw some oil on their smoldering tongues, or tell them they both made good points now let's get something to eat.

*****

Linda and I armed with shopping list and coupons headed over to the Stop & Shop. Linda, an excellent driver, unlike yours truly, drove her mom's ancient Pontiac 6000. Its engine was pushing a couple of hundred thousand miles, but it still had some giddy-up. The overall look of the car was a bad joke. One rear hubcap was left to adorn the worn black-walls with their rusting bolts. A general faded paint finish with patches chipped off, amidst splashes of corroding steel made it difficult for the unfamiliar to quickly determine that the car's true color was midnight blue. There was a dent on the passenger side that Linda had picked up during her first month of driving, totally not her fault. It was near Christmas and the Cherry Tree Shopping Mall's parking lot was jammed. The walking and driving were treacherous as powdery snow covered plowed packed streets of ice. After a day of shopping all I knew was what not to get Linda. She started creeping out from her parking spot when this beat up old Dodge Caravan turned the corner and began to slide towards us. The van in slow motion came sideways for my door. Crunch. My head bounced back and forth from my shoulders to the side window, giving me three lima bean size welts above my right ear. The driver, a forty-something year-old Hispanic, who spoke little English, looked frantic as he came out to inspect the damage. There must have been half-a-dozen kids under ten, a mother and grandmother. The oldest kid, a boy named Miguel, translated. Linda was all right and my head, I thought, would be fine. The front passenger door had some stick to it, but with a little extra muscle it creaked open. The father was soon in tears. Miguel explained that they had no insurance and that Papi, his father, would go to jail if we called the police. Soon Miguel's mother was out crying beside her husband. A baby girl cuddled in the mother's arms and another girl maybe four years old hung onto the woman's skirt.

Linda and I stepped aside from the mourning family and thought that the damage wasn't that much. I said something about being able to get some friends to knock out the dents. The father gave us both a long hug as he repeated, "Merry Christmas." The mother in choppy English kept saying we were very kind and that she and her family would pray for us. I thought I was going to start crying, looking at all those kids, how scared their old man was. The father then offered Linda forty dollars, all the money he had. She got all choked up, refusing and telling them to have a good Christmas.

Mrs. McCurry thought we were a couple of suckers and should have called the cops because somebody should pay to fix her car. I told her that with Tarzan's help, I thought, we could fix it. "Suckers, two young suckers," she said then flicked on an old black and white Paul Newman movie. Mrs. McCurry loves Paul Newman from the '60s. Linda said her mother would be fine. By the time I left for home she was saying how we did the Christian thing, especially with it being Christmas and the Pontiac was traveling on borrowed time.

A passion of Tarzan's is reconditioning old cars. I should say old car. Along the alley between his market and Peewee's Cleaners, kept under a protective cloak is Tarzan's pride and joy, a '61 fire engine red Plymouth Fury two-door hardtop. The Fury was Tarzan's first car, kept by his brother, Leo, when Tarzan went in the Army. After Vietnam, Tarzan drove it for a while. Then when he opened the market, he found the need for a small truck. He kept the Fury, for sentimental reasons he says. Over the years the New England winters and the summer sun took their toll on his once glistening set of wheels. Three or four years ago, while visiting his brother Leo down on Cape Cod, he went to a classic car show. He got the idea of restoring the old Fury and hoped this coming summer to show it off, maybe in Hyannis, maybe at the Fourth of July Summer Nationals in Worcester. A lot of times now, when business is slow, Tarzan will pull off the cover and polish up the shark grinning grill, or clean the extra wide white walls.

With Tarzan and Jose's help, I was able to knock out some of the Pontiac's dents. But it was never right. The front passenger door from the outside remains functionally useless. Inside the door works reluctantly for me, but won't budge for Linda. That being my usual seat I remain a bit leery of the door's cooperativeness in the event I should need to make a speedy exit. My getting into the McCurry mobile requires the front seat pushed as far back as it can go, with no foreign objects to jab my butt as I slide into position. Once my back hits the passenger side door I swivel my hips and retract my ever lengthening legs towards my middle. Linda then takes her position behind the steering wheel and the two of us wiggle our butts, as she presses hard on the seat's adjustment lever. Linda needs the seat fully forward, which leaves my knees locked in place against the glove box and my head scratching the roof.

Although all three of us have our licenses, Linda is the only one who drives frequently enough to feel like driving isn't any big deal. Since the LeBlanc's have been adjusting to living on Mr. LeBlanc's disability check, and what he gets for rents on the second and third floor apartments, getting Eric a cheap car and insuring it was out of the question. Eric like me is hoping that our after school and weekend jobs will generate the dough to get our own set of wheels and insurance. Getting canned at BK was definitely an unforeseen wrinkle in his financial affairs. Unlike me, Eric seems to be a natural behind the wheel.

Before I got behind the wheel of a car for the first time, I considered myself as being potentially, not just a good driver but more like an all-star, a NASCAR bound perhaps driver. God has given me all the tools, twenty-twenty vision, excellent reflexes, terrific eye hand coordination. Other skills, known only to me, which I assumed would serve me well, as I cruised the fair streets of Delmont and beyond, included: the ability to concentrate on one thing and do something totally foreign, like thinking about a pitch sequence during my last at bat while playing gin with Linda and Eric, not getting completely ballistic by everyday rudeness, which runs rampant in our city, and when lost or confused not being a chuckle head about asking for help. To date all of my talents have been of little value to me when it comes to driving. The reason for this, I trust, lies in the great under-mining of confidence that took place during my first driving lesson.

Being slightly older than Linda and Eric, I was the first of our trio to apply for and pass his Learner's Permit test. My parents, I think, believed they were supportive. Mom listed the dangers and responsibilities that went with driving a motor vehicle, speaking as if I were a time traveler from the 18th

Century. "The biggest cause of serious and I mean serious accidents," Mom announced in her, 'at best the world is a scary place' voice, "is speed and inexperience." She groaned about the stress of driving. It requires constant vigilance, with people darting out from between cars, crazies on your bumper, cars changing lanes, lights always turning yellow as you reached that critical point of should I speed up or brake. "An automobile is a dangerous weapon," she would slip in, giving me the eye, which said she suspected me of being the kind of person who would be less than constantly vigilant. At no time did Mom say, "I think this is a bad idea." Just one line like that and I would have closed up my Learner's Permit booklet pronto. Since, I started high school Mom has prided herself on letting me make my own decisions, within reason. She does however guide me with regular guilt injections in the form of saying, "I know you'll do the right thing." The right thing is whatever Elaine Alberti wants.

My father on the other hand took a different line regarding my becoming a licensed driver. He told funny stories of being Uncle Charlie's slave for a couple of weeks during the summer of 1977, while Charlie taught him how to drive his '66 Impala, which was a real babe catcher, according to Dad. There was no neurotic foreboding, Dad seemed to be looking forward to the experience as much as me. This all changed as he tossed me the keys to his '96 Mercury Grand Marquis to begin our first and last lesson. It was a sparkling, bright Saturday morning in April, the kind of day made for the commencement of great things. I was projecting a similar success story as what my father and Uncle Charlie had experienced. I saw, within the month, Dad bragging what a good driver I was and planning when I should go for my license. But, with the passing of his taxi keys Dad was transformed, like some fairy tale smiling prince into a shrieking loon.

"This isn't just a car, it's how I make a living," he said, standing on the passenger side with worry flashing out of his eyes, as I unlocked the driver's side door.

"I know." Did he think I forgot that he's a cab driver and this is his cab as well as the family's only means of transportation?

"I've never let anyone drive this. We got to be very careful." His head bobbed and I could sense his hands on the other side of the door twitching. "Be careful. We can't afford to have this baby in the shop."

I said, "Right." Wanting however to say, 'Relax, I know what I'm doing,' but as I squirmed about behind the wheel, it was as if this were my first time in a car. I could feel my mother's fears pressing on my shoulders.

"First thing is you have to adjust the mirror," Dad said, reaching for the windshield, identifying for me the rear view mirror, and sounding increasingly more nervous as he spoke.

"Can I move the seat back?"

"Isn't it all right?"

"Well, I guess." The seat was alright as long as I kept my legs bent.

"I got that seat set to give my customers plenty of leg room."

"Oh." Are we expecting to pick up fares?

"I'm use to being a little stuffed in," he said, dead serious.

"It is adjustable."

"Look, I haven't moved the seat in years. I don't know if you move it if I'll get it back to where it is. Is it that important?"

I was full with this is a big mistake, as I said, "No."

Our car was between a Honda Accord and a Toyota. I'm sure Dad looked things over and thought 'plenty of room even for a rookie,' however mysteriously this Grand Marquis, a full-size car to begin with, grew larger by the second as I started her up, checked my mirrors, and looked at Dad for a sign that this was still a good idea.

"Put it in reverse. You got to put your foot on the brake!"

"Oh."

"Just ease your foot off the brake." A little voice was telling me not to move my foot. "Just ease up on the brake. Go ahead. Go ahead. Danny!"

My easing felt more like an opening of a water faucet. The great Mercury ocean liner inched backwards, realizing I was looking straight ahead I panicked and slammed on the brake. Dad jostled, head twisted to view our backward motion, his chin diving into the headrest, "Just ease up on the brake." I did and the car rolled. "Stop, stop!"

Dad adjusted himself, eyes forward, commanded, "Put it in drive, in drive, foot on brake. Each time you shift you need to have your foot on the brake." These last words were said in a 'you dumb shit' tone. "Now cut your wheels towards the street. Look for Christ-sakes. Always look before you move, always." Nothing was coming. I inched out, wheels cut sharply. There was enough room to set up a picnic table between the Honda and us, but the Mercury's nose was growing again and I came to a sudden halt.

"You're okay," he said. I hesitated examining the distance, doubting his observation. "You're fine."

City streets do not remain static. In the blink between my stopping and starting a delivery van from Sophia's Bakery appeared without my noticing. I did not look, trusting in Dad's, 'you're fine'. The van honked, a lane of room was between us. I shuddered. "You got to keep your eyes on the road," Dad said and I felt like saying maybe we should do it another time, or with another father. Maybe Sunday at dawn would make more sense, less chance of colliding with the rest of the world who know where they're going and how to get there.

Dad looked around and said, "You're okay. Pull out. At the end of the street turn right. You got to stop." I'm not a numbskull Dad. Of course I'm going to stop. Did you think I was going to plow right onto Waverly Avenue, with its four lanes of congestion?

I crept, funeral procession speed, down Whitman and surprised myself with how easily I made it onto Waverly. I thanked God no one else needed to use the road as I generously borrowed from the middle. "Take the first right," Dad said, sounding like something was yanking on his draws.

"Stay to your right," he snapped.

"Parked cars," he said as if he just got goosed. I swerved into the center of the two lanes.

"Stay to your right!" I swerved back.

"Take your first right." I understood what my father wanted me to do. He wanted me to turn onto Oakmont, the first street on my right. I, however, for some unknown reason made as sharp of a turn as possible, while traveling at tricycle speed, into the alley that separates Gino's Bar from the empty, out of business Frank & Son Fish Market. Frank closed up about three years ago when he reached seventy. Frank is the son of Frank & Son. Tarzan says, he's holding onto hope that somebody in his family will reopen the place. Tarzan gives that as much of a chance as vinyl LP's making a comeback. The space between, Gino's and Frank's was wide enough for a car to squeeze down. If you ended up parking it there, the only way out was to roll down a window and climb out onto the roof. When Frank was in business at the alley's end there was room to park and turn around. Gino, with Frank's closing, uses the space for storage, which effectively prevents anything larger than a Vespa from turning around.

"What the hell," Dad in shock said, as I entered the alley.

"Where the hell are you going?" I had committed a monumental error and was compounding it by stubbornly driving on, knowing a blockade awaited us, but hoping it had been cleared. I could feel my father's red face as he said, "The alley's blocked."

I then inserted my foot in my mouth, "I know."

"You know, then why are we here."

I stopped the taxi a foot from a stack of barrels. I looked at my father who was mumbling to himself, "Dear Mother of Mercy." Dad took a deep breath and then asked, "Can you back it out of here?"

"Sure."

I put it in reverse and Dad chanted the new Alberti's drive song, "Keep it straight, go slow." Sweat poured out of him like a highway paving crew in July.

"Honk!' he screamed in my ear as the car neared the sidewalk. I slammed on the brake and gave him a, 'do you mind I'm in control here' look. I blasted the horn. "Go slow, honk again!" I did, freezing two elderly women at the alley's start. I waved them forward, and they waved back to us.

"Tarzan's mother and aunt," my father said, calmly. "Wave them on." I did, but the women armed with great handbags and handled brown paper shopping bags smiled politely and motioned for me to continue. We waved at each other three more times, I growing in self-consciousness with each greeting. Finally my father gave in and ordered me to back out further. Once the Mercury's front doors had clearance to open he stopped me and we changed positions. Dad drove us home and it was decided that he would pay for driving lessons.

Chapter Three

Like robots, Linda and I followed Mrs. McCurry's instructions. The cherries were dark, hard, and passed the taste test, two pounds came with us. The peaches, greenish golf balls, would take a week to ripen and earned a pass. Six medium sized, not-too-yellow bananas were snatched up. I showed off how Tarzan had taught me to tap a watermelon for sweetness. "Hold it like so, and give its belly a thump. If it vibrates and doesn't give a dead thud it's a good one." Linda smiled as I lowered a beauty into the wagon. Our cart filled with buy one get one free hamburger and hot dog rolls, ice cream, bagels, mustard and detergent, all matching up to the coupons Linda held like a full-house poker hand.

On the home stretch we split up. Linda headed over to the deli counter for franks and Swiss cheese and I doubled back with our half-filled shopping cart to the produce section to check out ears of corn for worms. I glided down the aisle imagining perfect swings on perfect summer days. I was crushing hanging curves. Mid-way up the aisle standing in profile, filling his family's order of butter and sugar sweet corn was Coach Inhorn.

Coach had been at Central since he got his teaching certificate twenty years ago. His face and neck were badly pocked and he had a way of looking at you that made you tuck your shirt in and swallow your gum. He was close to six feet tall with the start of a potbelly. Coach Inhorn taught social studies, mostly lower level U.S. History classes. Everyone called him Coach. This year I finally had him as a teacher, Introduction to Sociology. I imagined I would get preferential treatment knowing Coach often went to bat for students whose grades were nose-diving into that territory known as loss of eligibility. I saw myself catching up on sports trivia, daydreaming, and maybe using the class as an extra study, contributing every few days to a class discussion out of respect for the Coach. However, Coach surprised me after the first class, "Danny," he said, halting m at his desk. "You're a smart kid. I know how all my players are doing. You could find yourself with a scholarship, but a lot of schools, unless they see you as making a big difference in their having a winning season look at your grades. I don't give anybody a free ride. Show me what you got."

I wanted to ask him if I was giving him some vibes as to my previous plan to coast and bank on our relationship to steal a B, but just stammered out a, "Sure."

"Sometimes guys who have some talent think I'm going give them a free ride. It never happens. In fact knowing you're a smart kid, and a hard worker for me at practices I expect the same here."

"Sure."

Coach nodded and told me not to be late for my next class. Shit, my coasting senior year was getting a kick in the pants. I made, I thought, only one scheduling blunder that was taking Dr. Burnsides, Honors English IV class. Linda, who was pushing to be in the top ten in our class persuaded me with, 'It would mean us having at least one class together, and English is a snap for you. And Dr. Burnsides writes the best college recommendations and he's not as hard as everyone says.' When I whined, "How come everyone calls him Dr. Burnsyou?" She rattled off how five or six of the biggest nerds ever to attend Central did great and loved him. I countered with, 'Only freaking Einsteins like him.' She looked up at me all hurt and asked so sweetly, 'Don't you want to take a class with me?' I signed up.

"Coach," I said as he was ripping at the top of an ear of corn.

"Danny." I grabbed a plastic bag and began imitating Coach's corn inspection. "The ones that aren't too fat, but still full got the best taste." I nodded. "Did you see that new kid?" he asked eying the corn. "He's a sophomore, transferred from Boston. He's about as big as you, you six-four yet?" Coach gave me an approving nod.

"Maybe," I said giving a shrug.

"He's supposed to be quick, good shooter. His uncle and I played in the Park's League. I want you to take him under your wing, you being a senior." I must have had a constipated look of dismay for Coach's voice changed and he was now telling me how things would be. "I don't want him hooking up with some of the lunkheads who only show up to keep their probation officers happy. I figure between you and some of my other good kids he'll have a better chance. He's new in town, with you growing faster than the crabgrass on my lawn I think we might have ourselves a good year."

"He's a sophomore?" This was said in a way to communicate the weirdness of me, a senior, extending myself to a sophomore I didn't know, like the vast majority of the school's eighteen hundred, nameless strangers.

"Is that a problem?"

"No," I said, thinking only thing is I won't be in any of his classes, besides playing basketball we may not have anything else in common, and what does taking under a wing really mean?

"Good, his name is Louis Hunter, if you run into him or whatever, keep it in mind and keep this to yourself," Coach said, lifting up two bundles of corn and heading to the check out.

After the second ear of corn I stopped checking them. I had Louis Hunter on the brain. What is a Louis Hunter? What do I look like, a high school Statue of Liberty. I was feeling a pressure to please Coach and not sure what I really was supposed to do. I began to recount the corn in my bag, mumbling as a middle-aged woman with a glum mouth stared at me. Self-consciously, I began counting loudly and making erratic jabs of corn in the air before jamming them back in the bag, "six, seven, eight…." Her mouth grew noticeably sour and she turned her head. I thought, 'why did I have to see Coach now and who is Louis Hunter.'

Before I had reached twelve a pair of skinny arms came up from behind and wrapped around me. For a second I didn't realize it was Linda and, with Louis Hunter and unchecked corn rattling me, I broke away as if she were a mugger.

Linda, surprised by my force, yelled, "No Danny!" The packages of hot dogs and cheese she had clasped around my middle were propelled straight ahead, arching slightly then dropping like a jumper from the top of the key, swatting across the backside of the middle-aged crow, who's pissed off demeanor heightened with the attack of her butt by our wieners.

"Oops," I said to Linda, who, being ninety pounds on her fat days, spun away from me like a rag doll in a hurricane. I caught her with one-hand inches from wiping out a giant pyramid display of Bartlett pears. Seeing past me, she had a fly in your soup look.

"Did you throw these at me," the middle-aged woman stood waving the deli wrapped packages under my nose. Before I could speak she continued,

"You should be ashamed of yourself." The woman, looking hurt and angry, deposited the items in our cart. "This is a supermarket not a playground."

"I'm sorry," I said to her back.

"It was an accident," Linda said to the woman who seemed satisfied that we were a couple of goofballs and she had told us off.

We hurried to the front of the store to check out, giggling like little kids who have pulled a prank on an adult. As we were presenting our items to a thirty-something year old, dyed blonde with dark roots screaming from her scalp, gum snapping cashier, I told Linda about running into Coach. As I got to Louis Hunter I began racing and Linda had to slow me down.

"So there's a new kid and Coach thinks it would be good for you to try to be friendly with him," she said in a, 'what's the big deal' way.

"He's a sophomore."

"So?"

"Well, I don't even know him."

We went back and forth like this until the groceries were stored in the back seat and I climbed around her steering wheel and crunched my knees into place against the glove box. Our conversation moved from Louis Hunter to our having an indoor cookout at the McCurry's. We skirted around Eric's troubles with hope that he would wait to tell his parents about getting canned until he at least had something in the works. Mrs. McCurry was throwing Eric a lifeline. She would talk to her manager at the Stop & Shop about hiring him. For Linda, Eric's dilemma had a put up or shut up angle regarding her mother. Mrs. McCurry was constantly harping on Linda for not working with her. The money was slightly better but the idea of being side by side with her mother for an eight hour shift led Linda to conclude that eventually one of them would have to permanently disappear.

Mrs. McCurry, a woman long on experience in turning chicken shit into soup, gave us the best cheeseburgers and hot dogs I ever had. Into her hamburger she added an onion soup mix and a honey-mustard, on the side were mushrooms and roasted red peppers. I inhaled four, stopping for nothing. She boiled the hot dogs and then placed four at a time into this long handled wired tong, burning them black over one of her stove's gas burners. After corn and watermelon Eric and I waddled into the den to watch *Mystic River*. I was guzzling Pepsi to quench my salty tongue, one of the side effects to the McCurry burgers. I hoped the carbonation would create some gastric flux and I would let out a big burp, allowing room for the last two hot dogs.

Linda helped her mother clean up while I propped myself on the corner of the sofa. Eric sat across from me in a worn recliner with a broken footrest. Linda told us to start the movie because she and her mom had watched it last night. "It's so sad, but powerful," Mrs. McCurry said over the running dishwater.

"I dropped a bomb on my father, as I was leaving," Eric said, fast-forwarding the video, skipping over the coming attractions. I was hoping not to have this conversation now, full and bloated my world seemed just fine and I had neither the energy nor desire to take on the LeBlanc mess. "I didn't want to say anything in front of Mrs. McCurry." He gave a little self-conscious grin and continued, "One foot out the door as he's telling me to come home early to spend time with my cousins I say, 'Yeah Dad about five'. He nods and I'm amazed that he's not bullshit that I'll miss the major gluttony fest. So I say just like this, 'I got fired.'"

"And then you hauled ass over here." End of story, let's watch the movie, and wait for Linda to be here for she enjoys exploring the private latrines that pass for family relations.

"Not exactly," Eric's voice turned into Dan Rather when he's about to tell you something really awful has happened. "He said, 'What do you mean fired?'" I looked across inviting more. "He gave me this look like I told him I was doing heroin. He was wearing this stupid apron that falls to his knees. His I'm pissed off face comes on like his ears are wired. He hears Eric has a problem zap the switch goes on in his empty head. He's swinging this yardstick long barbeque fork under my nose. Is he going to stab me or just scare the crap out of me? Then he says, 'This isn't funny.'"

Eric stopped the video our eyes met and he eyeballed the kitchen area for a second before continuing, "I said something about the manager being an asshole, and he just flipped that fork up over his shoulder and starts yelling about how selfish I am, how I haven't a clue how hard it is to make ends meet. How I needed to go and beg for my job back. I'll get nothing from him if I'm not working. He's screaming how he busted his balls for us. Now my mother and Kenny are watching. My mother's saying 'Ray calm down', and he explodes on her. Tells her all this crap, like I just did something that guarantees spending eternity in hell." Eric shook his head and continued, "I tell him I'll find another job. He says in his, 'I hate your guts' way, 'Sunshine, you don't ever blow a job until you got one lined up. That's the way life works, Sunshine, if you care.' I hate him. He talks like he's looking for a fight, for a reason to beat on me.

"I tell him don't worry and that's when he goes nuts, screaming, 'Don't worry? Who the hell is going to worry around here if I don't?' I start to leave before he belts me, he had that look if I said anything it would be wrong, so I head out. He yells 'you better come back with a job, Mister.'"

"Shit," I said. All things considered Eric is here in one piece. He was able to hold onto this until after we ate. How bad could it really be?

"I figure I'll go home early. My father will try to keep it together in front of Uncle Willy. He'll cool down and just be a real jerk once we're alone." I nodded trying to look hopeful. Eric's voice lowered and his eyes darted from me to the kitchen entrance as if fearing the McCurry ladies would over hear him. "You know, I said after we graduate I was going to live on my own. Get a job and take some night classes." Eric slunk into his seat. "But if he pushes things I think I'll have to split." Eric looked again to the kitchen. We could hear Mrs. McCurry telling Linda to wrap up the leftovers. "You ever think of killing your father?"

I nodded confused and stunned. I wanted to make my friend feel better. I wanted to call to Linda, tell her the leftovers can wait Eric needs a sensitive ear to unload onto and mine are calloused and all backed up with hamburgers. "My father can be a real jerk when he wants to." I was blabbering fiction about my father, because as lost in his own world at times, I never once feared him. Sure there were times when I caught hell, but I knew he and I would be okay after the dust settled. Killing him? I never wanted to do anything, knowingly to hurt either of my parents. Had I hurt them, of course, but had I ever knowingly hurt them? I don't think so. Knocking off Dad, the Oedipus complex coming to life in my best friend, please Linda hurry.

"I never use to," Eric's voice flattened out as he continued. "I used to just wish I could avoid seeing him. You know disappear as soon as supper was over. But the last year or two I want to fight back. And when he talks like I'm something that needs to be wiped off his feet, errr. It makes me crazy."

It would be suicide for Eric to fight his father. Bad back and all Mr. LeBlanc was one powerful guy. "You'll be out of there in nine months. Nine months and we graduate," I said.

"I don't think I can handle it the way I used to."

"Hey guys," Linda called from the kitchen, "we're going to run out and get some strawberries for shortcake."

"Okay," Eric said. I could see he was glad that we would be alone. He had answered instantaneously like a *Jeopardy* champ. His 'okay' was met with their promising not to be long. "When he starts on me, part of me wants to fight back. Wants to tell him he's an asshole, a bully. But I don't then I feel

like shit, like I got no balls. Then I start hating myself."
"Hey, you got to play it loose. Don't let it get that far."
"It's hard Danny. It's so hard." I thought he was going to cry.
"Anytime you want you can come stay with me. Just like when we were little and afraid to walk home alone because it was dark."
"I imagine taking a big knife. You know like the one you used to cut the watermelon and plunking it in my old man's miserable heart. Then just like you split that melon, open him up from his nuts to his neck. Look inside, see if there's a heart. Or get his sledgehammer from down in the cellar, kapow! Give him one between the eyes then break the son-of-a-bitch's head open and see what an evil bastard's brains look like."
"Evil," I said, hoping he'd hear the way he was speaking and begin to calm down.
"What else would you call a man who brings kids into this world then goes out of his way to make them feel like garbage every time he sees them?" Eric was staring through me, the hurt and anger jumping out of him.
"When I think of evil, I think Hitler and Charles Manson. It's a small, select group."
"And Ray LeBlanc is what then?"
"A prick," I said.
Eric looked at me and a slight smile started in the corners of his mouth. "He may be just a prick, but I wish he were dead, or gone." The smile was lost as quick as it had started. "We'd all be happier without him."
"Don't think like that. Get that idea out of your head. You don't want that kind of crazy talk running around inside you." We talked until Linda and her mom returned with two quarts of strawberries, angel food cake, and whipped cream. Eric seemed better, the more he talked the less homicidal he sounded. I told him maybe next summer we could do some traveling together, or at least see if Tarzan's brother, Leo, could hook us up with jobs down on Cape Cod. I joked that killing his father wasn't worth throwing away his life. Eric just looked at me as if he were weighing the pros and cons; my assumption certainly wasn't a slam-dunk view. By the time the ladies returned we agreed not to say anything to Linda. She would worry herself sick, and Eric sounded like his old self, having retired homicidal Eric to some dark corner of his psyche.

Chapter Four

 Eric left after devouring seconds on the shortcake. I was glad he didn't stay to watch *Mystic River* with its friends betraying each other and knifing death scene. The last thing Eric needed was justification for murder. Mrs. McCurry bowed out, not wanting to see it again so soon after last night's viewing. Maybe in six months she'd be able to watch and not concentrate on remembering what was coming next, or silently mouthing the dialogue before the actors spoke, like she did with her favorite Paul Newman flicks. I stretched out on the couch, my calves resting on the far armrest. Linda curled up on top of me. Eric's mood seemed much improved by the time he left and I thought he just needed to vent. If a worried mind were suppose to suppress the appetite Eric's appeared to be a blank slate.

 I left soon after the movie, feeling as good as one can expect when all you've done is stuff your face all day and then cuddle up with the girl you love for a few hours. Linda the only person I knew who actually stayed ahead of her reading assignments, wanted to get some of next week's homework done before she went to bed. Linda was applying for every scholarship under the sun. She would see Mrs. Ruiz, her guidance counselor, every other week to make sure she wasn't missing anything that might help her land a free ride to a good school. Mrs. Ruiz had told her fifteen different ways that given her grades and limited finances a few colleges would make her an attractive offer. Linda only slightly recovered from her May SAT's. Scores I would have gladly surrendered my first born for. For a week after receiving her scores, Linda experienced migraine headaches and a level of irritability that had Mrs. McCurry threaten her with seeing the doctor.

At the door we said a brief goodbye, with Mrs. McCurry asking if I wanted to take some strawberries home. She had bought enough to make shortcake for the week. I gave Linda a friendly kiss goodnight. She would be over in the morning to get Eric and me for school.

Outside I could feel a buzz of activity coming from Waverly. For a Monday night, especially on a holiday, the street seemed to be jumping like a Friday. Maybe Gino's or the Capri had some special attractions, bringing the local regulars as well as some of the, what Tarzan called, 'uptown opera and symphony hall crowds,' out for a late summer night of fun in the old neighborhood. Because the three-deckers are packed so close together, parking is at a premium up and down all the streets running off Waverly. But because many of the apartments aren't rented and some landlords, like our Mrs. Leonetti, don't drive, you notice where there are usually open parking spaces. Then there are stretches along Waverly that when businesses are closed, like now, should have room for a couple of eighteen wheelers. Not tonight.

I passed Gino's. The smell of beer caught my attention. I peered through the dark-plate windows. It was clear from the sparse crowd that Gino's wasn't the cause for the invasion. Then seeing Tarzan's Market all lit up, I remembered him and Jose talking about this guy, Frank Martino. The Martino's used to live on Waverly. Their three-family's lot is now the Blockbuster Video. Martino, a lawyer, living on the edge of the City Council District that includes Fairview, feels sick about the way the city has neglected its older neighborhoods. The lack of a new comprehensive high school to replace Central, and an upgrading for Delmont General Hospital, had him thinking of running for City Council. Tarzan went on and on last week about how this guy was a fighter, a regular guy with brains. Not someone who was out to make a name for himself. He could win for he was a lawyer who could tap into barrels of dough. He was running for the right reasons. He wasn't going to let the same old hacks push the same old crap down our throats. I can't remember Tarzan ever being so impressed by anyone. Martino had contacted Tarzan, months ago about running for the district's council seat. Tarzan after hearing him out was ready to push the Martino bandwagon all over Fairview and beyond.

I walked into Tarzan's and there had to be seventy-five people jammed in up close to the cash register and deli counter. They were stringing out down the two aisles that held bread, pastries, and canned goods. The old Coca-cola cooler, which served as a table for Tarzan and Jose's chess games, had been dragged out behind the checkout counter. Standing atop the cooler in lightweight, summer, dress, tan pants and a white short sleeve shirt with a yellow and blue striped tie was Frank Martino, browned by a summer of weekends at his lakefront home. He looked too good to be from here. He seemed young for a politician, maybe thirty-five. He was speaking and all eyes were on him, except for Old Mike who was making sure everyone had a black and gold Martino bumper sticker and a flyer with family pictures.

I worked my way to the rear of the store looking over a sea of mostly older men's heads. I slipped behind the Tucci brothers, dressed in their gray work shirts and pants. The Tuccis were two old retired bachelors. Whenever I saw them, I shivered a little from guilt. They made their own wine. Tarzan would get for them cases of Muscat and Tokay grapes around mid September. They had barrels of the stuff down their dirt cellar. About four years ago Eric and I, bored on a Saturday noticed that the brothers were all dressed up, wearing their Sunday best, only time I ever saw them not in gray work clothes. They were two short, square men. Angelo, the older one, was maybe an inch taller than Joe. Both had an old country look and sound to them. Eric and I were leaning against somebody's car bored as could be. Surprised by their appearance, I called, "What's happening?"

The two old guys stopped and in broken English explained. They were going to their niece's wedding in Westborough. About ten minutes after they had backed their Buick onto Whitman, Eric and I began talking about breaking into their home. It would just be fun to look around. We heard stories about them, how they had to leave Boston when they first came to this country because of a family feud that resulted in Angelo almost killing one of his cousins. They had worked at the steel mill, but moved on to better jobs when it looked like the mill was on its last legs. Joe worked as a mechanic for the City's bus company, and Angelo operated a press at the newspaper. For the last ten years all they ever did was take care of their little backyard garden, make wine, and play cards at the Calabria Club over by Tillman Square.

The day of our first and only B&E, the apartment was locked up tight. I'm not sure if lifting an eyehook off of a cellar door counts for a B&E or just an E. We began to worry about the widow, Mrs. Lombroso, who lived on the second floor, hearing us as we tried to open the front and back doors, and made half-hearted efforts to raise a locked window at the rear entrance. We had talked each other into doing something that was dumb and I was feeling good about our failure. As we were leaving, I noticed on the back porch a low hung door under the rising staircase that lead to Mrs. Lombroso's apartment. I flipped the hook that secured the door and gave it a fingertip push. It opened wide. Eric's head, like an eagle on my shoulder, pushed me forward. I began to descend a rickety set of stairs, with my first foot landing on a narrow slat my pace slowed. Eric on my heels crept along creaking stairs. His breath wrapped around my neck. The musty smells and spider friendly light made me think with each forward step that this was a mistake. Small grimy windows scattered around this pit, shed webs of light across a massive wine press, to dark wooden barrels stacked along one wall, and dusty gallons of white and red wine along another wall. We stood taking everything in and then heard something. A footstep, I'm not sure but it ran through me like a ghost on Halloween. Eric started leaping back up the stairs and I climbed up his back trying to pass, knowing in a too scared to make sense way that someone or something was down there with us.

Eric bounded two steps at a time and I charged behind him. Then his left foot slipped off a step. His body fell, arms automatically leaning into the next step, breaking his fall. His left knee banged hard on a sharp edge. He swallowed his pain. His right leg sailed backwards as if he were preparing to kick a field goal. My head down, face near Eric's butt, I tried to run through him. His right heel met my nose and upper lip like a Flamenco dancer stomping out an excited finish. Eric too frightened to slow even after I yelled loud enough to get Mrs. Lombroso to peek out all her windows. I tasted blood then felt it on my lips as I ran after Eric. Despite the pain, fear, and blood I had enough sense to put the latch back on the door. We ran to the old steel mill without looking to see if there were any witnesses.

My upper lip split perfectly in half. The bleeding gave way to a swelling, making me look like a losing prizefighter. We came up with a story, of how we got into a fight with three kids, big guys, much older than ourselves, guys from outside the neighborhood. We held our own, surprising the bigger kids with our heart. The fight took place down by the old shoe factory near Spring Street. A couple of guys came out of a bar and broke it up before anyone got too hurt.

We agreed, what we had done was wrong and stupid. I felt sick, about sneaking into a neighbor's basement. My parents believed the fight story and told me to stay away from Spring Street. My mother put ice on my mouth and gave me looks of disappointment, ranting to my father about how the neighborhood, city, world is spinning down the toilet. My father asked for names and descriptions and seemed satisfied with vague answers of "really big," and "I don't know." My mother gave me a dozen variations of sticks and stones will break your bones. For about thirty seconds my brother Tommy thought I was cool. It was a couple of years before I could look the Tucci brothers in the eye. And now I felt nervous, trapped behind them as if they would read my mind, and realize that I had broken into their cellar on the day their niece got married. I took a few deep breaths and reminded myself that my fear of people reading my mind was irrational and that what we had done deserved a boot in the ass but it wasn't the crime of the century.

Old Mike saddled up to me and said, "Danny, give this to your father and mother. Tell them this is the guy who can help Fairview while there still is a Fairview." Old Mike then bubbled over, "This is a guy who's going places. He looks like Frank Sinatra and sounds like Mario Cuomo."

"Mario who," I asked straight-faced.

"Don't they teach you anything in that school?" Old Mike frowned and then snapped, "Ask your father who he is." He weaved through the crowd, making his way back towards the speaker.

"When my daughter Marci was born," Martino was talking as if everyone in the place was his friend. "There were complications. We almost lost her. She had a heart valve that was malfunctioning. Thank God, everything eventually turned out fine. She's a healthy six year-old who gives her big brother a run for his money. But, when she came into this world, this tiny little angel," Martino said, choking up a little. There was a chorus of ahs. Joe Tucci shook his head. Martino took a deep breath and continued, "Had to go through hell. Delmont General Hospital couldn't care for her. Our family doctor said you got to send her to Mass. General. Thankfully, I had the means that my wife could stay in Boston for the three months that was needed until our little Marci could come home. I remember when Delmont General was a great hospital. A hospital we could be proud of. I'm running because we deserve a first rate hospital in our city. Delmont General use to be on the cutting edge of new technology but for the last twelve years our hospital's budget has been cut to the point that now the Mayor and Council are considering closing it. I say we need to get our priorities straight. Every city deserves a hospital that you can have confidence in."

"You tell them, Frank," someone yelled out and then everyone started cheering.

"With your help I will," Martino continued. His legs rocked on the cooler, as if he were building momentum, getting ready to fly. "I graduated from Central High almost twenty years ago. That once proud institution of learning, at the time of my graduation was slated to close. To be replaced by a new modern high school. Something like, Kennedy High. Twenty years is too long to wait. A generation of kids coming out of neighborhoods, like this one have been short-changed. I say your tax dollars are just as good as those coming from the south and west sides of town."

"We're with you, Frank," another man called out.

"With your help I will fight for the money to build a new high school. Much is being made of the growing crime and drug problem in our city. What can be expected when the city continues to cut police budgets and closes up recreation facilities for our teenagers?" He brushed away sweat that was lining his forehead and continued, "The city is planning to sell the property that was once Delmont Steel." The room quieted and the Tucci brothers elbowed each other, their necks stretched upwards. "Edbert Link is getting ready to buy up the whole of it and turn it into a strip mall. It will be the death of Fairview. I've seen the cheap buildings and kinds of stores that generally rent space in places that Link is proposing. Five acres of land in this location, I say this is where the new high school should be built. Done right, it could be the first and a very big first step in re-vitalizing this community.

"I remember when Waverly Avenue was full of businesses, and people from all over the city would come here to shop, to eat, and we were proud of our community. There was no drug problem, there was no crime problem. Turning the old steel mill into a strip mall although better than keeping it a rat infested hangout for kids and drug dealers would change the face of Fairview forever and do nothing to meet the crisis we have at Central High. A new high school right down the street from us would be a catalyst for positive changes and have a ripple effect throughout the area. I ask for your help so that I may help the city we love."

Everyone cheered and clapped. People in the rear of the store began jamming the already claustrophobic front counter area. Tarzan, standing to Martino's left, beamed as everyone seemed eager to say something positive to the candidate and his host. Tarzan's eyes met mine and he nodded to my wave goodbye as I slipped out the door.

Chapter Five

"Your brother and father still aren't home," Mom said, sitting at the kitchen table with the Sunday *Globe* crossword, nearly completed. My mother is the only person I know who actually reads all of the newspaper. Her voice was full of daylong, fermented sourness, which made the Frank Martino rally at Tarzan's, a new high school, Link's strip mall, Eric thinking about killing his father, and my running into Coach Inhorn over a bin of corn all seem ridiculously unimportant. I guessed her mind had worked out hundreds of catastrophes for Dad and Tommy, and was now handing over the missing father and brother report to me.

I put the political flyer down beside the classified ads sections of the newspaper. She looked up, tilting the newspaper towards the table, allowing her hurt eyes to meet mine. I felt guilt for having abandoned her like Dad and Tommy. Lost for words, I went to the refrigerator, taking the last piece of cherry pie and a gallon of milk. I sat across from her at an angle that made ignoring me easy. I hoped five minutes of my munching and slurping in her vicinity would make up for her being alone all day. What I wanted to do was go to bed, or lie across the den's sofa resting tentatively on stacks of art history books, dog-eared journals, and scores of notebooks that catalogue ten years of my father's obsession. Or maybe, turn on the television and forget, but the sound of my mother's voice told me to stick around, she has much to say.

"I told your brother to be home by seven." Mom put the newspaper down, as I filled a large glass with milk. "I told him I wanted to go over his homework with him. Make sure he did it all." Mom rubbed her upper front teeth over her lower lip. She went on about how she didn't want him screwing up in high school as he had in junior high. I ate pie and did not point out that Tommy was screwing up long before junior high. She went on and on about wondering what does he do when he's out, expressing fears of drugs and hopes that he would turn out okay. I stopped listening. I had heard it all before.

"Does he listen to you?" I gave a, 'who me', look back and Mom ratcheted up her anxious plea, "I don't want to lose him."

"Lose him?"

"I can't talk to him. Your father tries to involve him but he intentionally screws things up. I smell pot on him most nights. God, you were so easy."

"Are they still working on the back-steps?" My father in his spare time was replacing the six wooden steps that led from Mrs. Leonetti's back porch to the walkway. Tommy and I gave intermittent spurts of help on the project. Dad in his typical scattered fashion kept neither of us, nor Mrs. Leonetti, informed of when he would tackle the job. This made it exceedingly easy to avoid helping him. Once working with him things went well enough. He would discuss some artist or work that he was enthralled with, and I learnt some carpentry skills. Dad was working at a pace that assured the steps would not be completed until well into the fall. He amazingly was able to complete one step each time he approached the job. This pleased Mrs. Leonetti for she was able to use her backstairs as the work progressed.

"Who saw him this summer? Ricky Tarello, and that bunch. And now with school he's like a phantom." Mom folded her arms across her chest and sat back in her chair. "It's after ten, where the hell, are they?"

"Tommy's probably at the mill." I would be willing to take out loans to bet on this. I could see him with Ricky and a few other sleaze bags smoking pot on the loading dock at the rear of the warehouse. Far enough off Waverly so their boom box of rap and heavy metal would not create a disturbance.

"What the hell would he be doing there? Don't tell me." Mom's eyes smoldered and her voice became small. "Don't they care?"

I wanted to say, Tommy was just going through a phase and he'd snap out of it. Dad would complete his book and get a job teaching at a university, and you would stop worrying and drive again. But the truth was, Dad and Tommy looked at us, the Alberti family, differently than Mom and I did. It wasn't better or worse, it just was different. Mom and I saw each other differently as well. It was more than just how we viewed the family and our responsibilities for at the bottom of it was how we viewed life and we were all on different pages, at times not even using the same book. There was no way for me to answer her. They did care. It just was most of the time what mattered to them was time zones away from Mom. Even when they agreed on a mutual concern the level of care was like contrasting marshmallows to walnuts.

"I'll go get him," I said, thinking it was the fastest way of my getting to bed.

*****

The night air was heavy, begging for rain that would not come. Sweat, which I hadn't noticed earlier, had glued my tee shirt to my back, as I marched towards the mill. Tommy needed a smack across the side of the head and maybe Dad did too. But, who was I to throw stones. I do my thing and it just so happens the things I love, sports are applauded, may help me get into college, may even help pay for college. What would the conversation be like if Linda and I were thinking of eloping, if Linda wasn't tied tight to Mrs. McCurry's apron and she wanted to stay out late most nights? It would be different if Dad completed something, just said to someone, 'hey read this.' If Mom knew how little work I've done in school all these years she might be thinking differently about Tommy. Hell the kid knows it's a school night; beginning of the school year, ten o'clock is Tommy pushing the limits, seeing what kind of curfew he can wrangle out of Mom.

Entering the mill's main entrance I could hear the faint sounds of a rapper. It and live voices quickly became louder. Closer, I could see two red flares as they dragged on cigarettes. The singer sounded like a wounded goose wailing, "The man is down because the man is brown. The day will come when the tables turn and who's gonna care if you were fair. You'll bite the bullet or catch it too, so like the wolves, run in a pack and attack." At first I could see four figures, two sitting on the loading dock smoking and two standing in front of them. Not sure who they were I thought maybe it was a mistake, maybe I should have brought a bat. The stink of recently smoked marijuana hit me like vinegar on an open wound. They acknowledged my approach as I neared. The two standing figures turned to face me. I could make out Tommy standing next to Johnny Post, a kid maybe a year younger than me. A kid with a reputation for being tough, liking to mix it up with his fists for the hell of it. Tommy was full of Ricky Tarello and Johnny Post. Johnny lived a few doors up from Linda. He stopped going to school a year before he formally dropped out. On the dock was a short stocky kid we called Butch. A little older than

Tommy and for the longest time, when I was younger, I thought Butch and his sister were retarded. They had flattened noses with wide spaced eyes like the kids with Down's syndrome. I don't remember how it came up but my father said if you ever saw their old man you'd know where those kids got their looks. Then there was Ricky, tall but shorter than me, wiry, tattoos on each bicep, one of a skull with a banner under it asserting 'HOW IT ENDS', the other a pair of dice and the heading 'I'LL TAKE MY CHANCES'.

"What's up Alberti," Post said. I knew he was sizing me up. I could feel his eyes studying my middle, my shoulders, and considering could he handle me, could he get in and knock the wind out of me, would my jaw hold up, would I fold. It had been months since we had seen each other, months in which I had grown and packed on at least thirty pounds.

"It's late," I said to Tommy. I could hear being pissed off in my voice.

"Late, the party's just starting," said Ricky, smiling a let stay cool smile.

"Tommy's got school," I directed this to Ricky and part of me was looking for an argument. I looked at the three morons Tommy was hanging with and figured a quick right to Post's chin and then punch out Ricky before his stoned ass got off the dock. Butch would probably freeze with his mouth open.

"It's early," Tommy said, and with it I felt his crossing over to Ricky.

"Let's go, you were supposed to be home hours ago," I said.

"To hell with school," Tommy said, backing away from me. Johnny Post started laughing. It was a phony laugh, done to encourage Tommy or heat up my collar.

I was ready to take Tommy by the neck and kick his ass all the way home if need be. Ricky gave Tommy a look, and Tommy shrugged and started walking towards me. I looked at Ricky and he smiled again and said, "Good seeing you Danny."

I nodded and began walking. Tommy kept a few feet behind me until we neared the mill's entrance. I wanted to calm down before I spoke. I could feel the anger easing out of my hands and neck. I slowed, allowing him to catch up. I would lay Mom's worries about Dad on him and ask that he not add to her load. For now, I would say nothing about his buddies, knowing he'd just hear what I said as an attack on his friends.

"I'm not some little kid who needs his big brother to come get him," Tommy said. His going on the offensive took me by surprise. I stopped for a second and looked at him, fought back an urge to let my feelings fly and kept walking. My lack of response must have put a charge in his backbone for he demanded, "I don't ever want you doing something like that again."

"You think this is what I want to be doing?" I yelled.

"Good, then don't do it again."

In front of the closed pharmacy we stopped walking. Maybe four feet separated us. I was fighting back the desire to give him a good smack along the side of the head. "You're driving Mom nuts. She deserves better." I was too upset to say much. I was afraid if he pushed it I might seriously hurt him.

"Go to hell."

I started walking slowly, taking deep breaths and telling myself to calm down.

"This is bullshit." I could hear Tommy hurrying behind me wanting to argue. I moved slowly, pulled between wanting to let into him and wanting to just get home. "You know nobody I hang with even has a curfew." I kept walking hoping Tommy would calm himself. "So tell Mom I'm not coming home." Tommy stopped moving and stood hands on hips.

"Let's go!" I barked.

"Fuck you."

That I was on a mission I was unaware of until Tommy flat out refused to move. "No fuck you," I said, springing with hands reaching for his neck. Tommy, ready for my attack, punched me hard on the right side the chest. He let loose a barrage of punches that landed harmlessly on my arms. My hands wrapped around his neck and I drove him like a shopping cart backwards, knocking him over a line of short hedges near the drugstore's entrance.

"I hate you," Tommy snarled looking up at me.

I took several deep breaths as he stood up slowly. "Come on," I said trying to signal I didn't want to fight. I didn't want to hurt him.

"I'm not going and you can't make me."

"Don't do this Tommy." I took a step forward. Tommy lunged into my abdomen and tried to bowl me over. I grabbed his head and easily tossed him down onto the pavement. A small cut started bleeding by his right ear. I reached down to help him up and he kicked me hard in the calf. I stumbled as he jumped up again ramming into my midsection. This time we crashed onto the sidewalk. A motorist slowed but offered no assistance. Quickly, I out muscled Tommy and held him down, my knees pinning his shoulders. A stream of swears and threats flew at me. I pressed my knees harder into his shoulders and told him to stop fighting, that I didn't want to hurt him. He tried to knock me off his stomach by heaving upwards with his butt and stomach. His fight slowly evaporated and I eased the pressure on his shoulders.

"I don't want to fight," I said, only slightly winded.

"Go to hell." Tommy, tensing every muscle in his body, gave one last great effort to free himself. My control was complete. It felt good to be so much his superior. A smile started in one corner of my mouth and before I could catch myself Tommy lifted his head a few inches from the ground and spit in my face. My left hand, which was resting on my thigh, swooped down and yanked Tommy's head down onto the pavement. My right hand gave him a slap in the face that could be heard across the street. The rage scared the hell out of me. I jumped to my feet, pulling Tommy up and spinning him in front of me. Tommy's momentum pushed him a few feet and I wrapped my hand on his shoulder guiding him forward. After a few steps Tommy on the verge of tears screamed, "I hate you. I've always hated you." He went on and on about how I was Mr. Perfect and he was the black sheep. How I was always pleasing Mom and Dad, with school, baseball, basketball, Linda, working, and it had always been, 'why can't you be more like Danny?'

As we turned up Whitman, Tommy back pedaling away from me started belting out at the top of his lungs, "I'm not you," and started crying.

All I wanted was for him to stop screaming how he hated me, and how his life as my younger brother sucked. That Tommy's crapper of a life was in large measure due to my, what he considered anyway, fabulous life, was news to me. I thought Tommy's dislike of me was more a general I hate the world attitude, which had little to do with me specifically. His disliking me, I thought, was similar to my disliking cottage cheese. I stopped and said, "Let's talk."

"Fuck you!" he said and ran ahead of me up the street heading home. I hurried my pace fearing Tommy would in my absence give Mom his, 'Danny is a monster who just beat the crap out of me for no reason', version of recent events. The sight of Dad's yellow taxi parked in his usual spot in front of our three-decker added fuel to my legs. A 'things are going from bad to worse' feeling lodged in my gut. I imagined my parents already commencing in, 'I'm tired of this life battle.' Her upset about his disappearance today will get lost in her arguing that he's letting her down, not pulling his weight around here and she's sick of it. Dad backed into a corner will feel unappreciated, ranting about how well he compares regarding the home front to artistic geniuses, whose lives are etched into his mind clearer than memories of their wedding day. Dad, feeling the victim, might retreat into the den to converse with some long dead master about how the demands of the modern age drain one's creativity.

I followed Tommy into our apartment, wanting to apologize more for having the feeling of wanting to destroy him, and punch his snarling face into oblivion than for what I actually did, but I also wanted him to apologize for the double barrel barrage of hate he heaped on me. Tommy's pissed off attitude sizzled from his scarlet smacked face. In the apartment's light I saw for the first time the growing welts along his neck. His eyes raged red like a rabid dog. For now, the less said the better.

Mom and Dad faced off around the kitchen table. Mom in her fed up pose, sitting back in her chair, arms crossed, and jaw locked for war. She lowered her voice, acknowledging our presence. Tommy sulked by her and entered his bedroom. Dad, also sitting back, lifted his chair onto its back legs, looking and sounding sarcastic, knowing that stance only served to fire up Mom. I slipped by, invisibly, into the den. I made room on the couch, moving a stack of cracking notebooks onto a stack of textbooks. I turned on the eleven o'clock news, keeping the volume low, pretending interest, positioning myself perfectly to hear every word of the Alberti debate.

"Did you ever think what I might want?" Mom asked.

There was a pause before Dad, sounding disinterested and sneering at the same time, asked, "Well what do you want Elaine?" I imagined his face turning ugly with smug superiority.

"If you don't know by now what's the sense?"

"Oh I know," Dad said, like he's a victim.

"How could you when all you ever do is think about some dead artist, while I'm struggling to keep us going." Mom calmly continued, and I'm thinking there is little hope that one of them storms off to bed before midnight. "You don't have time for me or the kids, or anything else. Did you have to use the whole day?"

Dad slow to respond, and I rooting for him to say he's sorry, or he's going to put his life work on the shelf and take up full-time the job of father and husband, but when he does speak the tone continues to be that of a great man talking to a moron, "I'm not going to get into this now."

"Why, the kids are old enough to hear what we've got to say."

"You want what Elaine?" Dad, slightly, raising his voice. I think he's upset that the kids aren't going to shield him from this confrontation.

"I want some of this load that is our lives to be gone. I can't take it any longer. All I do is worry about the bills, about our kids, about are we even going to be able to stay here. I need help. I'm tired."

"You don't get it," Dad said, sounding stronger.

"Oh I get it, I get to run around juggling a dozen things all the time so you can spend the day in Boston contemplating if we would ever have heard of Brahms if there wasn't a Beethoven."

The seconds of silence that followed felt eerie. In the past when Mom held Dad's great project up as a contributor to our economic or social woes he would retreat into his world of ideas and show through actions that this work he was undertaking was important enough for him to keep battling and not give an inch. He would brood and spend whatever time at home when not sleeping or eating in the den working on the project. His retreat would increase Mom's worries about Dad following in Uncle Dan's schizophrenic footsteps. These would be days or weeks of hell for me. Their misery was contagious and I was always the first victim. I would, if Dad's isolationism lasted, take on the morose attitude of Mom, finding myself increasingly asking for God's help and certain after a week of parental cold shouldering to each other that one of them would ask for a divorce. The tension inside of me would grow as my parents seemingly became comfortable with their cold war. Mom eventually would make some peace offering, either through conversation about a safe topic, like seeing a mutual friend, or taking requests for the night's supper. I would hear the white flag and smell the olive branches in her voice, and Dad always responded.

"You used to think this was important," Dad said, sounding hurt. I wished I were still out wrestling Tommy.

"That was before we had kids, when we were kids. We had dreams. Shit Sam, the world looks different at twenty then at forty. It's called life. I grew up, I thought you would too."

"Excuses."

I could hear Mom sigh. There was a longer pause and I was expecting Dad to come in here dragging his chin along the carpet. But, he continued sounding strong. "I still get excited about ideas. I can't shut it off. I still see colors when I listen to Schubert and Mozart. I still weep over works by Picasso and Michelangelo. I see trees and it's a Pissaro or Monet landscape. I walk into a church and its Beethoven's 9th ringing from every stain glass. I see a baby and it's Mary Cassat. Degas's dancers are getting ready for the ballet everyday in my crazy head, and Renior's family and children are my models, what I see in you and Danny and Tommy. And I do love you and Danny and Tommy, I just see all of this and more. I feel these great works, Elaine in my heart. I'm driving a fare and I'm somewhere else. I'm experiencing such joy, thinking about art and ideas. It plays out in my mind. Don't you think I know it all would be easier for all of us if I just packed all of it up and put a match to it? But it would kill me."

I felt sorry for the two of them. I wanted to get up and give them both a hug. Tell them they needed each other, that I needed them and that my world was spinning fast and the last thing I needed was for them to get divorced, or for Dad to permanently leave the land of the sane. Then, as I felt I couldn't hang onto all of my crap as well as their pile, my mother gave in with a gentle, "I know." I could hear her getting up, sobbing and then both of them saying they were sorry.

Chapter Six

Eric was sitting on the third step to our back entry, as I came downstairs to wait for Linda and our ride to school. I had left Mom and Dad in the middle of trying to get Tommy moving. It was as if last night's fireworks had no effect on Tommy. After Dad threatened him with a week of grounding, he dragged himself long faced from the bed to bathroom. I thought, it a fifty-fifty bet that Tommy would be late. The bright side was Mom and Dad were talking, and the tension from last night seemed now like a bad dream. This year's stated routine was for Dad to drive Tommy to Central and then Mom to St. Christopher's. The spoiled parochial kids had nearly an hour later start time than us.

Tommy, before graduating, or was it being promoted out of junior high, announced he would not share the school commute with big brother. This was fine with me, as I imagined Linda being all sweet and nicey-nice with my little prized asshole brother. I could see myself silently boiling over and then exploding into some kind of over-reactive rage, which would appear to even someone as knowledgeable as Linda to the inner wrangles of the Alberti's as a case of my being a jerk. What would have triggered my going ballistic on Tommy would be his subtle sarcasm to Eric and me. Given life as it is, I quietly thanked Tommy for helping my senior year get off on the right foot.

Mom, slightly more than Dad, was worried about our daily travel plans. Both of them had their fingers crossed regarding Tommy. They had hoped that by his surviving the summer and starting a new school he would become less of a rebel, and if not a student at least be less likely to get expelled. They had talked with me about Tommy's preference of not riding with me. I acted all worldly and said he was probably nervous about the new school and wanted to establish himself without being overshadowed by me. I told them that the way we were getting along it probably was better this way, less chance of my killing him. Mom took a fit, telling me she expected her boys to always be there for each other. That I, as the big brother, had to extend myself, to look after Tommy, to be the mature one and let petty squabbles die out without sparking World War III. I agreed, taking the path of least resistance, reassuring her that I would always be there for him, but right now talking to him was like talking to cement.

My father told me to just try and keep an eye out for Tommy. Help him along as best I could. "You're his big brother, whether you like it or not, and I'm sure he looks up to you," Dad said, as he headed into the den with a journal and notebook in hand, and a look that pleaded with me to be amenable. I nodded and thought he hasn't a clue of the size of the gulf between Tommy and me.

Eric greeted me by shaking his head, seldom a good sign. "What's up?" I asked wanting to tell him about my dragging Tommy home last night.

"My father and Uncle Willy were shit faced when I got home. Not a word said about my dismal employment condition. No, just a lot of droning on about Dad and Uncle Willy's wild youth. Stories I've heard so often I try to guess which one they will tell next as they begin roaring about the time they stole a model airplane out of Woolworth's, or took my grandfather's car on a double date without getting permission. But, it's only a matter of time before Dad comes crashing down on me about work."

"Maybe Linda's mom will find something out today."

"Well, I figure after school I'll head over to the mall, and out of the eighty stores maybe I'll get lucky, and somebody needs somebody who doesn't know how to do anything and is willing to do it cheap." Eric had lost any trace of humor as Linda's sagging old Pontiac made the turn up Whitman. "If he gets on my case, I mean really on me, could I stay with you for a few nights?" Eric asked. He stood for a moment waiting on my answer, as Linda pulled up alongside of us. Linda slipping out of the driver's seat to make room for my long legged entry smiled a hello over to Eric, who was standing waiting for my reply. I agreed with a nod. Our eyes met confirming it, as I began to slide inside. I nodded again before Eric got inside.

"You're sure," Eric said.

"Of course, but just try to be cool until June," I said, thinking it better to have a pissed off Mr. LeBlanc with no Eric to kick around, than a dead Mr. LeBlanc and Eric learning how to adjust to life at Walpole State Prison. I would, if my parents had it together enough, discuss Eric's mess with them and my offer of a bed. To my mother, Eric was always the good, saner influence on me, beginning I think in about fifth grade when she caught me jumping off our second floor porch onto piles of drifting snow in the backyard. Mom opened the apartment door hearing Eric tell me I was nuts just as I was about to leap. Mom screamed something, which served as a starter's pistol, and off I went. In recent years its Eric giving Mom answers she likes to all her questions, letting her walk away wishing I was more like him. My father generally voices the same opinion about everybody I know, 'he's a good kid.' And with Eric around so much I figured it might be days before he realized Eric was living with us.

Eric updated Linda on his situation and she volunteered her home as another safe haven if and when Mr. LeBlanc drove Eric to his breaking point. As Linda was offering this, her eyes kept rolling over to me as if trying to get from me an indication as to what was best. Since long ago I've felt that the three of us were friends closer than blood, I was completely okay with his sharing an apartment with my girlfriend. Eric had few options that would allow him to remain out of his house for more than a day and anything that avoided people getting murdered usually got my vote.

*****

Legend had it that Dr. Burnsides had begun his teaching career before there was a mandatory retirement age and he had been given a waiver, allowing him to continue teaching until he was good and ready to quit. We guessed he was seventy-five. He recited passages, committed to memory, from novels in order to make a point about another writer's work, or give exercises having you place characters from one story into another and rewrite the ending. For an old man he walked at a good clip, boasting his health came from doing what he loved, which was in his words, 'Opening our minds to great minds, and placing them in our hearts. And this is what I plan to do as long as I have a voice and the legs to get around this school.' What he did was teach the junior and senior Honors English classes, the Creative Writing elective, and the AP English. He began our first class telling us how his reading Hemingway, Steinbeck, and Fitzgerald as an undergraduate changed his life forever. His hope was as a teacher to impart both knowledge of the subject and a love for it. The reputation he had was that his inspiration translated into a torturous ton of work for his students. The pay off for some and this is what Linda banked on was a glowing recommendation from the good doctor and some guidance from him as to which colleges this letter would have the most influence. I was along for the ride so to speak, selecting Honors English IV out of my attachment to Linda. I did this despite a warning from my guidance counselor about the rigors involved as she handed me the summer reading list: *A Farewell to Arms, the Great Gatsby, Of Mice and Men,* and *The Confessions of Nat Turner*.

I read nothing that summer other then the comics and sports' page, tucking the threatening list into a notebook that was seldom opened during the school year, never mind July and August. I did develop a game plan for surviving Dr. Burnsides without any heavy lifting. It counted on Linda thoroughly consuming each book, her willingness to bail me out, the possibility that these 'American classics' had been made into movies, and my ability to pay attention in class and remember what was said; any combination of two or three of these factors should be enough to earn a C.

The first day of class I was intimidated by the size and gender of the class. There were twelve of us, who Dr. Burnsides dubbed his 'Apostles of Enlightenment,' a number far too small for me to get by with a smile and good behavior. No this would be one of those intimate learning experiences, which made finagling a passing grade through charm alone as likely as a rabbit persuading a fox not to have him for dinner. There were nine girls most were the brainy types, who manage to be on every committee as they glided through Central with cardboard smiley faces. There was stuck-up Lauren Edwards, who would go on to become class president. There were two spooky lesbian chicks, heavy into Goth, with black nails and pounds of metal decorating their round faces. Linda had informed me that they were lovers, deep into their relationship. She warned me, "They are brilliant, so don't try to be funny with them. They love to make jocks feel stupid." The two other guys in the class were nerds from birth destined to create the next Microsoft, make billions and probably have hundreds of guys like me working for them. I was out of place, trapped. I was in the wrong place with the wrong people. A dread came over me as I scanned my classmates that first day. Only this would be a five-day a week, nine-month gig that would repeat itself with me being the lone guy who doesn't get it.

Dr. Burnsides began the class by chatting about how pleased he was that the curriculum was changed so that we would have American literature as seniors. "You will be pushed," he said smiling. Then he went into the goals for the class, "To understand and take to heart the wisdom found in the readings." We would explore, discuss, read, read, read, and write so that when we graduated we would be ready for, "the demands of college studies as well as gaining an appreciation for the human condition in its many forms." Mid-way through the class he handed out the syllabus for the year. There were eight more books on top of the summer reading list. The summer books were to be his way of easing us into the course because after Thanksgiving the pace would quicken. His eyes had a spacey old man twinkle, and his voice was soft, as if he were coaxing wayward lambs back into the flock. I felt my social-life, as I knew it, being corralled into a straight back chair with a stack of novels stealing nights and weekends.

Dr. Burnsides gave us as an assignment due on Friday of that week. Write a three to five page paper, taking one of the main characters from any of the four novels from the summer reading list and discuss what you learned from this figure. I received the assignment and knew I made a terrible mistake. I saw myself visiting my guidance counselor and asking, groveling if there was any resistance, to be moved into a College Level English class. Linda after class, knowing my lame study habits, gave me a three-minute pep talk complete with an action plan as we walked to our next class. Before she headed upstairs to her Spanish IV class she smiled and said, "You can do it." I must have had scared written all over me as she gave me a quick reminder about *Of Mice and Men*.

I landed in Coach Inhorn's Sociology class and spent the first fifteen minutes re-evaluating Linda's ideas. She had told me about the summer reading books as she consumed them before July had finished. *Of Mice and Men* was really short with a good story, an easy read. It sounded pretty good. She said, over and over, it was the most readable book she ever read. That all the characters, big or small, were easy to get into and she knew I would like it. It was mostly dialogue. From Linda's review, I thought, even me with my inability to read anything unless there was a ball involved could read it in a night. I asked her to bring home a copy of the movie from work, which would knock pounds of pressure off me. She pulled my arm looking up at me like I was a naughty little boy and said, "But you got to read it. I'll get you my book." I agreed and she added another band-aid saying she would proof read my paper, making sure I didn't make any major errors. I had no choice but to give Steinbeck and Dr. Burnsides a shot, for quitting without going the extra mile now would be something Linda would always have, a memory of me as being too lazy to do something worthwhile, something that would help us grow intellectually, which to Linda was a big deal. There would be that separation always, Linda the student, the serious one, Danny the guy looking for the easy way, the good time, more interested in playing a game than improving his mind.

I launched into the sad world of George and Lenny from *Of Mice and Men* as soon as I got home from working at Tarzan's. Within the first half hour I could relate to the steady, caring, well-meaning George to such a degree that I read until midnight when George put a bullet in poor old Lenny's skull, saving his poor limited friend from mob justice. I did not need the movie.

My paper wrote itself. Linda was impressed. "You write so well," she cooed. The organizing of my ideas was personal, while on target with what George and Lenny had experienced. I saw my world as being George's and nearly everyone who was meaningful in my life, except Linda and Tarzan, were these needy Lenny's sucking everything out of me. There I was Mom's rock, Dad's sounding board, Tommy's parole officer, Mrs. Leonetti's errand boy, and Coach Inhorn's assistant in charge of wayward potentially high scorers.

I wrote in generalities about how George being a good person was always trying to do the right thing. He took on the responsibility of looking after Lenny when the easier way would be for him to go it alone. With the responsibility came a ton of sacrifices and there might not be much of a gain, however in the end you gain more when you do what is right. George was like every good father, brother, friend in life caring for those he loves without considering his own needs. As I wrote, I saw how I approached my relationships and, although wanting to scream at times, I sucked it up and hung in there.

Dr. Burnsides passed back the papers, saving mine for last. There it was in thin red ink an A, followed by a note in clear blue, "An excellent start, you captured the essence of the main characters, and translated their tale into the heroic struggle that each of us must deal with in order to be truly human and part of a community." I read his note a dozen times and wanted to thank him. I began to think again about all those people in my life who seem to steal my joy and felt sorry for them for maybe they too were running around with a full plate, and as I was grateful for Linda and Tarzan, maybe they were grateful in their own ways for me.

After Dr. Burnsides handed back the papers he talked about the quality of the works in general and then put the spotlight on my efforts. It felt wonderful, not like getting the winning hit or sinking the winning bucket at the buzzer, but more like the quiet pride when you make the team. The down side of this was

I had set the academic bar in Dr. Burnsides' class nose bleed high, setting I assumed unrealistic expectations that would require me to get on with the readings for the rest of the year and drop any thoughts of sliding along on Linda's skirt. I would be the go to guy in class until I tripped over my tongue enough times for the good doctor to show mercy and refrain from calling on me, unless I volunteered. To flounder for several weeks, perhaps a marking period, before he understood I was a reluctant apostle was more than my ego could tolerate. Therefore I had to give it my best shot.

Chapter Seven

"Come on, get up." I could hear the words as I struggled to fit them into my dream. There I was alone against five players from Kennedy and my four Central High team mates led on by a faceless Louis Hunter and Eric, who had somehow managed to make the team, having turned on me. Nine on one, with all of them growing larger, united in defeating me, rubbing my nose in it for being the lone loyal warrior for Coach Inhorn's Central Eagles. They were ferocious, laughing at my quaking knees. My heart was ready to eject from my throat. Coach's head swelling red, screamed war commands to me, as I inbound the ball to myself. Once the dribbling started, courage returned. I raced the length of a football field. With each bounce and magical footstep, I grew stronger, eluding defenders who would tower over NBA all-stars.

There was a tug on my big toe, and a voice outside the dream said, "Danny, get up." I ran faster weaving in and out between defenders. The hand on my foot became a series of defenders sticking out tripping legs to cripple my progress. Linda with Eric, now out of uniform, sat alone in the bleachers cheering. Inches from the basket, I was about to accelerate and begin my leap for an easy lay-up. Suddenly, the pillow from under my head was pulled out and crash. Eyes opened to my father.

"It's seven o'clock. We got to get going if we're going finish before noon," he said walking out of my bedroom.

On Wednesday night Saturday morning seemed far off and plans agreed on had a reasonably good chance of being altered or forgotten all together. It was with that mind set over a dinner of spaghetti and meatballs I consented to help Dad complete the backstairs. Tommy having missed supper also missed being drafted by Dad. He assured me we would be done before noon when I had to begin my real job at Tarzan's. He joked about needing three hands to do it right, telling me all he needed was for me to hold the boards steady as he cut, and that I would learn important carpentry lessons. From Dad's perspective I was lucky to have this opportunity, a view that was completely lost on me. But, given Monday night's chaos and the relative calm that followed, I was willing to comply with just about anything Mom or Dad requested, short of parading around town in a dress.

I had my breakfast of generic raisin bran and a banana. Mom had the look of conflicting bowels as she sat across from me with Mrs. Leonetti's checkbook, phone and electric bills. Mom usually wrote out Mrs. Leonetti's bills downstairs except on those rare occasions when the older woman was out of stamps and Mom was going to be paying some of our bills. That wasn't the case this morning. Dad, face shaven and the look of wide-awake nervousness, poured himself a second cup of coffee. "Don't worry about it, if we see that little weasel before three o'clock it's an omen. Buy a lottery ticket and perform some random act of kindness," he said. The weasel had to be Mrs. Leonetti's son, Joey. I assumed, Mom was writing the checks so that Mrs. Leonetti wouldn't have to listen to Joey harping on her for having to deal with the everyday affairs that come with maintaining a home, like paying your bills. Joey, according to my parents, was trying to make his mother feel incompetent, scaring her so she'd move into an assisted living apartment.

"What do you call this?" Mom asked not looking away from the last completed check.

"What we are doing can be seen as much mercenary as it is altruistic," Dad said, and I felt lost.

"I meant our lives," Mom said, rising an eyebrow.

Dad turned his attention to me and said, "Most of the work is done I just want the last three steps to set right, you know perfect. It'll show Joey boy that his mother has good sense letting us do what we do for her." I was busy munching and pretended interest in the back of the cereal box, which was geared towards eight-year-old boys, with its ravings about a free matchbox race car inside.

"You're not worried?" my mother asked in her 'what the hell is the matter with you?' voice.

"About Joey?"

"I tell you she was in tears last night," Mom said, her face getting gray and her wrinkly forehead began invading her eyebrows as she closed the checkbook. "Said Joey wants to take her out to see Meadowbrook Village. It's where three or four other old friends of her are living. He set up a visit for her for today. You know Joey, when he gets an idea there's no convincing him of anything else, worse than a baby who needs his bottle. She started crying when I said if you don't like it just tell him you don't want to move. He'll bully her into going. She knows it and knows there's nothing she can do to stop him. She said she knows it'll be only a matter of time once she leaves here that she's dead. She said something in Italian and then started swearing."

"Swearing," I said.

"She's scared," Mom said, apologizing for Mrs. Leonetti.

"Most of those places have long waiting lists," Dad said.

"Don't you get it? Even if she has to wait a year or two, she's going to be leaving this place. Joey will take over and the rent will double, or triple. There's no way we can afford to pay more, there's no way we'd ever find a place like this for what we're paying. It's driving me crazy. This neighborhood is going to the dogs. What we can afford the dogs don't want."

Dad took a long sip of coffee and I stopped hiding behind the raisin bran. "We'll be okay. One way or the other," he said, to calm Mom's fear. His words sounded empty, like when a parent tells a little kid to let them kiss their boo-boo.

"Just saying it doesn't make it happen," Mom said. "I'll take these bills downstairs and tell her you'll be finishing the stairs today. That'll make her feel better."

"One less thing for Joey to complain about," Dad said.

"Well, you heard what he told her last week how that job should have taken an afternoon and here it is two months later and still not done." Mom shook her head and continued, "Anything to make things look bad, leave it to good old Joey."

"Does he know what a carpenter would get for that job? The hell with him, just tell her we'll be done today, right Danny boy." I nodded and felt my world was getting one more yank. There was Mom and Dad at the control panel, as our lives nose-dived into the Atlantic with all the circuits shorted out. Dad, seeing the blue skies beyond the muck, saying stay calm we'll be okay, while Mom straps on her parachute.

CARLO MORRISSEY

*****

The first half hour of our rebuilding the backstairs was spent with Dad talking about how much was already finished. "Three more steps left. The runners are new we'll just pop off the old boards. Why don't you plug in the saw while I pop these stairs?" For a man who tried his best to avoid manual labor, my father was pretty handy and had a good eye for things mechanical. I think he was bitten by the 'I'm an intellectual bug' when he was in college and never recovered.

The extension cord for the saw had to run from the foot of the stairs where my father had set up a pair of sawhorses to the overhead light on the porch landing. My father complimented me on my height, as I easily reached the light socket. "Bet you can't wait for the season to begin." The season was basketball, for Dad knew where my love was even if he did little to encourage it. I nodded surprised he didn't follow up with some comment about my needing to use my brains.

I stood by as he slid a crowbar under a step and carefully lifted it out of place. Dad yanked on the nail's head and the wood screeched as if in pain. I thought of Eric, shadow boxing as to how to deal with his father. And there was my dad with all his half-baked ideas and I felt okay even if he hadn't a clue as to what was eating me up. He at least spoke to me in ways that made you feel okay. "See how these boards have worn." I looked and nodded. "Moisture gets inside the cracks and then come winter you get freezes and thaws. Getting spongy at the edges." Dad carefully removed the three old steps looking up at me as each one came free. Nothing was said until the last board was put to one side, "You're awfully quiet."

"Guess."

"You're mother worries too much," Dad said, as he measured a board for cutting. "Even if the rent did jump here we'll manage. Never know what tomorrow will bring until it gets here. No sense to worry about possible troubles, when we got plenty of real ones to keep us busy."

"Sure." I wasn't sure how we got by but I knew it was on a shoestring, and that string was old and worn. I suppose I was conditioned by a lifetime of hearing Mom complain about the lack of money. I automatically contributed most of what I made at Tarzan's to help her pay bills. What would next year be with me in college? If I got lucky with a scholarship then I might be living away from Delmont, if not, I could attend the State College and live at home. Either way, there would be expenses, and what I made working would probably get gobbled up on books or tuition. They would be short what little I gave them.

"You don't sound convinced."

"Just thinking about Eric," I said.

"What's up with him?" Dad asked, moving to the sawhorses. He laid an eight-foot plank across them and then pulling out his measuring tape hunched over the board.

I held the circular saw and stood a foot behind him, trying to summarize the weird LeBlancs. Not knowing how much my dad knew about Mr. LeBlanc and not sure how accurate was Eric's assessment of things, I said, "Oh nothing."

Dad looked up as he stretched out the tape measure. "Well, you look like it's something."

I shrugged.

"Is he okay?"

It was the perfect little question, posed in just the right way. If he were fine why would I be thinking about him, if it were good news why wouldn't I just come out and say it? A shrug would not suffice. "He lost his job."

"Well, those things happen, but he's a good kid he'll find another one." Dad turned back to his measuring and began to mark off where he was to cut, looking relieved.

"His father went kind of psycho on him."

"Oh." Dad looked up from the wood and took the saw from me. I moved around him to be positioned so I could hold the board steady. Dad kept his eyes on my face asking with his eyes for some details.

"His father told him he had to get another job or else. His father always rides him, makes him feel like shit."

"That's too bad," Dad said, sounding touched, "he's such a good kid."

"I told Eric he could stay with us if his father goes mental on him."

"Oh."

"I didn't know what else to say. I'm scared Eric might do something crazy. He really hates his father."

"How come?"

"He talks to him like he hates him everything is always a put down. It's like Eric is the biggest loser the way Mr. LeBlanc talks to him. He treats Kenny the same way. Eric is tired of being treated like dirt."

"Sometimes parents say things they shouldn't but it doesn't mean they don't love their kids."

"Dad, Eric can't stand to be near him. It's like they look at each other and you think they're going to war. It's worse than anything I ever saw."

"Worse than you and Tommy?" he asked, sounding disappointed.

"Worse." He took me by surprise, instantly I was back to Monday night holding Tommy down, wanting to unload punch after punch. Despite Monday's rage, I knew what I felt towards Tommy wasn't the same thing that Eric and his father had for each other. No mine was frustration and disappointment over what Tommy was doing to all of us, including himself. Didn't Dad have eyes? Couldn't he tell how much worry he was causing Mom? Didn't he understand the ripple effect of what he was doing? Mom gets a little crazy, she turns her anxiety onto Dad, who eventually turns to me for God knows what, a place to explore possibilities, an ally, someone to vent to and add to my already full plate.

"Don't know, you two went at it pretty good the other night. You know you're a big guy now, a man. You can't go off smacking Tommy. You could really hurt him."

"That's not what happened." I figured Tommy must have laid a pity party on Dad and he swallowed the whole story.

"Hold it steady," Dad said and zipped through the board. "So what happened?"

"He's running with Ricky Tarello and Post. They're both headed for either an early grave or jail. And Tommy looks at them like they're cool. They got the answers. He could care less about anything, or anybody."

"So what, you're going to beat him into making good decisions?"

I felt like my father was turning the tables on me and was blind to all that was wrong with Tommy. "No. You don't get it."

"What I get is that Tommy has had a hard time with things." My father hesitated and I thought he's trying to think up some foolishness that would in an easy to swallow way explain Tommy's stuffing his life down a sinkhole. "He's angry about a lot of things, part of it probably is because he's had to follow in your footsteps and he feels he doesn't measure up." I was tired of hearing about poor Tommy. I wanted to say, he needs a good kick in the ass. "It isn't easy being the little brother, and then to have a big brother like you."

"What?" I could hear the pissed off meter in my brain surging into the danger zone.

"Well, everything comes easy for you, school, sports, friends." Look at you, so tall, broad shouldered, like you can take on the world." Dad's words were like an opened safety valve and I could feel my jaw unlock. "You got looks and brains." I could feel myself blushing. We were inches apart. Dad looked up at me, his voice encouraging, yet his eyes seemed to see things differently. They seemed puzzled, as if trying to sort out the true Tommy and Danny. "Tommy will always have a struggle with the books. In life you can do a nosedive with the books and do well if you got the right attitude. See even there you got him beat. You're a lot like me. You see the good in people, in life. Believe me that attitude with your brains and looks you can go wherever you want in life."

My eyes squinted with disbelief and I said almost to myself, "I don't know." I wanted to say it isn't a bowl of cherries for me. I bust my hump most days and feel like the reward is that I get to get up the next day and do it all over again. I wanted to say instead of worrying about Tommy how about us talking about college. Like besides you telling me you want me to go, and you and Mom are flat busted and can't afford more than a pat on the back, can't we at least talk about it? How is it a smart guy like you can't give me, your son some advice? Should I try to get loans, if I don't get a decent scholarship? Should I forget about going full-time and get a job and take some night classes?

"And Tommy has to feel like he's miles behind you."

"He doesn't care."

"That's just his anger. I can't reach him. Tried talking to him a million times, that big stupid chip on his shoulder just gets bigger. Your mother is sick with worries about him and everything else."

"That's what I'm telling you, he's got to get away from Ricky."

"He's too big to just threaten him. He lies now about everything. I don't have the stomach for constant battles with the people I live with." I must have given him a funny look because he felt the need to explain. "I can go head to head with strangers. I can battle a hundred idiots a day, as long as they're people I don't care about. But you see when I look at you and your brother all I want to do is make sure we're there for each other, crazy, huh?"

"No, I think I feel the same way. But Tommy is a different animal. I don't think he'd take much notice of any of us, whether we were calling him home for supper or falling off a cliff. If he's busy or not interested you're on your own."

"It has to change Danny. For his good, but for all of us, it has to change." I shrugged not knowing what to say, feeling my brother was like one of those shipwrecked sailors, who swims ashore to a land of forbidden pleasures and when the rescuers, his people, having risked life and limb, come for him he tells them to get lost.

"You got to stay in his corner Danny. Stay in his corner." I wanted to tell him to forget it. Tell him Tommy's corner is crowded with Ricky and Johnny Post and a score of other morons. "You can do that?"

"Sure."

We worked for about another hour, saying little. Dad's attention turned to the business at hand. I found myself admiring him and fuming at the same time. Admiring him as he meticulously measured, cut, and guided his nails through the wood assuring no bruises, letting every stroke of his hammer fall square on its target. The job went incredibly well. The stairs were tight, edges clean. My father was proud. He would put a coat of wood preserver on tonight and tomorrow night. What got me steaming was a remark he made, 'make sure we're there for each other.' It took root under my scalp and flowered in my mind like poison ivy. The more I thought the more I felt sorry for myself, for in my view I was there for the whole lot of them and all I got in return was more of the same. Mom complaining about Dad, Tommy, money, Joey Leonetti, and the neighborhood, and then Dad looking to me for help or discussing his 'great project'. It was his using the 'we're' in his summarizing his view of our family, 'we're there for each other'. No Dad, I'm there for everybody, Mom's there for you and Tommy, and from where I sit it will always be that way.

Dad began rolling up the extension cord. I swept up sawdust that had flown six feet in either direction of the sawhorses. I heard a car's door shut. My father turned towards the street then screwed up his face like when he's eaten too many radishes. With the cord around his shoulder, tool belt restocked about his waist, circular saw in one hand, and a sawhorse in the other he headed back up the stairs. "Get the rest of the stuff," Dad said, moving, I thought, to avoid the approach of Joey Leonetti, who was now walking towards us. I bent over the pile of sawdust to sweep it into a dustpan and gazed up at Joey. It had been months since I last saw him. He was milky white under hairy arms and a face that always could use a razor. His balding crown had three sweaty fingers of hair crossing over from his right ear. He waddled, looking like he was in the uncomfortable finish to a pregnancy. His arms and legs seemed thinner than I remembered. A half moon of perspiration showed through his pale yellow short-sleeve dress shirt, cupping under his flabby man boobs. His breathing was heavy, as if the warm humid air plugged up his lungs.

"What'ya got?" he asked stopping for a second near me.

"Just finishing the steps," I said, feeling nervous, wishing we had already packed up.

"Good. They're okay." I wasn't sure if he was asking or giving an opinion. He gasped and hurled himself forward using the handrail to lift, as his heavy legs pushed off. I hoped the stairs would hold, moving behind him as one does an elderly person who you fear may fall. I followed him, lugging the other sawhorse, broom, and dustpan. Joey reached the porch, his breathing smoother, adjusted now to the little bit of exercise, as my father came out of Mrs. Leonetti's shed having returned the extension cord and sawhorse.

"Not bad," Joey said.

"They'll last twenty years easy," Dad said. I could hear irritation in his voice.

"We should be so lucky." Joey sounded phony, trying to be nice.

"We're just reaching our prime." I felt Dad was telling him, you may have enough money to live in a nice place in the suburbs, and vacation half way around the world, but Joey where it counts in the flesh and bone department I can run circles around you.

"Speak for your self," Joey said. Dad reached around him, taking the sawhorse from me and headed towards the shed. "Enjoy life while you can," Joey said over his shoulder to me as he started towards his mother's apartment. I felt sorry for both men. Joey huffing and puffing, looking like he'd have trouble wiping his butt, always angling for something according to Mom, something that isn't his, something he doesn't need. And Dad, able to do so much but trapped in his world of ideas, under appreciated and self-centered enough to disappoint everyone without being so self absorbed that you want to slam is face into a door. When you tally up everything, what you get with Dad is the home team losing in the bottom of the ninth, you're rooting for him but you know you're going home with a broken heart.

Chapter Eight

"I'm spoiled, what can I say," Old Mike said, referring to only enjoying his wife Clara's sauce. He sat on an old wooden chair whose back was missing two of the five supporting dowels. It was Old Mike's chair complete with paint splattered seat and legs, a remembrance from the last time Tarzan spruced up the place. Old Mike had finished working an hour ago, but hung around talking with Tarzan about things discussed all day and everyday: prices, his aching back, how his feet only brought him misery, how the neighborhood was going to pot, the Red Sox, and now Frank Martino's candidacy. Jose and Tarzan were in the backroom playing chess.

The neighborhood was buzzing with Frank Martino. He had according to Tarzan pulled off a gigantic political surprise on the Delmont City Hall pros. Old Mike said, "He pulled a Pearl Harbor." Tarzan explained how in every city election the District Councilor, Freddy Corso, who was in Mayor 'Inky' Butler's pocket, won with 35 percent of the vote. Inky a name the Mayor despised was called this by just about everyone I knew. The nickname was given due to his black slick hair, which according to Old Mike he had professionally dyed at the posh Sir Vuillard's Salon. The other reason for Inky's handle was his inability to balance a budget. The city had run record deficits and had required a state bail out on more than one occasion. Inky's power came from the thousands of jobs he had given people and the sweet tax deals he floated to the few remaining big businesses in town. Corso managed his wins because there were always two or three other Italians, an Irishman, and a Puerto Rican in the mix to split up the majority of angry voters. Corso thought he would not face any Italian opposition and with great confidence told Butler this would be his year. Corso, according to Tarzan, in twelve years on the Council had done nothing but kiss Butler's butt. Martino by waiting until Labor Day to announce and then filing his papers at the City Clerk's office the next day did not give Butler enough time to run a couple of stooges to divide up the opposition. It was amazing how Martino's bumper stickers and cardboard signs had taken over the neighborhood. Tarzan's Market had turned into a mini Martino headquarters. Amidst cases of tomatoes and bananas were black and gold Martino signs, campaign literature, and a box of two hundred bumper stickers, which we quickly dispersed to patrons. In every small business along Waverly Martino signs were on display. Even my dad put two stickers on his taxi's rear bumper and I convinced Linda and Mrs. McCurry that there would be no danger from showing their support for Martino.

The few Corso supporters in the neighborhood for the most part sheepishly kept their opinions to themselves. Freddy Corso had little to run on, he had been backed by Butler years ago because the mayor could control him. This opinion was entirely accurate and well established, making Freddy's backers defend him with lame tributes such as, "Freddy's a good guy," or "Freddy helped my cousin get a job."

Old Mike got into it pretty good one day with Freddy's Uncle Guido. Guido lived a few houses from Tarzan's place in one of the few three-deckers left on Waverly. A few years senior to Old Mike, Guido wears a sporty black beret and uses a cane, mostly to swat flies but he claims every once in a while his left leg starts to go on him. Guido came in and started things off complaining about the Martino sign in the front window. At first it seemed like harmless jabbing. Old Mike saying that the neighborhood needed a change and Martino, a lawyer would make us all proud. One thing led to another. Their voices grew sharper and stronger with each volley. Then Old Mike roared so loud, I thought the overhead fans would start rotating, "Your nephew hasn't done one thing for the neighborhood. Him and Inky should be thrown in jail."

"You're jealous that my brother's kid is so important."

"Important. Guido, he's Inky's fart smeller." Guido thought he had called him a smart fellow and agreed with Old Mike, smiling as if he had received a compliment. "What are you grinning at?"

"You at least see what a smart kid Freddy is."

"You're as goofy as he is. I said." Then Old Mike screamed, leaning over the counter, putting his face inches from Guido's ear, "He's Inky's fart smeller."

Guido stepped back and raised his cane as if he was going to take a swing at Old Mike, who began snickering from behind the counter. "May you go to the devil, you lousy bastard," Guido said shaking his cane as if victorious.

"Get out of here before I make you eat that walking stick," Old Mike snarled, and Guido turned around and walked out.

The routine was so ingrained into Tarzan, Jose, and Old Mike that once the chess game came out, Old Mike without a word stationed himself between the backroom with our local Bobby Fishers and the front of the store manned by yours truly. Old Mike would direct ninety percent of his remarks to me, while making some passing commentary to no one in particular about the progress of the match. It was the typical quiet Wednesday evening, a couple of newly weds, just moved into Fairview, bought a quarter pound of a half a dozen different cold cuts, making sure everything was tissue paper thin. After deliberating longer than what most couples do over where to go on their honeymoon, they decided on buying some of Tarzan's famous pepper salad. There was a spurt of kids running over for one or two items that their mothers needed to make supper, and the occasional stranger who ordered up a club sandwich. Between waiting on customers I was trying to read *A Farewell to Arms,* feeling an uncomfortable level of scholastic pressure from the nerds and little Miss Perfects who were as Dr. Burnsides put it, his apostles of enlightenment. I was feeling more and more, as Hemingway lost ground to Old Mike, that my flash of brilliance on the *Of Mice and Men* report was a major miscalculation; one I was afraid I would frequently regret over the next nine months.

Doing homework at Tarzan's, although a new experience, was cool with all parties involved. Tarzan told me when I first came to work for him, "You can always make yourself a sandwich, eat what you want but don't make a pig of yourself. If I catch you stealing I'll kick your ass all the way home. If you got homework and it's not busy do it here." This was the first time I took Tarzan up on his offer regarding doing schoolwork on his dime. Despite the feeling of being in over my head, Dr. Burnsides' class had created something new in me a desire to excel in a class that went beyond a vague feeling of it would be nice to ace a class. My view of schoolwork had always been that it should not interfere with life, which was sports, Linda, and screwing around with friends. Part of it was my not wanting Linda to think I couldn't keep up with her. And part of it was Dr. Burnsides. The old man had these eyes. They kind of twinkled right before he would call on me. It was like he and I were in league. His eyes telling me that he believed I was actually a gifted student. Once or twice during a class he would aim his glowing admiration at me and say, "What do you think Danny?"

There was no way in hell I could say, which nine times out of ten is what I wanted to say, "I dunno." No, he had conditioned me within the first couple of classes to be on my toes and to make sense of the discussions that filled the room for forty-five freaking minutes, five days a week. It was intense.

I knew what Old Mike was going to tell me, as he waited for me to ring up the customer. I wished he would follow the customer out the door, go home and let me dive into Hemingway.

"The best way, to really enjoy the Red Sox was watching it on the TV and listening to the radio guys." The radio was on a shelf right above Old Mike's head, strategically placed so that on busy Saturday afternoons, whether you worked the counter or got stuck in the backroom sorting tomatoes or taking stock of inventory you could hear every play.

Old Mike continued drowning out the home team's announcers. I wanted to wave my book under his long lizard nose and snap off a self important, 'do you mind.' "Clara, says I'm nuts. Either watch the game, or listen to it. Says the TV guys are better because they're on TV. It makes me nuts. Try to explain how the radio guys are real baseball guys. They live the game. It's their life, lucky bastards. Forty-three years we're married and she doesn't know a foul ball from a home run. She's going to tell me how to enjoy baseball. The greatest game invented. You know why?" Before I could give him the answer, which had been offered by Old Mike nearly every time baseball came up, he continued, "Because there's a spot for everybody, a guy can't run he can catch, a little guy like Rizzutto can make it to the Hall of Fame, you don't have to be seven feet tall or 300 hundred pounds to be a big leaguer. That's why its America's game. It's democratic. That's why people love it in the Caribbean and Japan. They're little guys, but they can be as big in their heads as Babe Ruth. Imagine that crazy Clara telling me how to enjoy it. It's like me telling you how to roller skate." Why Old Mike picked on roller-skating is beyond me, but his rant had a flow to it, which meant I had to look up at him and nod agreement or risk hurting his feelings.

Old Mike was big on respect, you respected your elders, your parents, women, and priests absolutely; government officials you respected to their face because they were mostly liars, but they might help you, and the first sign of respect was that you looked at a person when he talked to you. Old Mike drilled this into me on my first day at Tarzan's, teaching me how to wait on customers. "Always hand people their change, tell them thank you. It doesn't matter if it's your little brother buying a stick of gum, you say thank you. You look people in the eye when you talk to them and they talk to you. Not too long to make them nervous, just enough so they see you respect them. If you work with me you got to always show respect or I'll give you a kick in the pants so hard you'll feel it from now until Christmas."

I closed my book and looked over at him as he continued talking about the great Red Sox announcers from Curt Gowdy to Joe and Jerry. This led to a recounting of the Impossible Dream Team of '67, highlighting the tragedy of Tony C's beaming and Yaz's incredible play with bat and glove down the stretch.

Old Mike was trailing off about what a great manager Dick Williams was and how that's what this team needs, "discipline and fundamentals." I began slicing provolone for a customer, a stranger who looked lost, wanting Genoa Salami, provolone, oil, and thin slices of tomatoes, on a French stick. I had my back to the front door, thinking the guy was gay with his gold bracelet, rings, and thin tomatoes. Just as I was putting the provolone away, Old Mike roared, "What the hell happened to you?" I gave a half turn expecting one of the neighborhood regulars to be crawling in drunk or wearing a cast from some interesting mishap, but it was Eric. The left side of his face was puffy. His skin was swimming in shades of pale purple, scarlet, and grisly gray, which encircled hot white welts. His nose red with drying blood around the nostrils looked too sore to breathe.

Old Mike came over to him, yelling loud enough to break through the chess masters. "Jesus Christ, kid. You, all right? Look like you got attack by those Mexican killer bees. What the hell happened to you?"

The customer looked shocked, handing me a five as I rang him up. I was glad Old Mike was there. Eric's eyeballs were fuzzy behind tears lining up on his lids. "What the hell happened, kid?" Old Mike asked, sounding soft for the first time I could remember. I could feel Tarzan and Jose behind me.

"Those punks," Tarzan barked certain Eric had gotten the worse either from Johnny Post, Ricky Tarello, or maybe from their rivals a bunch of Puerto Rican kids, who increasing in numbers had begun to flex their muscles, as their roots began to dig into Fairview's concrete. These groups seemed to be bouncing back and forth between peaceful co-existence and raging hormones bent on destruction over some remark or look. Caught between the camps were kids like Eric and me, storeowners and families trying to deal with life's lumps without going out of their way to add to anyone's misery. I saw in

Eric's hurting face a different culprit. I imagined Mr. LeBlanc losing his patience on Eric's puss.

"Get some ice!" Tarzan ordered, and I scrambled to the icemaker near the rear exit.

"What happened?" Tarzan asked. Everyone moved with me to the backroom. Old Mike, staying true to form muttered how Eric's face was looking worse with time.

"My father," Eric said, embarrassed and scared.

"What the hell did you do to deserve this?" Old Mike asked, shaking his head.

Eric sat on Tarzan's stool, surrounded by the trio. I brought the ice over. Eric's face was bloated, swollen ugly, his left side distorted like a losing boxer. "Good," Tarzan said, taking the small bag of ice and directing Eric where to apply it.

"What did you do kid?" Jose asked.

"He's been on my case for not working, getting fired," Eric said, his voice growing calmer as he spoke. "He's an asshole, a real asshole." Old Mike reminded him that he was still his father. "You don't know. All he does is sit around and get drunk and figure out how he can break my balls. I had it."

"It's a misunderstanding, he was drinking," Old Mike said.

"No!" Eric exploded then matter-of-factly continued, "He hates me, treats me worse than a dog. It only gets worse with time."

"Look kid when I was your age," Old Mike started and Tarzan gave him a look that stopped him dead.

"What happened?" Tarzan asked.

"I come home excited because I got a job at Harper's."

"The fancy restaurant in the mall," Jose said. "They get twenty bucks easy for lunch." Tarzan looked at his friend skeptically. "What? I walked by the place on my way to McDonalds."

"They needed someone weekends, washing dishes." Eric sighed. "He's such a jerk. I tell him and my mom why I missed supper because the manager showed me around and I had to fill out some forms. He's totally shit faced as usual, so what do you think he says." We all look at him in sympathetic anticipation.

"'Isn't that lovely maybe you'll meet a nice guy there waiting tables Shirley.' Then he laughed like he's some big shot. The idiot thinks I'm gay."

Old Mike sighed and then mumbled, "What is it with you kids and all this gay shit?"

"Keep the ice there. It's looking better," Tarzan said.

"I hate him. Wish he were dead," Eric said, cold and tired of life. It was the voice of an old man, who had waged a losing battle for a half-century and was ready to die worn out and defeated. I felt weary and overwhelmed with fear. Maybe Eric was one of those ticking, teenage, time bombs that explodes onto the six o'clock news. And when the cops finish talking to everyone, after Mr. LeBlanc is laid out in the morgue and Eric is shipped off to Bridgewater State Hospital, the world finds out Eric had one friend, who knew his misery, knew the destructive potential and sat on his hands hoping for the best.

Old Mike spent the next ten minutes telling Eric stories about how his father use to throw whatever was close by when he was mad at him or any of his brothers. He tried to make Eric feel better with his own horror stories of growing up with a psycho father. "One day he was drunk. Not fall down stupid drunk, more fired up rotten drunk. He threw a boot at my head. Can't remember why, I duck and the thing goes out the kitchen window. The window was closed. Crash, glass ended up everywhere. Even in my mother's sauce. He got so crazy he chased me out of the house, running after me with only one boot on. I stopped running. Embarrassed, I let him catch me. Where was I running to? Eventually, we'd be together, and he'd beat the crap out of me. He starts crying saying he wanted to kill me, his own son. He bawled his eyes out. Kept saying he loved me. The next week I'm complaining about going to the store for my mother. Whack. A boot comes flying across the kitchen, hits me in the back of the head. Maybe your old man has got the same screwy way of showing he cares." Eric looked at Old Mike like he was from Mars.

"What?" Old Mike asked. Eric waved him off.

"If you ask me you guys are all too damn worried about a lot of stuff that you need to just let pass," Old Mike said. Eric's face was improving. The Everest welts sank under the ice pack.

"Aw shit," Eric shouted, lowering the ice and standing up with seventeen years of stockpiled tears ready to drown all of us in his misery. "It's everything."

"I know," I said over Jose and Tarzan's shoulders.

Eric shook his head and Tarzan placed a hand on his shoulder, settling him back on his seat.

"Too high strung, anybody can see that," Old Mike said.

"I get up wanting to blow his brains out." Eric's head dropped into his hands and he started crying, hushed long sniffles. Tarzan kept patting him, as his whimpering head drifted down between his knees. I felt guilty about Eric's condition, for having done nothing but listened and wished he hadn't shared the depth of his hatred with me.

"Christ," Old Mike said, wrinkling up his face.

"A few years from now kid you'll be glad you did the right things," Tarzan said, sounding calm and experienced. "Whatever happened tonight can be made right as long as you don't do anything crazy. If your dad was drunk he may not even know what he did. Probably hasn't a clue how you feel." Eric's head dropped another notch and his sobs became more muffled. Tarzan rubbed Eric's neck and shoulders as he continued, "It don't make it right, but sometimes all the things that have been jammed up our ass comes out onto people we love. The ones we should be kindest with we treat like garbage." Eric nodded and his head began to rise from between his knees. "It's a big piece of what makes so many people crazy. In a few years you'll be on your own, wife and kids, glad you did the right things." Eric sat up his eyes red, damp but no longer leaking.

Eric began explaining how he called his father an asshole. How his father approached him, right hand opened to swat Eric's face like a pest that flew to close, Eric charged, wrapping his arms half around his father's enormous middle. For a few seconds man and boy did an awkward dance, Mr. LeBlanc slowed by beer and unsure what was really happening. Eric full of rage and a growing realization that he had grabbed a hell of a lot more than he could handle hung on not knowing what else to do. Mr. LeBlanc with right hand programmed to strike commenced on slapping the left side of Eric's face and the top of his head until the kid dropped to the floor. Mrs. LeBlanc begged her husband to stop, fearing the worse. Mr. LeBlanc guided by his wife's pleas went off to bed. Eric dazed ran out, not sure if he would just keep running, jump off a bridge, or search out Danny.

The buzzer on the front door called and I automatically sidestepped past the group huddling around Eric. Standing in front of the deli counter looking sideways down the aisle leading to the store's milk case, looking as if she wanted to be anywhere else, was Mrs. LeBlanc. Her short hair was pulled back tight, allowing a little tail to hang at her back. Her faded blue, cheap, polyester pants stretched tightly around her expanding buttocks looked like they were about to unravel. "Mrs. LeBlanc." She sighed and looked away.

"Eric here?" she said still eyeing the distant milk cooler, her voice small and sad like Eric's.

"Yes."

"Is he okay?" she asked as if afraid to know.

"Yeah," I said, hoping Eric would come out and they could start mending their wounds.

She hesitated and looked at me. I tried to tell her with my eyes that I was sorry for her and her family. "Tell him to come home. Tell him its okay. Everything is okay now." She turned and walked out, head tilted to the floor, shoulders narrowing, and head dragging lower with each step. My eyes darted from her to the backroom entrance, hoping Eric would be standing there, calling to her, or she would stop and demand to see him, but she crawled out and Eric remained hidden in the backroom.

The ice did wonders for Eric's face. The swelling had gone down considerably, leaving only a little puffiness on the corner of his eyes. After washing his face, his color was back to normal. Eric stood staring at himself in the murky mirror over the backroom sink.

"What do you want to do?" I asked, thinking I should call home if Eric was crashing at our place.

"Kill the bastard," Eric said, moving back towards Tarzan, Old Mike, and Jose. From the looks on everybody's face he realized this comment needed explaining. He shrugged and said, "But that's how I've been feeling. But I don't know." Eric looked at me searching for help.

"You want to sleep over?" My offer brought noticeable relief to Old Mike and Jose.

"She said its okay. I should go home. The old bastard must be sleeping, his peaceful drunken sleep. He'll probably be conked out until morning. He was so gone he probably won't even remember nearly killing me."

"Maybe you should sleep over Danny's?" Old Mike said.

"Nah, but maybe if it gets crazy again, or I feel like taking him on again, I'll just go over to your place."

"You can stay with us," I said, thinking I had never gotten an answer from my father. Eric was probably waiting for me to say something, like, I talked to my parents and they're cool with you living with us. But I didn't say anything. I hoped the LeBlanc family would magically keep it together until we graduated and Eric could leave for good.

"Thanks, but I'm okay." Eric scanned the field of unbelieving eyes and said, "Really, this isn't the first time he's gone ballistic on me."

"At least for tonight," I said.

"You're sure?"

Chapter Nine

More and more my life was feeling like a scene from an old western. The disheartened lost wagon train, composed of everybody I know, keeps trudging along deeper and deeper into hostile Indian country. Miraculously, we keep surviving, but each time the arrows get a little closer and I start considering what my chances would be like going it alone.

Eric spent the night at our place. It had been awhile since the two of us shared a bed but the arrangement worked out better than I imagined. I was thankful he would catch at least an overnight break from his father. I explained things to my parents later that night and they both agreed it was better that Eric stay with us then risk another beating. That night Eric had a long talk with his mother over the phone. Eric told his mother he would not move out now, but he might sleep over our place more than at home. I heard him tell her, "When he quits drinking, or you throw him out that's when things will be normal."

Following Mr. LeBlanc's playing handball with Eric's head, my buddy's skills at ducking his father blossomed into an art form. Between the new job, which was harder work than I thought Eric capable of staying with for longer than a cup of coffee, hanging with Linda and me, sleeping over my house a couple of times a week, and camping out at Tarzan's most nights I was working meant Eric was hardly home. Harper's did phenomenally well on the weekends. They catered to upscale shoppers, who preferred sirloin to ground beef. There was enough afternoon business to keep Eric moving dirty dishes and laying out fresh linen from noon to four. From six to closing Harper's was becoming a favorite spot for the before or after theater crowd. Eric threw himself into the job, calculating the weeks until he would have enough dough to buy and insure a cheap set of wheels. The schedule at Harper's kept him out of Mr. LeBlanc's line of fire pretty much from Friday sunset to Sunday's last call.

The rest of Eric's waking hours were spent between school, hanging with Linda and me or down at Tarzan's. Initially there was no problem with his presence at the store, since the pre-beating Eric had often hung around with me, arriving near closing time and then helping out as I cleaned up the place before Tarzan locked up. As the post-beating days stretched out, I sensed growing awkwardness in the Tarzan to Eric blather. Nothing was said but the greetings as Eric entered became less welcoming, fewer questions about family and Eric's world were asked, and the one's that were seemed to be stiff obligations. When I was alone with Tarzan I was waiting for him to drop a bomb like, "Tell your friend to get a life," or "This isn't the New England Home for Little Wanderers." But he never openly complained.

One day Eric walked in, looking like he was ready to lose his lunch. Tarzan raised his head up from a barrel of pickled peppers he was sampling and said loud enough, to stop Old Mike's complaining to Mrs. Falco about all the good jobs going overseas, "How's life big guy?"

"Okay," Eric said, like a lost sheep.

Tarzan, now up and hovering over Eric, said, "I was talking to your father the other day. You know how wrapped up I am in this Frank Martino thing?" Tarzan was bubbling as he placed an arm around Eric's shoulder. His face lowered almost kissing Eric's. "Well your dad is just as tired of Freddy Corso as the rest of us." Mrs. Falco smiled goodbye on her way out and expressed an opinion that Freddy wasn't smart enough to get mixed up in politics. We all smiled back politely. Tarzan hands on hips continued, "I told him how you like to hang around here. How you keep Danny awake when business stinks. He said you were a good kid."

"Sure," Eric said with soured disbelief.

Tarzan, as if not hearing Eric's whine, continued, "One thing led to another and I asked him if it was okay if you helped out in Martino's campaign. I mean if you're interested."

"Sure like what?"

"Well Bus Antonelli is trying to get teams of people out canvassing the neighborhood, dropping off information about Frank. They go out before and after supper." Eric stared at Tarzan, giving what seemed serious consideration for this out of the blue proposition. "Figure it'll give you a better chance of meeting some girls than hanging around here with junior."

"Huh."

"I saw one of Bus's teams." Tarzan smiled and winked. "If I was twenty years younger I'd be out with them making sure those little cuties didn't run into any attack dogs. So what do you think?"

"You said you talked to my father?"

"Yeah, he thought it was a good idea. Said Freddy Corso's got his head so far up Butler's ass he can't see what the hell's going on around here. So should I tell Bus?"

"I guess."

"Good. The other thing, maybe it'd be too much with you working at Harper's and then if you walk around town with Martino's babes."

"What?"

"You know how's I'm always thinking about entering my Fury in one of those classic car shows." Eric nodded. "Well, I was wondering if you wanted to wash and wax it. The whole inside needs to be spotless, the white walls need a lot of attention and the chrome I want to sparkle like when the sun hits the ocean. You know gleaming. I haven't got the time. I'll never have the time. I'll pay you. But it got to look right. Figure we got four or five weeks before the frost is on the pumpkin and then I'll cover her up until Easter. Maybe if you get her looking mint again I'll find the time to look under the hood. I kind of promised my brother, Leo, that this Fourth of July I'd spend it on the Cape with him and bring the '61 Fury."

Eric looked puzzled.

"Leo's been bugging me for years. There are some things that happened in that '61 Fury. Stories that Leo and me lived through." Tarzan shook his head and his voice became far away.

*****

If Eric's life seemed to be improving my brother Tommy's was wiggling its way deep into a sewer pipe. He was leading the ranks of Central High's M&M's, the mainly missing. These were kids who arrived either very late, or like Tommy were dropped off by their parents with plenty of time to make it to home room before the first bell, yet nine days out of ten were waylaid by a pressing conversation, such as who had good weed, or whose rep was slandered. Other days a flash would strike and they would find themselves back outside enjoying one more cigarette before re-entering the creaking halls of learning. Their next major decision was when would be the best time to blow off school for the day. After the second day of school Tommy was but a name on a roster to his after lunch teachers, failing to show day after day.

Central High's two assistant principals, Mr. Eugene Carmody, a fifty year-old bulldog, with a smile-less face and neck bulging out from a tight white collar, and Mr. Wilbert Smith, a younger, taller, thinner, version of Carmody. The pair when not patrolling Central's corridors checking hall passes and disrupting the pleasure of those sneaking cigarettes in the bathrooms were scowling across their desks at discipline problems. Mr. Carmody had the reputation that he took no shit. He could wear down even the most hardened liar. Mr. Smith's rep was he caught you off guard, acting like your buddy for the first ten seconds before crucifying you. Our principal, Mr. Lakeman was an invisible force, who only interacted with students during school celebrations like graduations, senior prom, honor society dinner, spring play, sports award dinners, safe places that were almost guaranteed to bring him into contact with good kids. Most of us thought Mr. Lakeman chewed Carmody out and walked up one side of Smith's head and down the other regularly; why else would these two approach each day as if on a mission to save Central from anyone trying to have a good time.

Mr. Carmody had A through M of the alphabet. To my good fortune I had one fleeting contact with him until this year. That first encounter was during my freshman year. The baseball season was beginning and in my jubilation over having made the varsity team I entered school proudly wearing my new cap. Mr. Carmody from thirty feet away nailed me with a voice used on FBI interrogation training films, "Alberti, the hat."

My fear induced a spastic hand jerk, knocking the cap to the ground. I bent down quickly retrieving the offending cap and scooted off like a squirrel dodging oncoming traffic. In a rush of irrational anxiety, I leaped to the conclusion that Mr. Carmody would immediately inform Coach Inhorn of my breaking the dress code. For the next week I worried like a turkey on Election Day waiting for Thanksgiving to pass, waiting each time I saw Coach to fire off, "Alberti, what's this I'm hearing?" It never happened. Mr. Carmody had that frightening persona nailed and to his credit many student squabbles were settled peacefully due to his presence.

Tommy, as I would learn, had by the second week of school earned a private audience with Mr. Carmody. Tommy had like dog shit on a shag rug stuck to his two best junior high twin knucklehead buddies Quinn and Dylan Vernon. Quinn was a couple of minutes older but none the wiser. There was always a hesitation in the Vernon boys reply to anything more complicated than being asked how they were. They entered high school with boot camp shaven heads and a dedication to coasting through life. What the Vernon twins had in common with Tommy was an unwavering commitment to the belief that rules did not apply to them and it was far more important to follow your own half-baked ideas than to do what was expected. I soon learned that this trio of exceptional underachievers would on most school days blow the place after first period and in defiant slow motion amble down to Benny's Breakfast Barn. Benny's offered a stick to your ribs country breakfast for less than five bucks. The healthy portions and low prices attracted a strong early morning and weekend crowd, however by nine o'clock business was a sporadic drizzle of coffee and bagels to go and a few neighborhood retirees lingering over the sport's page and a second cup of decaf.

Benny didn't mind having a few Central High truants hanging around provided they paid for their coffee and kept the noise below the 'you little dopes are bothering me level'. Benny, a gruff old Navy cook, who looked like he won a string of battles, set kids straight from day one. "You're welcome here, as long as you act civilized." Benny's policy was better than contending with after-hours vandalism. Tommy and the Vernon boys liked the idea of having a mid morning coffee break at Benny's where their lunch money would keep them in a paying seat long enough to make the idea of returning to school seem ridiculous. From Benny's they would, unless it was raining, head over to Roosevelt Park, which was about a mile from the coffee shop. On rainy days they would stretch out their Benny visits until they were asked for rent money on the table. At the park they would tramp through the small wooden area, smoking cigarettes and believing they had the perfect solution to their parents' demands that they get a formal education. After killing the morning they would make their way over to the Vernon's apartment on the edge of Fairview. Mrs. Vernon was an assembler at the Delmont Electronics Corporation, working most days from noon to four. Mr. Vernon worked seven to three delivering orders for a local trucking company. In the Vernon's apartment the boys idled away the hours between MTV, video games, and heavy metal.

I had the misfortune of coming straight home from school the day Mr. Carmody caught up with Tommy. I had a couple of hours before work and thought about tackling Dr. Burnsides' latest assault on my equilibrium. He wanted us 'to become intimate' with Frederic Henry's, from *A Farewell to Arms,* sense of alienation. I walked in on my parents who looked harried and exhausted. The vibes they were sending were toxic and I moved past them as they grunted hello's through clinched jaws, replaying Mr. Carmody's message. Mr. Carmody's voice in my home was an instant explanation to my parents' green complexion. Bang! His voice squeezed on my temples, transforming me into a headache commercial whose relief was an image of Tommy marching off to the guillotine, manned by a smiling Mr. Carmody. The message he left was that he needed to meet with Mr. or Mrs. Alberti as soon as possible to discuss Tommy's poor attendance.

I flopped onto the den's sofa and immediately hid behind Hemingway. My attention fixed on the kitchen and Mom muttering protests about her not being able to take it any more and how there would be changes. Dad countered with a low humming mantra of "That kid."

They were soon in and around me. Mom jumped from Tommy being beyond redemption to our whole generation going to hell. Dad cleared his throat and sighed every time Mom paused. I wished for Tommy to materialize and stuck my nose deeper into my book. Thirty seconds later, Mom sounding now irritated by my indifference to their crisis barked, "Danny, what do you know about this?" 'This' was said with a freakiness that dropped Papa Hemingway onto my lap.

"What?" I looked up at my mother as the hurt this was causing her poured out. I sat up. Dad lifted a pile of notebooks and journals that I had been lying across, and plopped down next to me.

"You heard that message?" he asked.

"Look I don't see much of Tommy," I said.

"This is just beautiful," Mom said, and sat down across from us in a beat up heavy cushioned chair. "What happens after your father drops him off?"

"I don't know."

"Things have got to change around here," Mom said, sounding pathetic and lost.

"It may not be a big thing," I found myself shifting into damage control. Wanting as I looked at them to give some relief, though not believing anything I said, I continued. "How bad could it be? It's not like he's suspended or something." I went on yammering about it being early in the school year and a lot of freshmen get off to rocky starts then bounce back. Have a little conference with Mr. Carmody. It'll shake Tommy up. Students walk away scared for weeks. The man works miracles.

When I stopped they seemed to be breathing again.

Mom looked at Dad and announced, "There's no way I can get out of my classes, and you'd have to come get me." Mom seemed to have moved from the brink of lynching Tommy to being concerned with weaseling out of meeting with Central High's version of Godzilla.

"This is important," Dad said.

"I know, but, how would it seem," Mom said, getting up and pacing from her overstuffed chair to the kitchen entrance. "Everybody in that place knows everybody's business. Do you know what it would be like having to explain yet another school problem with Tommy? They already have him heading to juvenile court."

"Sounds like they know him well," I said, hoping to lighten the mood.

"That's not funny, mister," Mom snapped, stiil pacing. "It would be every morning having to give the teachers' room gossip bags the update on the Alberti problems. I won't do that. Sam, I can't just leave. Call this Carmody and tell him I can't be there until three o'clock."

"How about before school," I offered, thinking here's a solution.

Mom knocked my idea out of the parlor. "And start my day with a head ache, and be up all night worrying."

"Okay, okay I'll call Mr. Carmody. Is he still at school?"

I nodded.

"Danny, I want you to start taking an interest in your brother," Mom said, sitting back down, looking a bit more at ease.

Chapter Ten

A widely held belief among Central High students is that Mr. Zwerling, chairman of the Math Department, in a past life was a Roman gladiator, who retired from the coliseum undefeated. Mr. Zwerling, a bald brick wall of a man, as wide as he is tall, arrives a half-hour before the first bell and stands at the main entrance, usually in short sleeves. His jaw jutting, telling everyone this is my place; leave your bad attitudes on the sidewalk. His eyes trained by twenty years of scanning mobs of teenagers quickly zeroes in on clothing and earphone violations, as the daily flood of students march past him. His approach to correcting student misconduct is to the point laced with sarcasm that may be interpreted as a hope that the rule breaker pushes the issue. His verbal bombasts have left students dazed, as if they had been blindsided by a blitzing linebacker.

Linda, Eric, and I were rambling our way into the building. The leaves were just beginning to change. The weather clung to the last traces of summer. We were walking maybe twenty feet behind a tall kid with pants and sweatshirt falling off him. His Yankees' cap was tilting side ways and his arm wrapped around a big hair, stick figure, who must have poured herself into her low cut jeans. "There's a dress code missy that means navels aren't to be displayed. This isn't Revere Beach," Mr. Zwerling said, stopping the pair. The young lady tried to stare Zwerling down.

He continued with his chin challenging all comers, "Either come back with a proper top or go see your Assistant Principal. I'm sure he can find you something stylish that meets the school board's approval." Zwerling then shifted to her partner who must have silently expressed some attitude that needed adjusting. "Take your paw off the young lady. This is a place of learning not the tunnel of love. Hats off as always."

"You're cracked with that," the young man said.

"Mr. Hunter, what I am or what I'm not isn't the issue. What is, are your hands need to respect a young ladies space." Mr. Hunter slowly pulled his arm away from his girlfriend. Hearing the name, I stopped, letting Linda and Eric walk on ahead. This was Louis Hunter. He had the strut and voice of someone trying to impress the world on how bad he was. "What did you say, Mr. Hunter?" Mr. Zwerling was not about to let Louis mumble anything. No, Zwerling was in his element confronting someone who dared to not conform to his standard as well as the schools. Zwerling smelt blood. His voice sounded calm, "What was it Louis?"

"I said this is fu, crazy."

"What is?"

"You are, jumping on us before we're even in the building."

"Young lady what is your name?"

"Julie McAdams," she said, through a set jaw.

"Well, Julie McAdams, what will it be?" She turned around and headed back down the stairs. Her face lit up through the pile of makeup and her high-heeled waddle sparked with anger.

I moved beyond them but stayed at the front door watching and waiting to see how this would end.

"Julie," Louis called. She kept moving away from the school.

"I'll inform the office of your tardiness," Mr. Zwerling said in a voice that was loud enough to reach the fleeing student, yet remained strangely civilized given the din around him. He then turned to Louis and in a confidential tone said, "Louis it will be a long year for you if you think the rules are not going to apply to you. Now the next time you roll your eyes at me."

"I didn't!"

"Don't make it worse. Remember who sees you every day fifth period for Geometry." Louis lowered his head and his eyes met Mr. Zwerling's. To me it was clear Louis was not going to be some blind sheep among the flock. "The next time I see an attitude, the next time you resist following my directive, I'll accompany you to Mr. Carmody's office. Understood?"

"Whatever."

"Whatever." Mr. Zwerling began laughing and then as if a switch had been flicked his face became bigger, his chin more pointed, and his smile more perverse. "You are my project Louis. You are the student who begs for my special attention. And I will attend to you like you were my only student." Louis tried to stay cool, avoiding Zwerling's eyes. His gaze caught me staring down at him from the stairway and for a moment his old attitude came darting out. "Now get to your class."

My first tactical error in reaching out to Louis was getting caught gawking at him as Zwerling chewed him out. My second error was that I waited on the third step of the massive main entrance stairway for Louis, keeping my eyes on him as he became re-inflated with each departing step from Zwerling. By the time he reached me the cock of the walk strut was back.

"You got a problem?" Louis snarled.

"No but you do," I said as he came closer.

"And who are you?" he asked sounding more irritated.

I stuffed an urge to tell him he just made his second big mistake of the morning but imagined how Coach would want me to handle this. "Danny Alberti, and…"

Before I could say anymore Louis interrupted with, "You get your jollies off watching strangers get played by that loser." Louis walked by, closer than need be, as if asking if I wanted a piece of him. His eyes glared fiercely and I imagined later he must have had to use every ounce of control to not blow up with Zwerling.

"I thought you had game," I said to the back of his head.

Louis stopped and turned back. His face slightly distorted by simmering rage. "What the hell do you know about game?"

"I know if you want to play for this school you can't afford to piss off your teachers." I moved up to where Louis was standing, beginning to soften his hard ass face. He was a couple of inches shorter than me, with large able hands attached to long dunking arms. He had the face of a warrior and the body of someone who could run the court all day.

"What do you know?"

I felt caught, not wanting to betray Coach yet needing to reel Louis off the ledge before he crashed. "You look like you could hold your own on the court."

"You got that right." I started heading up the stairs and Louis followed. "But, I got nothing to prove to nobody."

"I just love the game and, figure, why not play with the best."

"Where," Louis asked, in a 'you got to be crazy voice', "in this shit hole." He wrinkled his nose.

"What the hell are you talking about?" I could feel my patience evaporating.

"I heard the Central High Eagles got their wings clipped and the state is thinking of scheduling you against some girl teams from Boston."

"So you think you're good?"

"I don't waste my time with losers."

I was close to my homeroom and didn't want to let this end on that note. "Maybe if you played with some of us you'd think different."

"Shit man maybe, but I hope to be either in Boston or Brockton soon." Louis then shared with me how he's trying to connect with his aunt who lives in Boston, or his older sister in Brockton.

I felt a weight being lifted as he spoke for I imagined even if I dedicated myself fulltime to keeping Louis Hunter in line it would be all for nothing. "Oh, well, if things change, and you want to see what I'm made of let me know," I said and we parted. Louis flicked his hand, giving me a half-hearted wave as he strolled slowly, as cocky as the only rooster in town. The wave was a minor victory. I thought, if his aunt and sister pull back the welcome mat I have something to build on.

*****

After school the magnificent trio met as we always did at Linda's locker. Eric was mildly excited as he was getting picked up at Tarzan's at three by a couple of Martino campaigners. According to Eric the babe situation was not as promising on the campaign trail as Tarzan had made it seem. The few knockouts he had seen were already hooked up with someone on what seemed a fairly permanent basis. There was however another motive driving Eric into performing free labor for someone he didn't know. Eric, realizing his options were few after graduation, thought, becoming known by a future city councilor might open a door or two for him come June when he hoped bussing tables at Harper's would become history. A job that paid maybe ten dollars an hour with benefits would go a long way in liberating Eric from his family. His post graduate plans seemed to be sharpening: land a job, maybe picking up garbage or cutting grass at the Parks Department, rent a room in the decaying center of town, take some night classes at Bunker Hill Community College, and save every spare nickel until he could first buy a car, then rent a decent apartment. The community college path to success crystallized after he met with his guidance counselor, Mrs. Rhinehart. She laid out expenses. Even at the state schools there would be a need for him to take out loans if no one at home stepped forward to help. Somehow the conversation went to Mrs. Rhinehart's daughter, Samantha, who after two years at a community college graduated with an associate's in physical therapy and started off making thirty-five grand a year, working at Delmont City Hospital. The salary sounded astounding. Eric over the next three days did exhaustive research on the Internet all of which confirmed in his mind that he wanted to make a career out of twisting people's limbs.

Once Linda got her old bomber moving, I spotted Louis Hunter walking with his begging for a kick in the butt attitude. This time he was with two other black kids, one was Jamal Kirby, who tried out for the basketball team last year but couldn't hack the idea that he would most likely ride the bench. Jamal struck me as a kid who might be really good if he hung in there. His interests seemed more into posing that he was bad. Not a tough kid like the gang that hung around Roosevelt Square, but a kid who aspired to being a pain in the back side to anyone who wore a tie or believed rules were made to be followed.

"You see that kid, the tallest one?" I said, as we drove by.

"The one with the Yankee hat," Eric said. Linda, wisely, kept her eyes on the road ahead, because for twenty minutes after the final bell within a three block radius of Central High you drive at the risk of some one running in front of you, cars darting out of driveways, horseplay spilling into the street, a new driver getting confused between brake and accelerator, a new driver more into his friends, music, cell phone, or whatever and plowing into you.

"That's Louis Hunter," I said, showing more dislike than I thought I had for him.

"Who," Eric asked.

"The kid Coach wants you to help," Linda said.

"He's a punk."

"Oh," Linda said, not surprised as that was a common way for me to characterize a widening pool of humanity.

"He gave Zwerling some grief, had his hands all over some slutty girlfriend. Real jerk, with a royal attitude, figures he'd team up with Jamal, hmm."

"So you going to talk with him," Linda said, her eyes moving between me and the road as we left the Central High danger zone.

"I did, he thinks this is a 'shit hole'."

"It is," Eric chimed in.

"But it's our shit hole," I said. "Somebody comes here with talent could make a difference and thinks he's too good for us. To hell with him, thinks we're weak. Said there are girl teams in Boston that could whip us. He's the kid Coach wants me to reach out to. Crazy."

"So forget it," Eric said.

"I can't. In Sociology class all I could think about was how or what I'd tell Coach. He's up there talking about when society feels helpless or norm-less, and I wanted to raise my hand and say, 'Helpless. Hey, that new kid thinks he's too good for us. He's got enough attitude to fill a detention hall. Sorry Coach not a clue how to get him to try out for the team never mind keep it together if he's any good. How's that for helpless."

"Let it play out," Eric said.

"I can't, I see Coach every day."

"So did you talk to this Louis?" Linda asked.

"Yup, heard first hand what a dump this is and how he hopes to move to Boston."

"If he's moving to Boston there goes your problem," Linda said, sounding like she was a hundred years old.

"That could take months the season gets started right after football. There'll be practices and tryouts before you know it."

"So was there anyway to talk to him?" Linda asked.

"I don't know, I'll see. Maybe he'll be in Boston before the season starts."

"So don't think about it," Eric said.

"It's just I feel I owe Coach, and if this kid sticks around, I'll find myself trying to be his buddy, when I really would like to wrap my hands around his throat, hmm. Shit hole."

Linda told me to chill out and Eric changed the subject to his father maybe needing another back operation. The doctor wants him to lose thirty pounds before opening him up. Eric described his father as a raving maniac when his stomach was full and feared a dieting Mr. LeBlanc would be lethal. With that happy thought Linda pulled up in front of Tarzan's and let me out.

Before I got all the way through the door, Old Mike barked from his chair behind the deli counter, "Thank God you're here. Did you get into trouble?"

I shook my head and asked, "Why?"

"You're late." I was early and looked up at the big wall clock above his head.

"I'm early."

"My corns are killing me. I got to go home and soak them in that Johnson's foot powder." I looked over the produce case and then the deli case. I had a lot of fixing up to do and hoped he would stay until I got most of the items out of the rear storage refrigerator.

"Where's Tarz?"

"He's in the alley admiring his baby. He says business is slow and disappears. My legs are shot. Thank God business is dead." Old Mike sighed from his chair. "Go tell him you're here and I need to take care of my feet. Christ they're killing me. Don't ever get old, kid."

I went back outside and around to the alley. Eric had washed and waxed the Fury the day before and Tarzan was cleaning the whitewalls with this solution that turned the grey circles around the hubcaps into snowy white tracts after about fifteen minutes of rubbing.

"Tarz, I'm here." He was crouching so close his face was nearly kissing the front tire.

"What do you think?"

"It's mint." And it was. Eric had the hood sparkling. The red seemed deeper and the few old pencil line scratches had disappeared for now.

"After the whitewalls we'll get the grill. Then it's going under the covers." Tarzan stood up and admired his work.

"Old Mike said he needs to go home and soak his feet."

"How you doing," Tarzan asked, gently rubbing a spot near the driver's door handle.

"Okay."

There must have been a whine in my voice because Tarzan turned and looked at me with a half smile and said, "You sure don't sound okay."

"Oh just got a lot on my mind."

"Like what?" Tarzan was now giving me his full attention.

I felt momentarily stupid and began pulling on the belt loops of my jeans. "Just things, nothing really but kind of like everything." As I spoke I saw a line up of everyone in my life except Linda and Tarzan, and I felt like I wanted a break from them.

"Don't let it get to you."

"It?"

"Life, Danny." Tarzan's words patted my back.

"How can you not, when it seems like everyone, well nearly everyone I know just keeps me busy doing stuff for them, or worrying about them. They're all so needy. It's like they're always yammering to me about something. You and Linda are the only people I know that don't pile a lot of stuff on me. It's like I got to be thinking about my mother, my father, my brother, Eric, his crazy family, Mrs. Leonetti, her creepy son, my teachers, Coach, and now this kid Coach wants me to keep an eye on, help out. And I know there's no helping him." I raised my hands in frustration.

"It's because you're good," Tarzan said, laughing almost to himself.

"Well, maybe I should start being bad, because the way things are I just, I don't know." I shook my head, exaggerating my despair, which made both of us laugh for half a second.

"Not like altar boy good. No, Danny what I mean is you got so much going for you everybody figures you can help them out. And because you do have so much going for you, you usually can help them. So they just get use to depending on you. So instead of complaining you should feel proud, or glad." I shook my head slightly. "Really Danny, it's the same for me. People are always asking me for favors or advice. I think of it as everybody I know is part of my team and I'm the star. I'm batting cleanup and they expect me to drive them home. Some of the guys on my team I wish they got traded, but they're family and with me until one of us die. So count yourself lucky that you're their go to guy rather than it being the other way around. It's just the way it is."

Tarzan gave me a long look. It was obvious he was serious and for a second I considered my life and said, "I think it's more like I'm a moon struck in an orbit around planet Loony-tune. I think I'm my own man, but as soon as I feel good about things one of the Loony-tune residents yanks on my chain and reminds me, Danny, gotcha."

"That's ass backwards." I stepped back and found myself leaning slightly on the Fury. Tarzan didn't notice and I quickly straightened up. "It's like the United States being pissed off because it has extra food to send to starving kids in Africa. Your friends, your family they lean on you because they know you can handle it. The crap is piling up and they know you can help them." Tarzan stepped forward and flicked my chest with his hand. "You should feel good that you can be there for them."

"I am, but."

"But it gets hard sometimes, and sad, and confusing." I nodded as he spoke. "But don't ever back away from a friend or family. Never Danny, because if you think about it, the biggest problem we got is that everybody is too busy for everybody else. Look at this neighborhood, people get two nickels together and they're running off to the suburbs, see their mothers and fathers once a month and get all bullshit because they're missing time on the golf course, or killing weeds in their backyard."

"So I'm just being selfish?"

"No, you're just being human." I nodded and felt better as we both headed back into the store.

*****

I bounced up the steps to our apartment with two big brown paper bags filled with milk, bread, lettuce, tomatoes, cucumbers, hot dogs, and cheese. Mom had given me her list that morning. I had thought it strange she didn't call to remind me, and figured she was testing my memory for things other than sports and Linda. I would put an IOU in the cash register for the family groceries and Tarzan would deduct it from my pay. It happened without comment, as I think Tarzan felt bad that more and more IOU slips were coming his way. I walked in on Dad at the kitchen table, scribbling in his notebook with two oversized art books opened: one to a painting of fruit that looked like the curves had been squared off and the other to the *Mona Lisa*. Dad looked up as I entered and said, "Perspective taking, I need at least one chapter on it."

I put the groceries on the small counter next to the sink and began putting the food away. Mom entered from the den. I could hear the television in the background, something about General Grant and the fortifications around Vicksburg. "You got everything?" she asked and took over, quickly depositing items in the near empty refrigerator. "Your father met with Mr. Carmody today."

"Oh, yeah, right." I had completely forgotten, thinking about Louis Hunter, Coach, Eric, and *A Farewell to Arms*. "How did it go?" I stopped behind Dad who was writing feverishly, and looked over his shoulder to read, 'How we get from DaVinci to Cezanne is critical in our understanding of Picasso.'

"You going to tell him or should I?" Mom said, shaking a cucumber at Dad.

"Tell me what?" I said, knowing this was bad. The combination of Tommy and Mr. Carmody, with Mom's, 'tell him' was not the way I wanted to end my day.

Dad looked up from the bowl of apples he had been examining and said, "Your brother's testing everyone, the school, me, your mother." I thought, 'what did the little knucklehead do now.'

"He got into an argument with Mr. Carmody," Mom said, taking a seat across from Dad.

"No," I said, for nobody argues with Carmody and remains in school.

"Tell him." I thought my mother was going to cry.

Dad pushed himself away from his books and crossed his arms, stuffing his hands into his armpits. "Mr. Carmody reviewed Tommy's attendance, or lack thereof. Tommy got all hot about his homeroom teacher, a Miss Andrews."

"Anderson." I corrected him.

"Right, Anderson. Well, Tommy claimed he was in her class everyday but Monday last week. Mr. Carmody defended the teacher, saying, even if he made it to her class, why did his second period teacher also have him marked absent." Dad sighed and said, "That's when Tommy started yelling that everybody has their minds made up so why bother talking."

"Yelling at Carmody?"

Dad nodded. "Yup, incredible, you just look at the guy and you snap to attention. I told Tommy to shut up and listen and he bolted out of the office."

"Is it drugs?" Mom asked. I shrugged and pursed my lips.

Dad looked at me with eyes that asked the same question. "Mr. Carmody is giving him a week of In-House Detention. I told Mr. Carmody we would ground him for the week. He said if Tommy showed the same attitude when he spoke with him later, then he would suspend him for three days."

"Should be for life," I said, taking a seat between my parents. Their heads swiveled in my direction. "Where is he?"

"He hasn't come home." Mom's voice trailed off and she looked exhausted.

"I don't believe it. Dad, this has got to stop."

"I know," Mom said and Dad nodded.

"He's probably with Ricky Tarello and those other bozos." I caught myself from ranting about Tarello and drugs, knowing it would be one more attack on Mom's weary nerves. I stood up and said, "I'll go get him."

Mom grabbed my wrist, not to restrain me but more to convey the importance of all this, and said, "I don't want you two fighting."

"That's up to him," I said.

Dad unlocked his arms and leaned forward. "We're losing him."

I looked down at them and felt so terribly sorry. They reminded me of people lost in a foreign land, needing help to make connections for the last train to where their brains made sense. Dad his face full of purpose but without direction. Mom, anxiously bit her lower lip, the hurt oozing out her eyes.

"I'll go with you," Dad said, searching my face for confirmation, as he started to rise.

Those four little words were explosive. I could feel my face flushing. Tommy and his new gallery of friends were squeezing the sides of my head. I would totally lose it if anyone said anything disrespectful to my father. "Maybe I should go by myself." Dad stood up and looked up at me. "It might be embarrassing you know, for him to get pulled by his father."

"Right, if he won't listen to you just come home. Don't fight with him."

"You can't let him off easy, Dad."

"No. I'll start picking him up after school," he said looking over at Mom who was now standing. She nodded. How long did they think that would last? How many days did Tommy make it to last period? How about setting him up with a probation officer, or one of those tough love juvenile boot camps?

"Danny, don't fight," Mom said as I left.

I headed directly for the old mill. I flew, half power walking half a fuming jog until I reached the mill's entrance. The long stretch of abandoned buildings had an eerie feel, as night settled on the rooftops. The warehouse loading dock was empty. My pace slowed. I ran possibilities over as to where Tommy might be: hanging over at Tarello's home, the little broken down park at the corner of Waverly and Blanton that was being taken over by Puerto Rican kids from that end of Waverly, or down the railroad tracks behind the mill, or maybe he decided to hang with the Vernon twins. He could be anywhere. Near the warehouse rap music and laughter muffled the occasional voices of Butch, Post, and Tommy. The paint chipped door was opened about a foot. I climbed up onto the dock. Streams of unsteady light spilled out. Raunchy old smells of dirt and urine, mixed like day-old puke with the newer stench of smoky wet wood, marijuana, beer, and cigarettes greeted me as I entered.

Laughter grew louder. The heat and light from the fire crackling inside a rusty fifty-five gallon barrel met me full force. Everything was cast in black and orange. Cans of beer were tossed about the floor. The boom box stationed behind Post was diabolically loud. I took them in before they realized I was there. The four of them on the floor playing cards sealed off from life in this dump. Butch, a cigarette dangling from his mouth, knelt on the cement excited as he beat the others. Post, one leg crunched under the other seated directly across from me, grunted a drunk-stoned acknowledgment of my presence. Tommy, lying face down, his cards held close to his nose. A cigarette wedged between two fingers, gave a glance my way and then dismissed me as if I were irrelevant. Ricky, close to the fire, legs crossed Indian style, his wormy face half shining in the fire's glow and half cast in dark shadows. Miller beer cans stood in front of each player. I fought back the urge to kick Ricky's ass.

"Tommy!" I shouted over the din.

Butch picked up the book he made. The others slowly turned my way. I zeroed in on Tommy and he defiantly raised his cigarette and took a long deep lung full. He was several feet from me yet the smoke he exhaled slapped my face as if he were calling me out for a duel. Post made an anemic nod in my direction. Ricky looked sideways at me and said over the roar of Eminen, "You want a beer?"

The offer surprised me. "Tommy you got to come home."

"No, not now," Tommy said.

"Have a beer Alberti," Post said, looking more alert.

"No thanks. Come on Tommy." I softened my tone.

Tommy took another pull from his butt and then flicked it against the flaming barrel.

"We're playing Hearts, partners," Post said, as if offering a reason why Tommy needed to stay. "Have a beer, it's early."

"Let's go, Tommy."

"Lighten up," Post said, somewhere between suggesting and demanding.

"Let's go, Tommy."

Butch put a card down to start play again. Tommy got up on his knees, focusing on the game. Post put a card down. Tommy followed. I took a deep breath, as Ricky played his card and took the book.

"We're going."

Tommy looked up and said, "Fuck no." I was surprised at my relief on hearing 'no' instead of 'you'.

"Let's go." I made sure my voice wouldn't be lost to the music.

Tommy looked up, and said, as if he were dismissing me, "Don't bother me."

I took two steps over to Tommy. He dropped his ass onto his heels. I reached for his neck with my right hand and Post moved between us. Tommy backed up on his knees and stood up. Growing balls behind Post, he shouted, "What the hell is your problem!"

"Alberti, the game's not over," Ricky said, all calm and cool. Post, sensing space behind him, stepped back. My fists were ready to cave in his face. I looked him in the eye and knew this crazy bastard wanted to get it on.

"Let's go Tommy!"

"I'm finishing the game," Tommy said over Post's shoulder.

"What say you join us," Post said, his face snarling, out of sync with his words.

"You need to come home," I said, ignoring Post, but keeping him in my line of vision.

"I'm staying." Tommy took a couple of steps back. I could feel Ricky behind me and Butch to my left.

"You heard him," Post said.

"This isn't your business," I said, looking directly at Post, whose eyes were getting wild, like a dog before it attacks. He stepped back and puffed up his chest. His head swelled and in the weird flickering darkness of the warehouse his face grew ugly and fierce.

"He's with us," Post said.

"Johnny back off," Ricky said, and Post stepped off to Tommy's right. "Alberti," Ricky said like we were old buddies, "you come in here, you're Tommy's brother and we try to welcome you and…"

I interrupted and took another side step so that I had the four of them in front of me, "Ricky save the bullshit. My brother is coming home now and if you want to try and stop me go ahead, but he's," I pointed over to Tommy, "coming with me."

Ricky glanced over to Post and gave a slight nod. Johnny Post came charging, fists flying. I saw the attack coming and head faked him. The first punch sailed by my chin. Post's second swing landed on my chest and then I used Post's midsection for a punching bag. His wind spent. He crumbled onto the cement floor. I turned to Ricky, ready to knock him next to his partner, but he was in stunned paralysis by the quick dismantling of Post. He made no move towards me. Butch came forward and before he got close enough for us to mix it up Tommy yelled, "Fuck it, I'm going." Tommy moved past Post who was on his knees catching his breath. Ricky and I locked eyes. He raised a hand that kept Butch at arm's length. I backed out, ready for all comers. Tommy, out the door, never looked back. Post now on his feet followed me and began taunting me with screams, "This isn't over Alberti, no way." I kept my eyes on him as I retreated for the outdoors.

Tommy flew away. His head down and hands dug deep into his jean pockets. My first impulse was to motor after him. It was a gut reaction to facing danger, the desire to be with family. After a few steps, watching Tommy making tracks without a look back, without, I supposed, even a thought that maybe those three losers are beating my brains out, maybe one of them was cutting me up, maybe his only brother could use some help, I slowed down. I turned back and looked at the warehouse, momentarily glad that no one was following. My hands were okay. My knuckles had some scrapes. I walked, growing angrier with Tommy, thinking of Dad's concern about losing him. From where I stood he was already lost.

I waited on the backstairs for a few minutes. I wanted to get over Tommy's leaving me alone to deal with his new buddies. I was afraid I'd go off on him.

There would be Dad yanking me off of Tommy, with Mom screaming about 'not raising savages', as I went off on little brother. I didn't want anymore surprises, anymore hurt. I wanted answers. How did Tommy go from being the family screw up to not wanting to be in the family? Dad felt like he was losing a son, I a brother. I never thought he would line up with guys who were trying to bust me up. Because no matter how bad Tommy screwed up, I knew in my heart I was there for him. I'd go to bat, or stand up to a hundred Johnny Posts for him. It was automatic.

Tommy went straight to bed, giving Mom and Dad 'whatevers' to their outline of the New World Order. They both looked defeated and tired when I came in. I gave them the abridged version of Tommy's making it home, saying only they were playing cards by an open fire.

"He's so angry," Mom said.

"He wanted to stay there. Nobody likes to get pulled from their friends," I said.

"You didn't fight?" Mom asked.

"Me and Tommy, no, he just needed some convincing."

Chapter Eleven

Dr. Burnsides had us, after the second week of classes, move our desks to form a circle. 'Now, that we're more like family. This will reduce our inhibitions on our great voyage.' Some of the girls gave their usual ahs and ohs, as sucking up was a constant state of mind for a half dozen of them. All I know is my anxieties soared into a major panic. Linda plunked her desk dead center opposite Burnsides, leaving a space next to her for me. I stood frozen for a moment, holding onto my desk. Then I gave her futile eye and head signals to slide over. She just sat there, smiling contently, leading me to greater self-destruction. The two other guys in the class Dane Sederstrom and James Buckman wisely took seats to Dr. Burnsides extreme left, keeping themselves out of his line of vision at least eighty percent of the time. I muttered, "Over there" to Linda pointing with my nose to the extreme right side of the forming circle, but Cindy Licciardi and her cousin Jasmine wandered over there giggling about Cindy's latest plans for the upcoming weekend. Cindy was always coordinating parties, but never invited Linda and me. We stood her up last year and she formed the opinion that we were losers from Fairview. Last spring she invited us to what she said would be 'so cool' over her house. At the last minute, she called saying that everyone was meeting at the Sound Barrier, a dance hall specializing in under age entertainment. The Sound Barrier lived up to its name, playing every thing super loud and fast. We skipped it, as the ten-dollar cover fee to have your eardrums meet somewhere behind your nose was too much for us. To Linda's right Lauren Edwards, wearing a clingy top and a micro mini, slithered into the chair. Lauren recently broke up with her boyfriend of the past two years. She was doing a good job teasing half the football team with her long legs, lashes, sweet smile, and get-lost answers when things went beyond flirting. To Lauren's right sat Charlene Smith, nearly six-foot tall, light skinned African-American, who looked like she had American Indian blood in her. She was looking at Ivy League schools and opinions were plenty that she would end up at Brown on a full boat. Next to Dane and James sat the Gothic lovers, Theresa and Tamara. They settled in at the point where the circle arched towards Dr. Burnsides. Theresa looking dangerously gaunt now had a spike do, while Tamara's head looked like she had just visited the barber at a Marine boot camp. There were no options but to sit directly across Dr. Burnsides, as Carmen Garcia took the seat nearest his right and Katie Vincent the one on his left.

Linda loved our places in Burnsides' circle. Without exception each day as we dragged our desks to form it the arrangement held true. There we sat looking straight into Dr. Burnsides' long soft wrinkly face. Some days we created a wide orbit. Other days my out stretched legs could play footsies with Burnsides. Today was a small cozy circle.

Not able to sleep, after mixing it up with Post and the gang, I laid up forgetting about Tommy as I finished *A Farewell to Arms*. Not only did I read it, but I now had two fictional figures to identify with, George in *Of Mice and Men* and Frederic Henry in *A Farewell to Arms*. As my eyes closed, I was comforted by the thought, 'I had my headaches, but at least the person I loved wasn't dying on me'.

"Everyone," Dr. Burnsides announced, "take out some paper. I want you to think for a few minutes about why Frederic Henry is heroic." After a minute or two everyone but me had their head down, filling up lines, I'm sure, of insightful sparkling gems worthy of a Cliff Note summary. My mind works slower than the rest of the class. I needed some time to get a handle on the idea of Frederic Henry, the disillusioned American whose girlfriend and baby die, and he's left walking alone in the rain, as heroic. He was tragic. George and Lenny were tragic in the Steinbeck novel. What was heroic? Then it hit me why they were heroes, for in this world, the world of George and Frederic just trying to have some peace, to live, to love without having to kill someone, without having life crush you was hard, maybe impossible, but these characters gave it their best shot. They did it with dignity. They were just regular guys, battling to survive crazy situations. They weren't Schwareznegger or Vin Diesel heroes, but they were bigger and better. They wrestled with monsters that all of us will face someday if we live long enough. It was a wow experience.

I just kept trying to imagine what I would do in Frederic Henry's situation. I didn't know. Not a clue, but I would want to face it like Henry. What I managed to write was 'Why is Frederic Henry a hero?'

"Good, good, good," Dr. Burnside said. "I see you've all been digesting Hemingway," he said, staring at me a few feet away with my empty sheet of paper, "Danny, what do you think of our Lieutenant Henry?"

Everyone turned in my direction. I looked over to Linda who gave me her concerned poor baby face. "What makes the good lieutenant heroic?"

I nodded and nodded. My head was churning with ideas. I clearly saw Henry as a hero, but I was seeing everybody in there own way as a hero and I knew that would sound ridiculous. Dr. Burnsides gave a little, "Ah." It was his signal that he was disappointed, that he was losing patience, that he would ask Lauren, or Tamara, or Charlene, or my Linda to help me out. Come on Danny you know this, I told myself, but my tongue was silent as my head nodded.

"Katie, could you help Danny?" Dr. Burnsides neck turned like a snapping turtle about to lock onto an unsuspecting victim.

"The world is out to get him," I mumbled. Dr. Burnsides looked back and a slight encouraging smile began to form. "He just wanted the simple things in life." A hint of approval in Dr. Burnsides' eyes and my voice was stronger. "He was sick of the war and the dying." Dr. Burnsides was now pulling the words out of me with kind knowing eyes. "He just wanted to be happy with Catherine, have their baby. The world had gone nuts. It was a world war. All he wanted was not to get killed, and love his girl. What everybody wants. Not too much to ask, but what does he get? He's alone. The people that mattered are dead. It stinks."

"And why is that heroic?"

"Because throughout it all there's no bellyaching, he remains a man. He knows he can't change the world, but he can try to live with dignity. Keep his values. Do the right thing. It's a lot like George in *Of Mice and Men*."

"Bravo, Mr. Alberti. And what is the right thing?"

"It depends. For George it was not having his best friend abused and killed by a mob. For Henry it was trying to find peace and live with the woman he loved. I think for each of us we have to find it for ourselves."

"Interesting," Dr. Burnsides said and turned to the class, "other ideas?"

I AM THE MOON

*****

There are alleys on each side of Tarzan's market. One alley is home to the '61 Fury. It is parked exactly in the middle, allowing both doors of the hardtop to open enough without catching the sides of the buildings, so that even my long legs can manage an easy entry. There is nothing else in this alley and everyone knows it is off limits. The other alley leads to the store's dumpster. Taking out the trash, breaking up boxes, and keeping the areas clean are part of my job. When I arrive to work if there aren't too many customers and Tarzan has nothing specific for me to do, I check all the display cases and then make a run to the walk-in refrigerator and get what is needed.

Eric and I walked in, finding Old Mike leaning on the deli case waiting on a customer. He greeted us with, "I need provolone, Swiss, Genoa salami, pressed ham, boiled ham, mortadella. Our boss is killing me. Tell him this is a business not a hobby." Old Mike said loud enough for Tarzan to hear him. He stretched his long neck over the counter and, as if sharing some personal secret, whispered to the customer, "These young guys today can't be satisfied with one thing. No, it's politics, old cars, the horses. It's everything, but what puts bread on the table."

I walked behind the counter, dropped off my books, and went into the back room. Tarzan had trays of cold cuts, cheeses, sliced tomatoes, and chopped lettuce. Fifty loaves of fresh Italian bread were cut in half and Tarzan was filling them with mortadella, salami, and ham. "Hey Danny," Tarzan greeted me.

"Mike needs a bunch of stuff."

"Good. Mike needs to go home, as soon as I'm done here. His legs are bothering him. I think it's his sciatica." I nodded. "Is Eric with you?"

"Yeah, he's out front. Tell him if he wants to make a few bucks I got that chrome cleaner."

"Sure. What's with all the sandwiches?"

"A donation to the cause," Tarzan said.

"Donation?"

"Yeah, Frank Martino called for some sandwiches for his workers. I asked how many and said, don't worry consider it a donation to the cause. You can deliver them around six."

"How's that going?" The little bits I got from Eric were mainly around how the few hot babes were total airheads, who were already hooked up with other airheads. Eric did spend one day with Bus and a couple of guys putting up a hundred gold and black Martino signs, mainly in the outlying nice single family home part of the district.

"Everyone is thinking he's a shoe-in. But Inky Butler isn't going to let one of his boys go down without a fight. I figure something will happen between now and election to make this thing even nastier than it's been and closer than most people think. Rumors are going around that Martino has a drinking problem, one DUI about ten years ago. I told him, don't worry. Keep asking for a debate on the issues. You ever hear Freddie Corso talk?"

I shook my head no.

"Martino's best weapon is Corso. The guy sounds like a taped message. You know when you call a company and you get the recording. It's all pleasant and nice but you're aggravated because it isn't human. Freddie Corso has no answers all he's got are excuses." Tarzan shrugged and started separating slices of salami. "I can't believe we might get somebody who cares about the neighborhood."

I smiled, not knowing what to say, for the neighborhood was the neighborhood. I didn't have any ideas as to how Frank Martino, Inky Butler, or Freddy Corso could make a difference. I left Tarzan to his sandwiches. Eric agreed to work on putting the sparkle back in the Fury's grill. He was quiet on the drive to and from school and seemed droopy as he went in the backroom to talk to Tarzan about what he wanted done to the car.

There was a rush of customers as I returned to the front counter with the meats and cheeses Old Mike needed. In between waiting on customers, I got the front deli case looking good. My efforts had filled a few cardboard boxes full of trash that needed emptying. When Old Mike finished telling Mrs. Casaverdi how his Clara makes braciole, I asked him if he needed anything as I headed outside with the trash.

Old Mike was a whole lot less irritated after I told him what Tarzan said about his going home after he finished making the sandwiches. I thought I'd check on how Eric was doing and went his way after dropping off the trash. I found him admiring his work. He had applied a milky solution to the front bumper and grill, and was waiting soft cloth in hand to wipe her clean.

"How's it going?" I startled him.

His body reacted and then he recovered, "This?" I came around to the front of the car and took a look. "Smell this shit," he said sticking a little silver can under my nose.

"Woo! What the hell is it?"

"I don't know but, after getting a whiff, I read the directions three more times." Eric looked down at his handiwork. "Says, let it stay on for five to ten minutes. I think it's been long enough." Neither of us had a watch. I nodded and he started rubbing in semi circles, removing the stuff, and leaving a shimmer that was better than new.

"That stuff is something," I said. He kept wiping and the shine intensified. Eric worked harder on the grill as if trying to recover the gleam on a hundred year old penny. "I'll finally get to see Martino Headquarters, got to deliver sandwiches."

"It's nothing special." Eric his head down walked to the back of the car as if he were on a mission. I leaned against the building and watched. He shook the little can violently and then poured some of the toxic liquid onto another rag. He began slowly applying the nasty cleaner to the rear bumper, taking special care not to get any of it on the paint. He was meticulous, but his motions and expressions told me he was pissed off.

"Maybe you should wear gloves," I said.

"Yeah," Eric moaned and I knew there was something he needed to talk about.

"How's Harpers going?"

"Okay. The waitresses believe I'm retarded because I'm busing tables and would rather do that than wait on the slobs who come in there to eat. At least at Burger King everybody feels the same, whether you're making it or eating it, you're at Burger King. People at Harpers, they look at you like you're a pathetic freak, a loser, and the manager. A Nazi, who says anytime anyone complains, 'You don't like it, screw.' He says it like he wants you to screw so he can get somebody else in there. Somebody else who's begging for a job, who'll kiss his boots, and say thank you as the Nazi creep kicks him in the ass."

"You staying," I asked.

"Sometimes I think its better having a job you hate but need, because then you got something else to be rip-shit about. It puts your anger onto a different target." Eric stood up and snapped his fingers. "Bang."

"Maybe you shouldn't smell that stuff," I said trying to be funny.

"I was going to ask you about moving in, but then your brother Tommy declared war on the rest of the Alberti's, so I figured the last thing you guys need is another problem."

"I thought it was going better."

"When I'm at work, which sucks, or school, which sucks even more, or here, or over at your place, it's okay. But he's home all the time, worrying about this operation and drinking more. My mother says he's scared. I tell her it's him or me and she doesn't say anything." I didn't know what to say. "Yesterday, he saw my pay stub from Harpers, one hundred-eighty-three-dollars. You'd think I hit Megabucks. He says I need to give him half. I was stunned. How will I ever get out of there if I got to give that bum half?"

"What'd you say?"

"Nothing, I wanted to just tell him to go to hell." Eric's face saddened, his eyes glistened with tears. "He says you show me your check if you want to stay here. I just nodded. I hoped it was the booze talking, and he'd forget." Eric shook his head. "I give my mother fifty dollars a week. She needs it. We worked out a deal. If she's short I'll give her more if I got it. If I give him half she'll see none of it. God I hate him." I looked at the bumper and searched for a solution, but came up empty.

Eric started cleaning the rear bumper and got the same spectacular results. "What do you think?"

"Looks good."

Eric looked me in the eye and sounded like this was the most important question he ever asked, "No, I mean about me staying with you guys."

"I'll ask."

"Thanks."

"Hey, Alberti," I knew the voice and cringed. Ricky Tarello was standing at the alley's entrance. "Thought that was you," Ricky said, then posed, silently as if to say, 'Hey man look at me. I'm special. I'm the man.' But the man froze when his top dog got a beating.

Eric and I turned. Eric knew all the details about last night as I filled Linda and his ears with everything from the build up to and then blow by blow description of the Alberti-Post bout. Linda kept saying she didn't want to hear it, yet her whole body seemed twitching with excitement as she drove. Every time I paused Linda would chime in with something about Tommy needing counseling. Eric said nothing just patted me on the shoulder when I finished.

Eric stood hands on hips. "Ricky," I said, thinking you little weasel, what have you got for me, a knife in the kidneys.

"I thought we could talk." He was in tight worn jeans and a denim jacket over a gray tee shirt. He wasn't moving and I thought maybe Post and Butch and who knows what other cock roaches he might have waiting on the other side of the alley.

"Sure," I said, thinking there's nothing to talk about, except you leaving my brother alone.

Ricky entered the alley and I figured keep him at least four feet away. Make it so if he reaches for a blade you have time to react. He walked slowly, eyes riveted on me. He hadn't changed overnight. One quick right to his bony chin and knife or gun whatever wouldn't do him any good.

"So this is the prize kept under the covers," he said, trying to sound light and forcing a grin from his yellow teeth. He stopped more than arm's length away from me.

"She's a beauty," I said, tapping the Fury's hood and kicking myself for not just tearing into him for last night.

"I wanted to say about last night. Things got crazy." He was talking in a calm controlled voice. Here we were face to face after I left him too scared to fight, and he's talking like he's the guy in charge. "Don't know how it got so crazy. It must have been the beers. You know?"

"Whatever."

"See, it's important us guys from the neighborhood stick together. You know what I mean?" Ricky scratched at his cheek as if he were drawing out more information to help him.

"Not really Ricky."

"The spics are invading us. They got the park and are moving closer and closer to us."

"I got no problems with anybody."

"For now, but you wait. They're opening up little restaurants down near Spencer and Hancock Streets."

"I don't go down there."

"Me neither, but what I'm saying is they're coming up here."

"Ricky I got no problem with some Puerto Ricans I never met," I leaned slightly on the Fury and then pulled away quickly, afraid I might scratch her.

"All I'm saying is there are fewer and fewer of us guys who were born here and we need to stick together." He lightened his tone as he continued, "So no hard feelings."

"Shouldn't Post be the guy talking since he had the big ideas last night."

"He was wasted."

"He didn't seem that bad."

"Earlier we did some freebies, were blasted, then drinking all night."

"With Tommy!"

"No, take it easy. He came later, had a beer."

I imagined Post, Butch, and now Tommy sitting around getting high, listening to Ricky talk, some racial crap and I was getting more agitated. "Ricky, listen my brother Tommy likes hanging with you guys. I don't know why but he does."

Ricky interrupted, "Good kid."

I raised my hand to stop him. "He's off limits to you guys. I don't care what you do in the old mill, but you do it without Tommy."

"I'm not his pops."

"Well, I'm telling you." I could feel my heart pounding and my mouth drying.

"It's a free country Alberti. I don't tell nobody who they can hang with." He spoke in this calm almost quiet voice.

"But I'm telling you." I waved my index finger at him like an angry parent telling Junior to clean his room.

"Is there an 'or else' to this?" Ricky smirked making me feel stupid.

I took a deep breath and said, "It'd just be better for everyone."

Tarzan, wondering what happened to me, came up from behind Ricky and demanded, "There a problem here?"

Ricky turned and Tarzan looked through him with a loathsomeness that hurt. "No, just admiring the wheels." Ricky was still being Mister Cool.

"That right Danny?" Tarzan asked, keeping his eyes on Ricky.

"Yeah, the car is really looking good," I said.

"What do you do with yourself, Ricky?" Tarzan asked.

"You know, just hanging out?"

Tarzan stepped forward and lowered his voice as if he didn't want any stray ears picking this up. "I hear things about you and it isn't good."

"Can't believe everything you hear." Ricky's voice cracked a little and his hands, at his sides, acted nervous. Cool evaporated in Tarzan's shadow.

"Well, I hear from different people Ricky that you're selling pot and cocaine." Ricky hissed and wrinkled his forehead. "And other shit. And I believe them."

"Believe what you want." Ricky started to walk around Tarzan.

Tarzan grabbed Ricky's arm and with a yank, as if guiding a wayward child, brought him in close to him. "If I ever see or hear that you're selling any of that shit down here I'll boot your ass all the way home."

"You're crazy," Ricky said, mustering up a whole lot more defiance than I ever heard anyone give Tarzan.

"You got that right," Tarzan said, squeezing his arm before pushing him away. Ricky, his head tilted down, walked out slowly. When Ricky rounded the corner Tarzan said, "That kid is trouble, has been all his life. I don't want him around here. Was he trying to sell you some shit?"

"No," we both said.

Tarzan said, "Good." I felt myself relaxing. Tarzan stood for a while studying the Fury before we all went back inside the store.

*****

Eric took a ride with me over to Martino Headquarters. Driving Tarzan's van made me feel like a baseball bat was rammed up my butt. Tarzan said a thousand times, the only way you get good at something is with practice. But whenever he gave me the keys he always said, 'Be careful.' I wanted to say that when I drive I'm extremely careful 99 percent of the time. It's that lousy moment that I decide to change the radio station, give eye contact to my passengers, or reach for a can of soda that a light changes, or somebody decides to cut in front of me. But it's getting better.

We spent the time dissecting Ricky Tarello, agreeing there would be more trouble if Tommy kept hanging with those clowns. Martino's Headquarters was in the old Lancaster Pharmacy, which closed about ten years ago. It was in the south end of Main Street, at the western fringe of our district. This end of Main Street showed the slow rot of urban neglect. About every third storefront was boarded up, or was being used for something that represented several steps down from the business that was there a few years before. The support for Frank Martino was overwhelming. Nearly every store had the black and gold posters displayed in their windows and many of the boarded up properties were plastered with Martino signs. Scattered about were Corso's red and white signs. Corso seemed to be relying on several large billboards, strategically placed at busy intersections throughout the district. The billboards had a picture of Freddie talking to an elderly woman who was sitting on her porch. There was a caption to the left of the woman that said, 'Re-elect a Councilman who cares, Vote Corso.' The Corso campaign ran regular newspaper ads that gave in less than ten words his position on key issues. Old Mike said Freddie was trying to buy the election.

I parked across from Martino Headquarters in the empty lot where the old Fitzpatrick's Clothing Store had once stood. "You going to talk to your parents tonight?" Eric asked as I turned off the engine.

"I guess." I looked over and Eric was holding onto the door handle with one hand and clutching his left knee with the other. "If there isn't anything crazy going on, you know."

"Because, I'm thinking there's no way I can stay there and pay for his good times. No way. I know I'll," Eric paused and then as if substituting a word said, "blow."

"Don't do anything stupid."

"You got to talk to them, because I don't think I'll last at my place."

"I just don't want to say something if they're all bent out of shape with Tommy."

"I know." Eric's face darkened and he crossed his arms. "I just know I can't handle it much longer. I hate him, can't look at the bastard."

"Stay over tonight."

"Nah, if you talk with them it could be screwy with me there." Eric uncrossed his arms and began pressing his palms on his knees. "You're going to talk with them?"

"Okay, okay, unless Tommy pulls something major."

"I think more about it," Eric said, looking at me.

Fear was gripping me and I kept my eyes straight ahead. "What?"

"Cutting his throat, and slitting him from his balls to his mouth."

"Come on."

"Danny, I have one happy memory of him. I was nine years old and he took me and Kenny to the movies. Disney, *Song of the South*. The whole time there, going and coming home he didn't yell, not once. He didn't make fun of us. Back then he used to call us his two stupid monkeys, Monkey See and Monkey Do. It was said like he meant it. There wasn't any joke. It was how he referred to us when he wasn't pissed off. Usually we avoided him because he was always pissed off. It was torture. Everything was wrong and he'd yell until you cried and then he'd say now I'll give you something to cry about and wham! He's slapping you across the room. Then it was get out of my sight you little baby. Or he'd say to Mom get these girls out of here. But that day he was nice to us. It was like he was glad to be with us," Eric's voice trailed off, "the only time."

"I'll talk to them. Don't do anything stupid."

Eric nodded. I closed my eyes and fought back tears.

Chapter Twelve

I jogged home after work with a dozen of eggs for Mrs. Leonetti cradled under my arm. Eric decided to stay at Martino Headquarters and get a free meal. He was certain someone there would give him a lift home after an hour of knocking on doors and spreading the word. He seemed less down once he started mingling with some of his new campaign acquaintances. There were dozens of people standing around talking and drinking coffee. Some guys kept eyeballing us as we brought in the sandwiches and I thought they were there for the food. A couple of middle-aged women were on the phones jotting stuff down. As I was leaving, Frank Martino came in and we almost collided in the doorway. He gave me this big hello and said, "Big Dan, Tarzan's main man." It may sound dumb but I felt better that he remembered me. Until I got back to the store, I was trying to figure out how he knew my name and settled on the idea that Tarzan must have told him that he was sending me over with the food.

Mrs. Leonetti was a second grandmother to me. Everything in her apartment was where it should be. The aromas from what she had made that day, garlic, oil, cheese, mint, parsley, peppers, greeted you usually before she opened the door. It was always welcoming. My mother would complain that at her age Mrs. Leonetti put her to shame as a housekeeper.

Her sweet old eyes seemed so happy to see me, as her outstretched arms and hands reached for my face. I bent down and she caressed my face and said, "Danny, you're such a good boy." She then kissed my cheek and hugged me. It was always that way on first seeing each other.

"Come in," she said, taking the eggs from me. "How much do I owe you?"

"A dollar," I said.

"Only a dollar," She said, looking surprised. It was always the same look of astonishment whenever I told her the price.

"With my discount, you know."

Mrs. Leonetti went to her change purse and pulled out two neatly folded dollars and took my hand. She placed the money in my palm and as I started to protest she said, "You do me a big favor. It's hard for me to go out at night, even to Anthony's store." She always called Tarzan Anthony. She was the only person I knew who did.

"It's nothing, I had to come home."

"Sit," she said and tugged on my sleeve. "I made a carrot cake for my Joey. He said he needs to lose weight. He got mad. Sit. I told him when you got married your diet changed and you got fat. Don't blame me. He got more mad. Sit down."

"Okay." I sat down at the kitchen table where a beautiful carrot cake waited. It had thick cream cheese frosting and slivers of carrots decorated the top. Mrs. Leonetti's was the best, loaded with raisins and diced walnuts.

"You want some hot chocolate?" she asked, cutting me a slice that could easily serve two people.

"No."

She walked over to her refrigerator and said, "I'll get you some milk." I nodded, as the first delicious bite landed in my mouth.

She handed me a large glass of milk.

"It's great," I said.

She sat down across from me. "You're such a good looking boy. Your grandfather, your forehead, and nose yes its Lorenzo Alberti. As you get older you'll look more like him. It happens to all of us. We grow into our parents," she sighed, "poor man, Lorenzo."

"Poor," I asked.

"Oh, to lose a child," She said, shook her head and I recalled the story of Uncle Larry and his tragic car accident. I nodded and took a big swallow of milk. "There is no pain like that."

She looked admiringly as I chewed. "Do you know the story about the Alberti and the Petruzzi Families?" Her maiden name was Petruzzi and I had heard bits and pieces over time about my great grandfather saving Mrs. Leonetti's father's store during the great depression. Before I could say anything, she told me how her father came to this country from Bari in southern Italy. He went to work at the Baines Nail and Screw Company, which went out of business before I was born. How he worked like a dog and managed to save enough to open a business in 1928.

"Twenty years after coming to the greatest country in the world, my father opened Petruzzi's Market. It was a lot like where you work. They had fresh meats and cheeses, fruits and vegetables. I was just a baby when he opened it, but my mama would tell the story of how papa cried before he opened the door for the first time. I never saw him cry, not even when my brother Rudolph died from the fever.

"Your great grandfather, Roberto, was a saint in our house, a saint. You know about the Great Depression from your history books?" I nodded. "Well, I know it from living. When it was real bad I was too small to remember, but my brothers and sisters told me the stories. Men stood all day waiting for a chance to work, day after day. There were lines for bread, coffee, flour. Grown men passing around a cigarette like it was gold. Everyone was poor, but we had fun. I don't know if you kids with your computers and telephones are as happy as we were with nothing but each other."

She looked forgetfully for a moment and then continued, "My father opened his store in 1928, more than a year before the trouble started. His market was where Gino's bar is. We were doing so good, my older brothers Joe and Frank worked with my father. They told me all about it, the customers, special orders. He had jars of licorice and would bring some home on Saturday nights. Then the bottom fell out, and nobody in this neighborhood had even two nickels to rub together. People joked, its okay to have holes in your pockets because there's nothing to put in them. My father gave out too much credit, thinking people would soon be working, but it didn't happen that way. Some people never recovered. They lost everything. That would have happened to us if Roberto Alberti didn't give my father three hundred and twenty-two dollars. That's what papa owed the bank on the store and he had nothing but bills. When you have nothing three hundred dollars might as well be a million.

"Your great grandfather had some money. He was working, right through the depression. He had a job with the railroad. They cut their work force in half. The men who were lucky, like your grandfather, great grandfather, worked all the time, eighty hours a week. They killed those men but at least they could feed their families."

I finished my cake and she said, "Have some more."

"No, I haven't had supper yet."

"You want some pasta fagioli?"

"No, I should get going."

"It's all ready. I just have to heat it up. Remember when you and Tommy were little and you'd have lunch with me. You loved my chicken soup." I got ready for her to tell me how one day when I was about six I told her she should come live with us so we could eat her soup everyday. She told the story as if on cue and then asked, "Some nice pasta fagioli?"

"No, I'm sure my mother has something for me."

She smiled as if remembering where she left off and continued, "But your great grandfather just gave my father the money. My father promised to pay him back but instead as long as we had the store your money was no good. Your great grandfather said, when my father tried to pay him, 'You are the neighborhood. Without your store how many families would have died.' That's what my Joey doesn't understand. This is my life. This house, this neighborhood, these stories, that's what I have."

"I should get going." I stood up and turned towards the door.

"Take some cake for your father and brother."

"Okay." It was a carrot cake that cookbooks could feature. I figured after supper another piece would go down nice.

She got up to get a paper plate for the cake and I noticed sticking out of her book on horoscopes a pamphlet about Meadowbrook Village. She saw me staring at the book and said, "I know you're not suppose to believe in this stuff, but sometimes I have weeks that seem to be exactly as the stars predicted." She smiled and shrugged.

"No, I was looking at that thing from Meadowbrook Village."

"Look at it." She cut me a piece of cake that would leave her next to nothing.

"That's too much," I said, pulling out the colorful brochure.

"You boys are growing." Then she looked skeptically at the paper in my hand and whispered, "What do you think?"

"Looks nice," I said, spreading the brochure open, looking at pictures of old folks being served lunch, as if they were at a fancy restaurant, another picture of three old ladies shopping at a department store. Across from the pictures was a list of services provided, everything to keep an old person living on his or her own. I flipped the brochure over and saw more smiling seniors being helped by smiling Meadowbrook staff. There was a picture of an old man showing someone his bedroom, and another picture of someone's grandmother getting her hair done at the Meadowbrook salon.

"I couldn't cook there," she said sadly.

"Oh."

"I wouldn't see all my friends." I thought most of her friends are dead. She patted my hand. "I wouldn't see you and your mother and father."

She drifted into her chair like a sheet of paper blowing off a desk.

"You don't want to go?"

"I got so many memories here, this house, the neighborhood. I wouldn't be able to make my cakes and cookies, my soups. Who would make you risotto? What would I give you if you ever came to see me?"

There was a long pause. I scratched my thigh with one hand and rubbed my nose with the other.

"When my kids were young I thought how wonderful to have this big three-decker. Either Joey or my Lena, or Louisa would live here. Maybe all three and they would take care of their old mother and father. I imagined three floors filled with my children and grandchildren. But nobody wants old people. Nobody wants this old neighborhood, except for the few," she looked up and gave a mischievous grin and said, "who enjoy a nice piece of homemade cake."

I raised my eyebrows and touched her shoulder. She grabbed my hand, squeezed it gently, and said, "While I'm here, I'm alive. A place like that would kill me Danny. Kill me as sure as anything I know." She let go of my hand. "Within the year I'd be dead. I'd miss it all so much. You know, don't laugh, but after I watched the six o'clock news tonight I was thinking about you, coming here with the eggs. Seeing you enjoy my cake. You must think I'm crazy."

"You should live where you want."

"Yes, but we die where they put us." She reached up to kiss me and I lowered my face. "I'm sorry I shouldn't talk to you like this."

*****

With the first crack of our apartment door I could hear the blasts of Nine Inch Nails coming from Tommy's room. The kitchen table was in transition from supper. A loaf of bread and butter was at one end, used paper napkins were in front of Dad's place, and crumbs dotted about where Tommy ate. The sink was jammed with dishes and pots sitting in tepid suds. After adjusting to the clanking quacks coming from Tommy's room, I could hear the television in the den. Politics. Mom must be getting her daily update of the sky is falling from CNN or some other downer broadcast.

"Mrs. Leonetti gave us some cake," I shouted, putting the cake on the table.

"There's chicken and potatoes in the refrigerator."

I pulled out the leftovers and gave them a finger test. A minute in the microwave and this won't be half bad. The longer I was in the kitchen the easier the music was on my ears, but the more annoyed I was that I had to listen to his depressing noise. I filled a glass with milk and got some utensils, deciding to join Mom, as it would be easier to ignore the political debate she was enjoying than Tommy's moaning cats.

Mom, in her overstuffed, threadbare chair that she had threatened to get rid of years ago, looked up from papers she was correcting. She gave me a sideways glance and little shake of her head, which said to me look at this mess. The coffee table in front of the couch was overrun with Dad's papers and notebooks. The couch had two piles of books that had spilled over into each other. Smaller volumes jutted up from between the cushions. There was room at the end of the couch closest to Mom for me to sit. I placed my milk on top of a *Scientific America* journal, which featured an article on the blending of sound and light. I was used to balancing plates on my knees. Thankfully, what was left of the chicken was legs, which I could manage with my hands.

"Where's Dad?"

"Oh, he couldn't think here." She pointed her nose towards Tommy's room.

I frowned and took a mouthful of potatoes.

"We agreed. We'd rather have him home listening to whatever he's listening to than out there drinking." Mom's voice tailed off on drinking, and I heard her fear that Tommy was into more than downing a couple of beers.

"Dad picked him up?"

"Right after school, then your father swung by and picked me up. It was the longest ride home I ever had. Says he hates us, and his life. Never knew suck could be used so often without losing its venom. He looked like he was boiling the whole time." She closed her mark book and put it on a stack of papers on the floor to her left. "I told him one week and then you can go out after school until suppertime."

"What's he been doing?"

"You're listening to it. He came out for supper, looked at me like he wanted to kill me." She gave a look of disbelief and said, "Why is it you kids always make me out to be the heavy."

I almost choked on a piece of chicken as I held back a laugh and said, "Because you are."

"Really," she said, her eyes narrowing in on me.

"Don't get mad, but you remember what you tell us and zero in on us. When there's a problem you're like a hawk. Nothing gets by you. Dad can only hold us to something for a day, two at the most then he's wondering whether Beethoven or Mozart had more influence on the Rolling Stones."

"Right," She giggled. "What do you think?"

"Tommy?"

"No about classical influences on Mick Jagger."

"You got to hold the line. Ricky Tarello is poison, more problems than Tommy knows."

"I remember Ricky when he was little. He was such a sad little boy."

"Well, he grew up into a sad little punk, who's mad at the world."

"Just don't know sometimes."

"Well if Tommy has his way he'd be sitting on the loading-dock at the old mill all day everyday, so just stay on him."

"Okay boss," she said, her eyebrows arched and a silly giggle followed.

"All I'm saying is Ricky Tarello is into more than just drinking beers and playing hearts."

I lifted up a chicken leg and greedily began tearing into it. Mom shut off the television
and looked like she wanted to talk.

"How's Mrs. Leonetti?"

I took a swallow of milk. "She showed me the pamphlet from that place."

"Meadowbrook."

I nodded. "She doesn't want to go there."

Before I could finish, Mom flashed with anger and frustration. "Well, she may not have much to say about it. Her little weasel son has plans for this place and the first thing he has to do is get his mother out of here. He could care less about her happiness. No, he's got ideas of selling this place before the neighborhood goes completely down the toilet." She shuddered.

Mom didn't want to know what I thought. She had a ton of worry running around playing tag between her ears. "Joey," she continued her right hand punctuating the air for emphasis "will drive her crazy with his constant pushing. He's like a baby who needs to be fed. He's relentless. Always was a spoiled brat.

"She was crying this morning. Made the little bastard a carrot cake and he started yelling at her about his cholesterol and blood pressure. He said her cooking, always making him cookies and cakes, is going to kill him. I thought,

'Please do us all a favor, and do it quick'. He said he didn't come to eat cake; he came to see if she looked over the application for Meadowbrook. He'd die if he knew she tore it up, threw it in last week's trash. She told him she didn't know where she put it, so Joey starts up with see this is what I'm talking about, you can't be alone. You'd forget your name if it wasn't written over the doorbell. She was crying the whole time. Your father thinks we should report him for elder abuse." Mom shook her head. "It makes me so mad, the little creep."

I nodded and chewed as she talked. Finally, as she broke off, I thought here's my chance to change the subject, for I had over the past few years heard the Joey Leonetti bashing so many times that I knew nothing ever came of it except to make my parents more depressed. "Eric's having big problems at home."

"That poor kid, he's another one. No luck. Has been swimming up stream since birth."

"It's getting real bad." I put my plate of chicken bones on the coffee table not worrying about Dad's papers.

"Why, what happened?"

"More of the same, but Eric's working to save to get out of there and his father wants half of his pay."

"Well, they probably need the help."

"He helps plenty, gives his mother plenty. But you know his father will blow it all on booze and lottery tickets."

"You don't know what goes on in the LeBlanc home."

"I know enough that Mr. LeBlanc is an alky who gets his kicks out of screwing with Eric and Kenny. And Eric can't take it. He just can't take it." Eric hating his father, Eric wishing his father was dead, thinking he could kill the bastard, thinking more and more that way was dancing around on the tip of my tongue. "Mom, he's ready to crack."

She sat back in her chair and closed her eyes.

"You see it all the time, how families blow up. Somebody just can't take it anymore and they snap. Well, Eric may be that somebody."

"He's such a good kid," Mom said, her eyes still closed.

"Mr. LeBlanc just rides him, has all his life. Why have kids if you're going to hate them."

Mom turned to me her eyes open and her voice exhausted. "It never starts that way."

"Well all's I know is Eric is ready to snap." My arms opened wide as I pleaded. "He needs help."

"He seems okay when he's here."

"Right, we eat and then disappear into my room, or lie on the floor and watch a movie." I could hear the trembling in my voice. "You don't hear the problems. You don't hear how bad it is." She pursed her lips. "We got to help him before it gets real crazy there."

"What?" There was more life in her voice.

"You see these kids who can't take it and they snap. They get their revenge, that's what I'm afraid Eric is going to do. Get his revenge. End up on the news like some psycho."

There was a long pause. Our eyes locked and I felt overwhelmed with pity for her, and Eric, and Mrs. Leonetti, and Tommy, and everybody, because our world was coming apart.

"I'm tired Danny. I don't have the strength to deal with your brother most days, what do you want from me."

"Can Eric stay here?" I asked looking at my feet.

"Where would he sleep? What would his parents say?" I looked up. Her left eyebrow arched in a way that told me she was against it.

"He's okay on the couch, or crashing with me."

"And his parents," she asked.

"Mom, they don't care. Have you ever heard them tell him, 'no you can't sleep over here?' Never, not even when we were little."

We went back and forth for awhile. Mom was weary and took time to realize that the LeBlanc's had moved to a new state of crazy. If they were a country, the situation would be described as the oppressed underclass is getting fed up and ready to revolt. Plans are under way to assassinate the tyrannical dictator. Mom finally surrendered with "I'll talk to your father."

"Can Eric stay until you guys decide?"

"Sure," she said, quietly like when you've been up all night and need to rest your brain.

Mom reached down for her papers, signaling the conversation was over. I went out into the kitchen to deposit my dirty plate and glass when Dad entered. He looked pleased at me and walked by, dropping a notebook on the kitchen table. He went directly over to Tommy's room. There was no hesitation. He knocked once and opened Tommy's door. Without the door shielding us the driving bass was ushered under my feet and rollicked up my back.

"It's too loud Tommy!"

I braced for an argument, but instead was treated to a mille-second of silence. Then Dad said, sounding as neutral as Switzerland, "You don't have to turn it off."

"It sounds like shit that way."

"Your choice," Dad said, walking out, tilting his head in Tommy's direction, "poor boy."

I was certain that Tommy was fishing for the earphones that were lost somewhere in the piles of clothes, papers, CD cases, and junk collected over his short life.

Mom stood in the doorway between the den and the kitchen. Dad began, hesitating, reminding me of when I need to give an oral report, how those first words stick on your tongue. "I was up at Atkins Pond, trying to sort out the best way to start."

"To start," Mom said, sounding like she had heard this before and hadn't the patience or strength to hear it again. I imagined she was hoping to talk to him about Tommy or Eric, and there's Dad still with his head in the clouds.

"I think I got it worked out. All this time my approach was wrong." Dad leaned back against the counter near the sink. "I need to organize around contributions that have been essential to the evolution of Western art."

"I'm tired Sam." I could hear her disappointment as she turned and started to retreat for the den.

"Something wrong," Dad asked, looking at me.

I reached past him and got my glass and filled it with milk. I started, "Eric needs to."

Before I could finish Mom said, "Wrong! God Sam, look around."

"What?" Dad moved towards the den.

"We've got nothing. We live from week to week. And it's only a matter of time before we'll need to move. You watch. You'll see." I could hear Mom sitting down. Unconsciously, I sliced a large piece of cake and began chomping. "Joey's been pushing hard on his mother."

"I'll start working weekend nights." Surprisingly, Mom didn't counter with her fears that he would be robbed or murdered. "I'll start this week. They're always looking for guys on Friday and Saturday nights." I could hear Dad sitting down on the couch. "What else?"

There was silence except for the sound of my chewing, which reminded me of the clock that ticks in those thriller movies, telling you the seconds before you blow up with the bomb that's handcuffed to your wrists.

"Between Tommy and Joey, isn't that enough."

"Look it'll take time for Joey to move his mother. It'll take time for him to raise the rent or sell the place or whatever. They can't just throw us out."

"But that's what we got after twenty years."

"What do you want?"

"I just thought by now we'd have more," Mom said, sounding hurt.

"You mean things?" Dad said, as if it were an absurdity.

"I mean maybe we'd own our own home. Maybe we could help Danny with college. Maybe I don't know."

"He'll be all right." Dad lowered his voice and I had to strain to hear him. "He's got brains and looks, we're lucky."

"Sure, but I wish we could help him," Mom's voice trickled off. I wanted to hear more, wanted to thank her for the kind thoughts, and thank Dad for his confidence and compliments.

Just as my parents were getting ready to knight me, Tommy's room exploded with raunchy lyrics and a deadly beat. The whole house trembled and the sudden onslaught of noise knocked me back in my seat and hunched my shoulders up to my ears.

"Lower that Music!" Dad's shout was lost in a sea of bass guitars and drums. Dad and Mom both shouted from the den's entrance.

Dad walked to Tommy's room and gazed over to me. I raised my eyebrows as if to say he's all yours. Dad pushed the door open. What was said was buried in the room. Then the music stopped and Tommy yelled, "I hate this place." Dad walked out and Tommy screamed after him, "I hate you."

Dad, standing in Tommy's doorway red faced but his voice managed to remain calm, said, "Keep the music low or keep it off. Other people live here."

"Go to hell!"

I short circuited. The next thing I knew I was reaching over my father, yelling at Tommy to shut up and apologize, or I'd kill him. Tommy just kept swearing at us. I remember calling him 'a piece of shit', which my mother later told me hurt her deeply. I also remember telling him something about ramming his head up his ass. Dad pushed me back into the den. I didn't resist, as I had enough sense to understand the last thing we needed was for Dad and me to get into a wrestling match. Tommy, as Dad escorted me away, made various obscene gestures mainly concerning grabbing his crotch while making guttural noises. I looked at him and didn't see my brother. No, he was the little traitor who probably had hoped his new buddies would put a big hurt on me. I wanted to drill him a couple of times and let him know that, him and a half a dozen Johnny Posts were nothing. Guys I could chew up and spit out without working up a sweat. I plopped down on the couch. Mom sat in the easy chair. Tears crept down the side of her face. Dad went back into Tommy's room and it wasn't clear what was said, but the shouting and music was over for the night.

Chapter Thirteen

Leaning up against the family taxi, waiting for Linda and Eric, I was dressed more for a day at the beach than school. The only clues I was a student were my bagged lunch, Sociology textbook, and a three-subject notebook, its cover a tapestry of blue and black doodles. A heat wave hung over the Northeast, making the first week of October feel more like August. Some trees more gold than green made the summer temperatures seem absurd, especially when trapped in any classes on the south side of Central High, where four of my six classes met. There was nothing to break the blazing sunlight, whose beams washed the dingy, watered-down, earth tones of our classrooms. Of the twelve foot long multi-paned windows that opened at all, most could only be raised two feet as the school had child proofed them more than a generation ago after a student tripping on LSD jumped from the second floor stairwell. He ended up keeping a team of orthopedic surgeons busy for months, mending fractured pelvis, both legs below the knee, collarbone, and ankles. The city, fearing future lawsuits, came up with a bunch of band-aid solutions to a school that should have been condemned. A safety audit was completed and of the thirty-two items recommended the only ones they enacted were the safety locks on all the windows, safety screens bolted in place, and fiberglass shields that jutted out from the sills on the second and third floors. The shields were an added precaution on the upper floors for those rare occasions when a person determined to kill themselves decides the best place to do it is in an over crowded high school by unscrewing the rusted bolts that hold the screens in place and crawling out the two foot high opening, and then finally jumping onto diseased dwarf shrubs or crabgrass. The ventilation problem attracted an inordinate amount of complaints from kids and teachers from about Easter to the last day of school. Depending on what kind of September we have, groans triggered by the warm, stale air usually begin by eleven o'clock on the first day of school and continue until the first frost hits.

Linda and Eric were very late. I contemplated going back upstairs to give her a call when the rest of my family trickled out to the taxi. Dad led the way, head down, tips of his ears red, grim faced as if on a forced mission, whose end was certain and painful. I straightened up as he climbed behind the wheel of the Grand Marquis. Tommy, hands wedged deep into his jeans' pockets, followed a dozen paces behind. If Dad's look was determined resignation then Tommy's was of a defiant con on his way to the gallows. His upper lip curled as he looked over to me before scowling into the back seat. I wanted to tell him to chill out. It's only school. Mom, her right shoulder tilted towards the sidewalk from the weight of her school bag that grew heavier with each passing week, clutched three textbooks to her chest, as her pocketbook dangled dangerously at her elbow. Mom looked like she had witnessed a murder. I opened the door for her. There was nothing said. I figured my leaving the house ten minutes earlier had saved me from another Alberti firestorm.

I learned later that Tommy had pulled an, 'I'm quitting school when I turn 16 routine', when Mom asked him if he had made his lunch, which of course he hadn't. Dad told him if he quit he couldn't live with us to which Tommy, I guess, remembering the last family wedding we attended, broke out with a rendition of *Celebration*. This triggered a retreat by Mom into her, 'I can't take this any longer' feeling sorry for herself and angry at the both of them. I guess the three of them independently decided that the best course of action was to say no more and get on with the day.

Linda pulled up as Dad pulled away. Eric was a no show. It was a mystery. No call, nothing. Linda had blown the horn and waited. Blew the horn after five minutes and left, not wanting to wake neighbors, and fearful that Mr. or Mrs. LeBlanc would come out and give her a ration of grief. Not that they had ever done this, it was just that the senior LeBlancs had become monsters in her mind, as Eric told one dreary episode of family life after another. Linda knew she couldn't handle being near Mr. or Mrs. LeBlanc not even for a quick knock on the door. She thought she might scream some compassionate plea to them to stop torturing their children.

I filled her in on Eric and his needing out of the zoo. We agreed that Eric wouldn't do anything too crazy. I said this as not to have Linda turn into a worried knot, but I thought just maybe something of extraordinary horror could be awaiting the next person who entered the LeBlanc residence. I imagined, Eric sticking the biggest knife he could find into his father's gut and then after gaining his attention repeating the action a dozen times while cursing why his father couldn't keep his acid mouth shut. She stopped tapping the steering wheel with her left hand when I told her my parents would talk about his staying with us. That my house probably wasn't much better than Eric's, but at least Eric wouldn't be walking around with a bull's eye on his back.

Central High has two parking lots in the rear of the school. A teachers' lot, too small to handle the more than one hundred staff, who keep the place humming, is adjacent to the 'Faculty Only' back entrance. The overflow of teachers find creative ways to moor their vehicles, as most have a genetically based aversion to parking in the midst of their charges. If we parked on the lawn, sidewalks, and fire lanes like our wise mentors I'm sure at a minimum warnings would be issued and if the practice continued the privilege of bringing a car on campus would end as soon as the matter passed from our principal to Mr. Carmody or Smith's desk. The other lot was for students. It always has tons of room. It is a mix of asphalt and grass shaped like an open hand with its fingers leading to a small field where the football and baseball teams sometimes worked out. Real practices happen about a mile from the school at our home field, the Colonel Nelson Briggs Memorial Park. At the far end of the student lot is a twenty-foot high embankment that fences it off from Walker Street and a row of single-family homes, whose owners do everything in their powers to keep contact with the Central High student body at a minimum. High walls, gated wrought-iron fences, unleashed German shepherds, alarm stickers on front doors, neighborhood crime watches, and calls to Delmont PD are part of the Walker Street Neighborhood Association's war on crime. All of which makes the Central High student body feel like we are the enemy.

Linda parked aside of Shawn Haynes's yellow Cutlass. Shawn swore up and down that the car was never used for public transportation and his Olds was more a canary yellow than the shade of mustard used for my father's taxi. Shawn was my height and a ferocious rebounder. I know Coach Inhorn had plans of Shawn, Riley Davis, and me giving him some height, speed, and experience up front this season. In the backcourt Javier Pagan's speed and ball handling, and Lyle Woodhouse's long bombs would balance us big men up front. With a kid like Hunter and junior Mickey Coughlin coming off the bench, there was no telling how far this year's Eagles would go. Shawn was a senior who needed five years to graduate. He was okay with that as long as his girlfriend, Latoya Gimble, came back with him. If not Shawn would go the GED route.

Two months before our first game, major cracks were showing on the projected Central High Basketball Team. Riley Davis, at six-foot-four, was my main competition for the center spot. Riley had the shoulders to block out far taller guys and I figured he'd get the nod over me. But Riley's world was spinning out of control, and now he hoped his uncle could use his political connections to save him from jail, or at a minimum expulsion. The story I got from Riley, and a half a dozen others who were there that night, sounded like one dumb idea led to another and then another, and another. The problems stemmed from our first football victory, two weeks ago Friday. A 12 to 7 nail-biter over Valley Tech. Riley played tackle and defensive end, and had the game of his life, 7 unassisted tackles and 2 huge QB sacks. His trouble started after the game when a dozen guys and their girlfriends decided to party behind the school. As the drinking increased the collective noise from car stereos, boom boxes, and loud mouth youths under the influence made its unwelcome way to the Walker Street homes.

Riley and, six-foot, two-hundred-eighty pound, Roosevelt 'Rosy' Sylvester, his co-anchor on the offensive and defensive lines, decided to have some fun with quarterback Cameron Corbett, who was making out with his girlfriend in his parents' Toyota down in the faculty parking lot. Cameron had not joined the others in the beer-fest. He ended up back at the school because it was a convenient spot for him and his girlfriend of the past three months, Kelsey Marie Doyle, to neck. Kelsey lived less than two blocks from Central, and to Cameron the less time driving meant the more time kissing and grabbing. Cameron, a junior, took over at quarterback before our first game and his head increased a full hat size with each passing week. He was wiry and an elusive runner, who seemed more suited to be catching rather than throwing the ball. The accuracy of his passes dropped off dramatically on anything over twenty yards. It was as if he just threw to a jersey without differentiating between receivers and defenders. If our Eagles were to win anything it would be owing to a running game and strong defense.

Riley and Rosy stumbled down from the student lot and thought they would scare Cameron and Kelsey Marie. Have some fun and invite them up to the real party. Without a plan and juiced up on a case of Coors, the two oversized pranksters sidled up to the Toyota. Riley banged on the driver's window and Rosy pressed his buffalo-size head against Kelsey Marie's window. Cameron and Kelsey Marie were at a point where clothes would soon be falling off. Unbeknownst to Riley and Rosy a disgruntled Walker Street resident had called the cops complaining about the noise coming from the school parking lot. Delmont PD received the call around the same time Cameron rolled down his window and told Riley to leave them alone. Rosy called over to Cameron, "Come on hot stuff, you don't think you're too good to be with your teammates." Kelsey, who had a reputation of being the queen bee, looked at her snagging Cameron as quite the prize, only heard 'Come on hot stuff'. She gave Rosy a dismissive glare. Rosy responded by rocking the Camry and hollering, "Stuck up bitch."

Cameron, I suppose, felt the need to defend Kelsey but knowing that either Riley or Rosy, even drunk, could bat him around all day, tried to reason with them. Words were tossed about, at first joking, but as Rosy's rocking intensified Cameron lost his sense of humor. One thing lead to another and at some point Kelsey staring at Rosy demanded to go home because as she screamed, "I'm tired of being around a bunch of juvenile assholes."

A very drunk Riley said, "You think he's an asshole?" He pulled down his pants and mooned Kelsey and Cameron, while repeatedly yelling, "This is an asshole!" Timing is everything. As Riley centered his big white ass and took a bow, two Delmont police officers pulled into the Faculty Parking Lot.

That was the last football game for Riley and Rosy. The charges included underage drinking and creating a disturbance. Riley was also charged with gross and lewd behavior, and indecent exposure.

Lyle Woodhouse's problems created fewer rumors and jokes than Riley's. He began working more and more hours at his father's Shell station on Hanover Street. Mr. Woodhouse had some mysterious infection that began in the summer. It took months for the doctors to figure things out. The older Woodhouse lost about forty pounds and was in and out of the hospital from the Fourth of July until right after school started. Lyle and his older brother Lincoln, who graduated from Central last year, pretty much took over the family business. I think Lyle had one of those 'ah ha' experiences as he realized that at five-foot eight no matter how good a shooter he was he was not going to be dribbling for the Celtics and that he loved getting into his grease covered overalls and monkeying around with cars. Once school started Lyle maintained a fifty-hour a week work schedule at the garage, as he went on an every other day school attendance plan. Generally, he showed up on Tuesdays and Thursdays. By the first week of October he had missed twelve days of school and was nearing the limit of absences allowed for the year.

Lyle told me that his father was feeling better, but that he still wasn't up to the long hours needed to run the gas station. That he was thinking of quitting school and taking over the business with his brother. Lyle had been the kind of student who got C's because he was a nice kid who showed up. It was a certainty that if he kept going as he was he would either drop out, or not have the needed grades to suit up for the Eagles.

Shawn's window was wide open, an oversized '76ers cap looked out at me. His back didn't budge as Linda's cranky door announced our arrival. I was surprised that he didn't look our way and give a quick 'What's up'. I thought, what the hell, and reached in and pushed his shoulder. There was a pause. Latoya backed into the far corner of her seat. Her long narrow face seemed fragile. Sunlight caught her large hoop earrings and a damp smudge of her makeup at the corner of her eye. Shawn looked over his shoulder and said, "Yo."

"Yo, you're going to be late." I tried to sound concerned, as Latoya usually gave me a ridiculous smile and a 'Hello, white boy.' It was our joke, going back a couple of years. One day a bunch of us were talking about inter-racial dating and she said if she ever thought of trying it out I'd be the first to know.

"No biggie, I got Tisdale first." Mr. Tisdale taught Introduction to Computers and Computer Programming. The Intro course was a work at your own pace class intended during the first quarter not to turn you into a computer phobic. This was Shawn's second go around with Mr. Tisdale. They had worked out an arrangement that if Shawn showed he had mastered several skills then he could work on individual projects. Shawn interpreted this to mean he could use the class as a study. I had visions of Shawn repeating the class next year.

I leaned in and Latoya looked in the opposite direction, as I asked, "How you doing Latoya?"

She shook her head and eked out, "Okay."

I raised my eyebrows and Shawn straightened up giving me his full attention. "I'll catch you later man."

"Sure." I patted Shawn's shoulder and my face asked for more information. "Later."

I rapped his shoulder a little harder and swung back to Linda. I took her hand and we headed towards the building. "What?" Linda asked, reading me right as she always did. I looked down at her and wrapped my arm around her shoulder feeling lucky. Lucky I had her, and lucky I would be graduating.

I squeezed her shoulders and bent down kissing her lips. She readjusted the books that were cradled in her left arm. "What's with him?" Her head motioned back to Shawn as we turned to the main school entrance.

"Latoya, I bet." My free hand dropped from her shoulder and rested on the curve of her lower back.

"What?"

"Her mother has hooked back up with her step-father, George. He's a real nut. One day he's all mister-nice-guy the next day he's like Saddam Hussein. Then he starts drinking and he mellows out. Latoya hates the guy, 'cause when he's in his Saddam mood he smacks her mom around. Crazy." The last time Shawn said anything to me was a week ago. George was vowing he was a changed man, had found Jesus. He and Latoya's mom were going to the Baptist Sunday services together. Shawn talked about killing the guy if he touched Latoya. I figured it was all talk, but now thought that's probably the problem in the yellow Cutlass.

"She must be crazy." We were near the front steps and Linda with urgency said, "Remember your guidance appointment." I had forgotten, and my face told her that. "You need to ask her."

"Sounds like begging."

"If there's a good, small, liberal arts school that both of us can get in."

"And afford." I had narrowed my sights on UMASS, UCONN, and Worcester, Salem, and Framingham State. The two universities, because of their good, sometimes great basketball teams, were my first choices. The others I thought made sense because of their locations and costs.

"Yes, afford, but she should know who gives what kind of help to what kinds of students." Linda had had it with me on this subject. There was no way that she was going to a large university. A constant movie played in her head of us trucking to classes at autumnal tree lined campuses composed of ivied covered brick buildings in some sleepy New England town, far enough away from Delmont to make us feel like we could be anything we wanted to be. A small college most likely with horrible baseball and basketball teams that set records for consecutive losing seasons at a Division III level. But who cares, we'd be together. When I said we could be together at UCONN, she jumped like I just asked if she wanted to start shooting heroin. 'UCONN, it's not a college it's a city. I want to go someplace nice and small.' It's as if nice and small was a single concept that did not allow for the pairing of nice with big. No, it had to be nice and small. Linda was thinking Williams, Amherst, Connecticut College, Bowdoin, Bates, Brown, and Dartmouth.

She should aim high but I figured if she were going to Amherst or Williams I could be practicing my jumpers or hitting a curve at UMASS. I could drive up on the weekends and it would be close to perfect. Linda would hear none of that, imagining college weekends in the library cramming just not to drown. 'If we're lucky we might be able to get a late night pizza or something.' She was excited about the idea of being challenged and the more she talked the scarier it was getting for me.

"You remember the schools?"

"Yah but." She looked up disappointed. "All I'm thinking is you're near the top of our class. I'm like fifty places back."

"You're a great athlete." She poked my side and sounded like a parent giving a whiny kid hope.

"There's probably a million guys going for a hundred free rides, I've never been that lucky."

"Just ask." We were inside and soon to part; Linda heading to her first period class and I would turn right down the main corridor for my guidance counselor, Mrs. Thorndike. Linda gazed up with a reassuring smile, putting me right back on top of the world. We kissed and she darted for the stairs.

Mrs. Thorndike was a short old woman with thinning orangey brown hair, and tiny grandma glasses. I heard her groaning one day last year to Mrs. Ramirez, Linda's guidance counselor that she would keep working until her husband retired, which sounded like it was a long ways off. She was like a lot of the older staff at Central, saying whatever was on her mind, saying it in a don't waste my time, cut to the chase way, which made me feel like I had a mouth full of nails. On top of this, getting time with Mrs. Thorndike was like having an appointment with some medical specialist, who made you feel fortunate she could squeeze you in. I understood Central was a huge school with only four guidance counselors, down from five when I was a freshman and six when my mother taught here.

As I approached the guidance area Mrs. Thorndike was walking into her office with a large Dunkin' Donuts cup. Her rose color lipstick left a mark at the lid's opening. Her eyes widened with my approach. She motioned with her head for me to follow her into her office. On the office door was a poster of a team of mountain climbers braving a snow-covered peak. Over their heads on a bright blue sky was the inscription 'Success is one part inspiration and nine parts perspiration'. Her desk was cluttered with stacks of papers behind which were a series of photographs of her children and grandchildren. Everyone in the photos was blond and smiling except Mrs. Thorndike, who seemed stiff and cold even when playing with babies. I sat in the green cushioned chair aside of her desk. Behind my head was a poster of London's

Globe Theater. Directly across from me at eye level was a dark foreboding poster of Rodin's Thinker and in black block lettering, 'All Great Things Begin with an Idea'.

"You're taking the SAT's next month?" Mrs. Thorndike asked as she pulled out my folder from her desk's file drawer. I nodded. She flipped through some papers and said, "Not bad." She looked over the top of her glasses and said, "If you keep your grades up you should have no trouble getting into UMASS or University of Connecticut." She sounded like she was dismissing me.

"I was wondering." Her head turned from the papers and cocked in my direction. "If there were some smaller schools I could get into."

"I thought you wanted to play sports on the big stage." She liked to say 'big stage', and this time her saying it made my dreams of making a Division One varsity team seem foolish. "Coach Inhorn thinks that might be possible. He thinks you could get some scholarship money."

"Yeah," I said, nodding.

Her head swayed gently and she said, "Let me see, let me see." Her finger ran down my transcript. "The state colleges would be no problem."

"How about Amherst or Bates," I asked, hesitantly.

"Bates?"

I nodded. "Well, it's not so much Bates, but schools like Bates." I was sweating. Of course it wasn't Bates, since I had never heard of the place until last month when Mrs. Ramirez told Linda to shoot for the stars, and Bates was on the list of great small New England colleges. I could feel my tee shirt sticking to my underarms.

"You'd have to bring those SAT scores up about eighty points. And I think you got a couple too many C's." She could see my disappointment. "Those schools are very expensive and they're not into sports as much as UMASS. Not sure what kinds of scholarships they might offer. But I could see you fitting in at UMASS or Worcester or Framingham State. Good schools Danny. You'd probably get a decent financial aid package but it's the getting in to a place like Bates, or Amherst."

"Do you have a list?"

"List," she asked.

Now I really felt stupid as she looked at me like a nose just popped out of my ear. "You know like good smaller colleges that I could get into."

"Danny, you need to decide where you can best do the things you want to do in life. I thought playing basketball and baseball at a big school was important." I nodded. "I thought you wanted to stay kind of close to home, but live on campus." I nodded. "And that costs, unless you get some kind of terrific scholarship." I nodded. She looked up at me knowingly and said, "Your girlfriend doesn't like UMASS."

"Well, it's yah." I felt so dumb.

"Linda McCurry," she said doubtfully. I nodded. "Danny, you may not get into the same school as Linda, even if you both try to figure what a school wants and you kids match up nicely. It still might not happen." She looked back at my transcript. "What I tell all my students, don't worry about what someone else is trying to do. You have to figure out what's best for you. And unless something has changed I think UMASS and UCONN make the most sense."

"I may apply to some of those other places."

"Why?"

"Just to see, I don't know."

"There's an application fee you know?"

"Oh."

"Some are fifty dollars, some more."

"Oh."

"Danny, do some talking with your parents, with Coach Inhorn." I nodded with my eyes and she wrote me a pass for my first period class.

*****

"There is a relationship between economic power and political power or influence," Coach summarized his twenty-minute talk on power elites in America. He had explained how politicians need money to campaign and those with extra cash contribute, expecting, at times, special consideration when laws are being passed. While the great majority of us, the have-nots, are on the outside looking in. I was thinking as much about my meeting with Mrs. Thorndike as I was about Exxon-Mobile versus environmental activist groups. I had filled Linda in at lunch about my meeting with Mrs. Thorndike. Linda was up in arms, ranting, as she waved a Red Delicious apple that was too big for her hand in front of my face, about how it was Mrs. Thorndike's job to help me apply to whatever school I wanted to go to. "She can advise but she should respect your wishes," Linda fumed. All I said was that she wanted me to talk to my parents and Coach. Linda knew Coach's position and feared he had brainwashed me. Although Mrs. Thorndike didn't say it, I got to feeling like Linda and I would be attending different schools next year.

Coach's desk was covered with papers. A middle section about a foot square was left clear, allowing space for him to write. To his right was a three-by-two, sturdy, wooden table that Coach sat on throughout most of the class. Sociology was an elective, only juniors and seniors allowed. From his perch he had a good view of all twenty of us. By the end of the first week of school he had a good read on everybody. I sat center aisle four seats back, with Shawn to my left. It was clear from the start Coach had higher expectations for me than the others. Whenever a class discussion became lost in the silent abyss of twenty unprepared, memory defective adolescents my skin would crawl knowing Coach would give me a quick eye and if I said nothing it would be, 'Danny what do you think?' And I never disappointed, no, I always had something to say. When my gallivanting mind wandered off a cliff Coach would throw me a lifeline, dusting off my ideas and somehow connecting them to the point he wanted to make.

Coach finished by comparing America to a buffet table where corporations and special interests are allowed to get up first and are given giant platters to fill. Then those people connected to this powerful first group go up and fill their plates, which are smaller but they aren't complaining. Last to eat are average, working people who are given salad bowls and hope the first two waves of chowhounds have left something for them. He then wrote our assignment on the board 'Does the idea of power elites change your view of America? How? Why?'

Everyone pulled out their notebooks and found a clean sheet of paper. I was thinking we grow up believing that everyone is equal, but some people are more equal than others. It's not a racial thing anymore. It's a money thing. And the have-nots, that is everyone in this room, and everyone I know can only hope that they can improve their lot a little bit and be happy, while the truly powerful have the world as their play thing. I sat staring at the paper. Nearly everyone wrote with the practicality of getting this done so there's one less homework assignment. But I sat thinking, too many ideas to write anything down. My paralysis registered with Coach, who gave me the 'you're letting me down look' and said, "Come on, this shouldn't be hard. Between the book and my jabbering, it should write itself."

My brain was in a freeze.

After a minute, Coach came prowling up one aisle and down the next. He looked at each student's work and mostly nodded or said, 'okay.' Coach stopped at the last row to my left. As usual Joshua Fontaine and Manny

Delgardo, a couple of slackers, had done nothing. I could hear Coach explaining the assignment and asking Manny to explain to him what they were to do. There was mutual agreement. Coach pointed out in the textbook the page with the pertinent information. I was next.

"I see you've been busy," Coach said, looking down at the blank sheet of paper.

"Been thinking," I said, twirling my pencil.

Coach put one hand on the back of my chair and one on Shawn's chair and leaned forward. "Don't make it harder than it is."

I shrugged. "I've been thinking about next year."

"I think things look good at UMASS and fifty-fifty at UCONN. They'll wait and see what kind of year you have. But baseball and grades will get you someplace. And you should do okay with the financial aid if you can't get a good scholarship. But if you have a good year on the court, who knows."

"Well, maybe I'd like to see someplace smaller."

"Smaller?"

"You know have that small school experience." I didn't know what the 'small school experience' was, but Linda was sold on it.

"Danny, you get a shot at UMASS or the Huskies and you could be playing for a National Title. Come on, don't get stupid on me." My eyes riveted onto the blank sheet of line paper in front of me. I could feel my cheeks redden. "I got people coming to see you and this other banana head." Coach pushed Shawn's shoulder and Shawn grinned appreciatively. "People from there as well as URI, maybe BU, and BC," Coach said, trying to keep his voice down.

"Oh."

"Think big and who knows Danny maybe you'll put Delmont on the map." Coach straightened up and placed his hands on his hips like when he's getting ready to rip into someone. "Donald McLemore six years ago had your talent but didn't have the grades. Angelo Casagrande, eight years ago had everything. He was beautiful, but a little bit short for Division I. George Peloquin, my second year here, had everything but the desire. Don't screw this up. God gave you a growth spurt. Do you know how crazy and wonderful this is? You go from a five-foot ten shooting guard to a six three or four guy with tools, and shoulders. God gave you brains and now a body that people will be interested in. Don't get screwy. It's your life here, your life." Coach slapped my shoulder and I wanted to salute, or kneel, or something. "You need to show people this year." Coach smiled and it felt so weird. For the first time in my life a man I admired was looking at me like I was really something. I nodded. He was right. This was my chance. Coach would kill me, or he would be so disappointed I wouldn't be able to look him in the eye if I didn't do what he wanted. Someplace small seemed like a whacked idea. Someplace small would be throwing away my future. A future that included, according to Coach, a role in a NCAA Division I Championship, which would make his life more meaningful, and afford me upon graduation opportunities in coaching somewhere, and perhaps a look by some NBA teams, not to mention baseball and an equally mind boggling slew of dreams and possibilities that could happen only if I rose to the occasion at UCONN or UMASS'. Six months ago I would have been happy anywhere, but now with the schools Coach was talking about why not shoot for the stars?

*****

Linda didn't have to be at Blockbuster until four. Her mother's birthday was Saturday and she wanted to check out some stores at the Independence Mall. I had the day off, as Tarzan was playing less chess and working out front more. This would happen about once every couple of months. Tarzan would feel like he was losing touch with his customers, or complain to Old Mike about overhead, or waste, or how he had to teach us how to do our jobs, and presto! Tarzan would be this smiling bull out front greeting everybody, cleaning everything, and making sure every display looked like something out of those fancy, colored, Sunday newspaper flyers. By the end of the week Tarzan usually got tired of listening to old ladies complaining to him about everything from the price of tomatoes to medical problems. My hours would increase, and Jose and the chess set would start reappearing.

Mrs. McCurry was really into oriental things. There was a knick-knack shelf in her living room with a green ceramic pagoda, a bronze Buddha, and a bunch of tiny wooden Chinese guys carrying buckets of water, and Chinese dolls the size of Barbie in silky robes serving tea to an old man with long whiskers.

Linda had her eye on a Chinese tea set on sale at the Fragrant Lotus. It was marked down to thirty-nine ninety-nine, from fifty-nine ninety-nine. The Lotus specialized in Far Eastern goods. The cups had gold trim on the lip and stems. Each cup featured a different exotic flower. The teapot showed a field of lavender colored flowers. In the distance were blue-mountains and a peach colored sky. All of it looked so delicate, you would never think of using it.

"I talked to Coach today." I could hear scared sheep wandering into my voice.

"About?" She said as we turned out of the school parking lot.

"About this whole college thing." She glanced my way and I could see her cute little jaw tightening. I sighed. "He makes a lot of sense."

"What did that man tell you now?" She shook her head and goosed the old Pontiac.

"In all his time coaching there have only been a couple of guys that have been good enough to get a serious look by a big name school, a school that can really compete."

"Danny." Her voice was scolding. I knew I should have kept quiet until after hashing this out more at home. "I thought you wanted to be where I am."

"I do."

"But he's pushing UMASS and UCONN."

"Do you know what it would mean if I could play at that level?"

"God, Danny." She pouted.

"This could be my chance to make it big."

She kept her eyes straight ahead. Her skin seemed to be sizzling. Every move seemed an irritation.

"If you go to Amherst, or Williams, or Bates, or wherever, they're all in New England."

"You don't understand," she said through her teeth.

"You don't seem to understand what baseball and basketball mean to me." My arms waved as I spoke. "It's my dream Linda. And Coach thinks if I have a great year there could be a place for me at a big name school."

"And that's why you want to go to college?" she asked in a way that if I said yes I would be confirming that I was an idiot.

"Yeah, not just for that but it's a big reason."

"What about what Dr. Burnsides told you?"

"What?"

"That you see Hemingway's true intentions."

"I was lucky. I took a wild stab at it."

"The only one on target in a class full of brains," she said.

"I was lucky."

"Danny, college can give you, us a start at doing good things. The focus has to be on who we'll be four years from now."

"I know." I saw myself signing a minor league contract with the Red Sox, or being invited to the Celtics rookie camp.

"When we're done with college what will matter is, the degrees we have. Not what your batting average was."

She hasn't a clue of what it means to play at UCONN, or any team that can get to March Madness. She hasn't a clue that I would trade ten years of my life for a big league scout to offer me a minor league contract. "It's what I want." She shuddered, automatically. The Pontiac turned into a freezer. She drove in a quiet stew. I tried a few times to explain, but my tongue dried and my head ached. I wanted to tell her that we are two different people. It will be okay because we got this love that doesn't mean we're joined at the hip, but we would never do anything to hurt each other, whether we were living together or a million miles away.

Nothing more was said until she parked the car and looked over to me as she was getting out. "Maybe we could see some of these places."

Independence Mall was one of the few things that Delmont did right, two floors of stores, restaurants, and movie theaters. Through the main entrance the world of gray concrete and black asphalt changed to a brilliant mosaic of red, white, and blue walls and floors. The ceiling was a rosy plate glass that warmed everything beneath it. There were seven water fountains around which were benches for tired shoppers to catch their breath. Because of the natural sunlight real trees and flowers made it feel like a park when you were window-shopping. Linda led the way towards the Fragrant Lotus, which stood a few doors down from the Mall's food court. Seeing the signs for Wendy's, Friendly's, Nathan's Hot Dogs, Sbarro's, Manchu Wok, and D'Angelos' made me think of Harper's and Eric. Harper's was on the opposite side of the mall next to the movie theaters.

"There it is," Linda said jabbing a finger up towards the treasured tea set, which sat on a shelf just above my head. Linda had forty-five dollars and was hoping the set would have been further reduced. No such luck. She spun a little circle around the center aisle counter that displayed ornamental fans, bronze dragon platters, and jade jewelry. Her eyes jumped from the glass case to the shelf above us. On her third circumnavigation around the aisle a middle-aged Chinese woman in a gold silky pantsuit and fiery lipstick asked in perfect English, "May I help you?"

"I really like that tea set, but the price is more than I can spend," Linda said, looking up at the prized article.

"You have very good taste." The Chinese woman looked Linda in the eye. "That was imported from a small factory near Shanghai. The colors will never fade. You can drink a million cups of tea and those flowers will look as fresh as the flowers in your garden." She smiled and nodded looking up at the tea set as if greeting an old friend.

"Yes it's beautiful. My mother loves this store." The woman smiled warmly at Linda. "But it's a little bit too much for my budget."

"It is beautiful." The woman said and looked at me for support. I nodded and began examining the fans to my left. There was one depicting a bunch of young girls dancing around this fat guy.

"Well, thank you," Linda said still looking up at the tea set.

"I have had that set a long time." Its value grew as she gazed at it. "Maybe it needs a new home. If you want it, give me thirty dollars."

"You sure," Linda said.

"Yes, how is that?"

"Great. Thank you."

The Chinese lady carefully repacked the tea set into a box, which despite seeming too small had enough room for everything. Linda clutched the white plastic bag with the outline of blue lotus blossoms that held the tea set and locked her other arm around my bicep. As soon as we were out the door she motioned with her head towards Friendly's and said, "You want a sundae?"

"You buying?"

"I got a coupon," she said, snuggling up to me. We were in synch floating through the mall.

"Eric!" Across from us coming out of Wendy's was Eric. "Eric!" He stopped and headed over to us.

"You won't believe the beautiful tea set I got my mom," Linda said unable to contain her excitement.

"Where were you, buddy?" I asked as Linda released my arm.

"I overslept then figured I'd get out here early. I'm working four to eleven tonight. Thought I'd apply to some other places. Maybe not have to deal with as many jerks." Eric hissed.

"I thought I'd just hit everyplace from here to Harpers."

"Anything new at home," I asked.

"They got on my ass for over sleeping, but neither of them got up before eight. They didn't realize I was still in bed until long after nine." Eric twisted up his face and shuddered. "Then the asshole tells me to get to school. He grabs my neck and shakes me awake. I knocked his hand away and he flings the covers off the bed. 'Get your ass to school, Sleeping Beauty.' I threw on some clothes and started walking here. Made a few stops along the way. Put in applications at Stop & Shop, Food Warehouse, Gleam Car Wash, and

Lowman's Bakery. Do you know Lowman's is the oldest bakery in Delmont?"

We both shook our heads.

"Three old Jewish women and an old baker, I think they need some young guys to do the lifting. It must have been two hundred degrees where they make the bread."

"Harpers that bad," Linda asked.

"Oh, I figure if I can get something full-time with benefits, I'll quit."

"Harpers?" I asked.

"Harpers and school," Eric said, giving a cynical smile, "then move out."

"Don't!" Linda screamed as if she was being attacked.

Eric shrugged and frowned.

Linda jabbed Eric with her free hand. "You're too smart to throw everything away."

"Throw what away?"

"Your future, now don't be crazy," Linda pleaded.

"I'll get my GED and still take classes in the fall."

"What about graduation?" Linda asked.

"I'll be there to cheer you two on, and then we'll go over to the Capri for pizza and celebrate. I'm buying."

"Eric, don't be crazy," Linda said, giving me a sideways glance.

"Nothing crazy about it," Eric said calmly, "I figure in a month working full-time I could afford a room near Martino's Headquarters."

"Ick," Linda said, wrinkling her nose.

"Well, I can't stay where I am. Somebody will end up at the emergency room or morgue."

"Eric!" Linda stomped and again looked to me for help.

"And what I get at first would be just until I can afford better."

"You can stay with us," I said, feeling my parents would never allow Eric to move into a room at the Y, or over Goody's Pool and Billiard Parlor. The two places I knew that rented rooms down there.

"You sure," asked Eric, his eyes opened wider and his jaw relaxed.

"Yeah, I mentioned it last night to my mom. I'm sure it's okay."

"What they say?" Eric showing a trace of a smile, not the cynical one but the kind he uses when he's about to beat me in hearts or put down a triple-word score in Scrabble.

"My mother needed to talk to my dad."

"So maybe it's not okay." Eric's smile evaporated.

"No way will my father not be okay with it." I nodded, trying to convince myself that what I was saying was the truth; that the Alberti's would be waiting with open arms for him.

"I'll talk to my mother tomorrow." Eric's face and tone returned to its old somber state.

"I'll let my parents know that you're moving in for awhile."

"In a few days?" asked Eric.

"Sure," I said. "If it works out you don't have to drop out."

"Right," Eric agreed. He reached over and we shook hands and hugged. Then he hugged Linda and I thought she was going to start crying.

Chapter Fourteen

The sweet sickening smell of marijuana seized me like a cold shower in January, as I opened the back door of our apartment. "Hello! Hello!" My mother's school bag and books were on the kitchen table. Books slanted into her bag in an uncharacteristic jumble. "Hello!"

The pot stink was growing as I felt a cool draft of autumn air coming from our front porch. Near the porch's entrance through the screen door I saw Tommy, rocking in the shadows, completely oblivious, head phones tied to his brain, Walkman blasting, allowing a murmur of croaks and cracks to the outside world.

I swung the screen door hard, wanting to knock Tommy into life; that is my life, our family's life. It whacked his elbow. He jumped and turned towards me. Eyes widened with horror. He turned back smugly to view the street below, dismissing me the way irritated adults look at other people's spastic little kids playing in the super market.

"Hey!" I yelled. Tommy resumed gyrating to the music. "Hey," I said, pushing his shoulder.

Tommy turned to me, his face screwy with anger. "What?"

I yanked the right headphone out.

"Shit!" Tommy removed the other headphone. "What the hell's your problem?"

"You smoking pot?"

"You see any pot?" It was said with what was becoming Tommy's 'go to hell attitude'.

"No, but I smell it. And I'm sure it's not Mom or Dad smoking it."

Tommy shrugged and started to put the phones back on. I latched onto his right arm and brought it down to his side fast and hard. He glared at me but didn't move. "Where's the pot?"

"I don't have any pot."

"Where's Mom?"

"They took Mrs. Leonetti to the hospital."

"Hospital," I said, and thought the worse.

"We got home and she was complaining about chest pains or something. Dad kept saying better to be safe." Tommy clucked his tongue, as if to end the conversation.

"She's all right?"

"She thought it was nothing, but they scared her into going."

"So you decided to have a little party." I was thinking about Mrs. Leonetti while wanting to rip into Tommy.

"You need to get a frigging life."

"You're going to stand there and tell me you didn't just smoke some grass." Tommy rolled his eyes.

"This place stinks with that shit."

He sniffed. "Can't smell nothing." Tommy shrugged and put his phones back in his ears.

Before the phones were back in, I said, "You're becoming a real loser." I headed back inside afraid more talk would lead to my attempting to knock sense into little brother.

I opened windows in the kitchen and den. The longer I was in the house the less noticeable was the stench, but the angrier I got. I flopped onto the couch in the den and on the coffee table were three stacks of my father's notes. The piles of books, notebooks, and journals that usually resembled a scattered jigsaw puzzle were organized into tidy rows under the coffee table. Across two tiers of notes on the table were thirty typed pages. In the left top corner was 'Alberti' in the right top corner was *'Art That Matters'*. Dad was more than serious. He was writing.

I picked up the manuscript and started reading. Dad began his masterpiece with a defense as to why art matters. He described the world without music, the visual arts, and literature. He described the great spiritual experience he had listening to Beethoven's Ninth Symphony inside old St. Thomas's Catholic Church. I remember that night. It was years ago. Dad running around the house saying things like, 'Beethoven has actually been to heaven.' He wrote about how Harper Lee's *To Kill a Mockingbird* did more to improve his understanding of race relations in America than all the history books he had read in school. Of why Lee's book along with *The Confessions of Nat Turner* and Jackie Robinson's biography should be required reading for every American. On and on he went giving examples of how art inspires and informs.

Think of a wedding or funeral without music. Think of every building erected without the individual grace and style of a learned architect. All of his little comments and long rants over the years were being laid out eloquently. I couldn't believe how well he wrote about something that I thought was a waste of time. The thirty pages were Dad's passionate plea, which had been smothering our home since before I was born, that civilization's best chance at surviving was by developing what he called the 'humane heart' in all of us. This wise and compassionate heart is nurtured best through the arts. On the last page, he began discussing how literature informs humanity better than psychology about the effects of mental illness on individuals and families.

I put the manuscript back on the pile of notes. I thought about giving Tommy another shot at seeing things like ninety-nine percent of the world did. I told myself 'Just talk. Don't go in there thinking you're going to change him'. The marijuana seemed to have been blown out with the cross ventilation I engineered an hour ago. I took a couple of deep breaths and slowly opened the screen door. Tommy was rocking back and forth. The music coming from his headphones seemed louder. He must have sensed my presence, as he slowly looked my way. Pissed off as usual, he mouthed, "What." His scowl told me to go to hell.

I motioned for him to remove his headphones.

He complied, looking terribly bored with me.

I looked away and said, "Let's talk."

"What for?" he snapped, rocking and fiddling with the headphones as if anxious to get back to his music.

"Because I don't like what's happening with us."

"Save it."

I shook my head and stepped closer to him. "Shit, Tommy, doesn't this bother you?"

A slight smile, almost a smirk, started as he let out a quiet sigh.

"It's like you don't care."

"Wow, a whole minute before the great Danny Alberti started lecturing his loser brother." Tommy looked up smiling. "Like I said, save it."

My ears were now pounding, my neck sweating, my face felt like the skin was too tight. "Well, next time you want to smoke that shit in here I'll let Mom and Dad air out the house and figure out them selves what you've been doing."

"Is that what you wanted to tell me?"

"Shit, no!"

"Come on. This is whacked." Tommy's head swirled in little circles, keeping beat with the music that squeaked out of his Walkman.

"You just don't get it."

"Get what," Tommy shouted.

"Without a high school education you'll be doing lousy jobs for lousy pay." Tommy shrugged. "You think guys like Ricky and Post are your friends, but they're just a couple of losers looking to take down everybody."

"Who I hang with is my business."

"Who you hang with says a lot about who you are. You hang with losers, gee Tommy what the hell do you think is going to come from that."

"A good time, some laughs. Maybe you should try it. Maybe if you got your head out of the clouds you'd see what's real around here." Tommy laughed and started to turn away.

"It's a big joke to you." I waved my hand in front of his face, stopping his retreat.

"No," Tommy said raising his voice. "Look we live here, a dump. The neighborhood will soon be overrun with Puerto Ricans, and Ricky is the only guy who is thinking about how to protect what's ours. You see what's happening just up the street. God damn Ricans think they own Waverly."

I couldn't believe what I was hearing. "It's a big world Tommy, big enough for everybody."

"Well, from where I see it they're going to start moving down this way and we'll be ready."

"What do you mean?"

"Shit, you're the one with the brains you can't figure what'll happen."

"Use your head Tommy. You want to get out of this dump, then, start doing something to help yourself, like get an education."

Tommy paused as if considering what I said. Then he fired back, "GED will be fine."

"Last time I checked they weren't just handing them out."

"Whatever." He hissed through his teeth and I wanted to strangle him.

"Whatever, that's a great comeback." I could feel myself heating up. I was trying to tell myself to calm down but as I spoke the volume increased and I started jabbing Tommy's chest with my hand. "Well, think about this, whatever, every time I see you with Ricky Tarello or Johnny Post I'm going to march your ass home. Got it! Because they're heading no place good and you don't need to take the ride with them."

Tommy backed away from me and snapped, "Go to hell."

"No, I think I'll go to your room and see if I can find your stash."

"You mess with my stuff I'll kill you!"

The threat calmed me, for I wanted nothing more than for him to take a swing at me so I could slap him around. "Hmm, sweet dreams baby." I smiled and headed inside.

"Hey, what the hell's going on here," Dad hollered from the kitchen.

"We're out here," I yelled back, thankful for hearing his voice. I was now in the hall that separated the kitchen from my parents' bedroom. "How's Mrs. Leonetti? Where's Mom?"

"Your mother's still at the hospital. They're keeping her at least overnight. Run some tests. She's feeling better."

"Good."

"I just came by to get some of her things. Your mother's waiting until Joey gets there."

"Oh," I said, looking away from my father.

"You guys at it again?"

"No," I said.

"Sounded like Tommy was going to kill you, and you, what? Taunting him?"

"It was nothing."

"Look, a lot's going on, I need you to be, as they say, part of the solution."

"Sure," I said.

"We shouldn't be too late. There are cold cuts in the refrigerator, or you can make some hot dogs and beans."

Dad sniffed, looked betrayed and asked as if not believing, "What's that smell?"

I shrugged.

"I hope it's not what I think it is." Dad looked around at the open windows. Although seasonable for October, it was a far cry from Indian summer. In a hushed voice he said, "Marijuana."

"I, I. don't know."

"You don't have to say anything." He walked past me and out to the front porch. "Tommy, Tommy!" Dad was roaring. "Shut that off."

I stood frozen in the hallway, wanting to hear it all and wishing I were somewhere else.

"What, now. I can't even listen to music." Tommy snarled.

"I smell pot." Dad was loud, but sure of himself.

"Don't look at me," Tommy fired at him.

"Who should I look at?"

"Why does it have to be me? I don't see any grass around here," Tommy said, sounding tired and fed up with everything.

"You telling me Danny's smoking that shit."

"Is that impossible?"

I took a deep breath and waited for Dad to set him straight. "If I find you smoking that stuff you'll be grounded for life."

"I don't smoke it," Tommy screamed.

"Well, you smell like you do. This house smells like you, or somebody was smoking it."

I had drifted to the back door and could see them clearly in the late afternoon light. They eyeballed each other intensely. I was invisible, hoping Dad would reach him and if not then see what a boot in the ass would bring.

Dad lowered his voice and said, "You only get one shot at being a teenager. Don't screw up your whole life now. One chance to make the most of it and then it's playing catch up, and believe me catch up gets harder and harder the longer you keep screwing things up."

"That's it, that's all you ever think about," Tommy yelled, his arms flailing. "What a screw up Tommy is. Why can't Tommy be like Danny? I hate this place, and everyone in it."

"Great!" Dad's shout startled me. "You can hate it here and hate me all you want, but until you're eighteen I'm responsible for you and you'll live by our rules." Dad quickly turned and almost walked into me. "I'm going upstairs to get Mrs. Leonetti's nightgown and toothbrush, and whatever." Dad was now in the kitchen. I trailed him wanting to tell him he was doing good, doing the right thing. "I trust I can leave you boys alone and nobody's going to get killed, and the police won't be waiting for me when I get back."

"Don't worry."

I flopped down on the sofa and stared at the coffee table loaded with Dad's project. It was clear to me that Tommy would keep pushing us away and by the end of the year he would dropout of school. He was now completely under the spell of Ricky Tarello, and this was gnawing at me. This crazy talk about Puerto Ricans moving in the neighborhood was nuts, but added new wrinkles to the mess. Tommy would be trouble without Tarello. With him I shuddered, imagining Mom and Dad making holiday visits to Walpole to see their boy, the angriest kid in America. The more I thought, the more hopeless it seemed.

"Tommy, I'm going out," I called to his shadowy figure rocking on the front porch. I thought I'd pay Tarzan a visit. Get some advice. I hit Waverly and instead of going to the store I crossed the street and marched over to the old mill. It was getting dark. Most families were sitting down to their suppers, but I thought Ricky and company would probably be sitting in their cave catching a buzz.

Late October, even before the clocks fell back an hour, the sun seemed to just drop out of the sky after six. By the time I made it to the warehouse hangout, the sky was sparkling with stars. When I got to within shouting distance of the warehouse's loading dock a thin figure slipped back inside. Too short and scrawny to be Post or Butch, Tarello was gaining disciples. Before I reached the platform, Post, Butch, and the Carando brothers, Steve and Jeremy presented themselves. They held similar poses: legs spread about a foot apart, hands on hips, and even in the darkness their faces looked soured.

As I got closer, Steve Carando, who was my age, but I hadn't seen or talked to since junior high, looked liked he had a closed knife in his right hand. Steve had spent time in DYS for a half dozen robberies before he turned fifteen. The Carando family lived on the corner of Hornsby and Waverly, above a Chinese take-out place, where Waverly becomes more Hispanic. Since my junior high days, I hadn't given Steve much thought. I assumed he was locked up someplace. His under nourished brother was trying to look tough. Butch had something bulging from his waist. I thought the worse as Post folded his arms across his chest and said, "What do you want?" Getting shot by Butch the retard, or stabbed by Steve, who was voted least likely to succeed by our eighth grade class, seemed a likely end to the day.

"Where's Ricky?"

"He isn't here," Post said. I braced myself for an attack. I figured Post knew he couldn't beat me in a fair fight so they would take the four on one handicap and grow a pair of balls.

"Well tell him something for me." Post tilted his head as if considering my request. "If I find anymore pot on my brother, or any other drugs, I'm holding Ricky responsible."

"Your brother is a big boy," Post said, sounding as if he enjoyed my predicament.

"I know where he gets it and I'm holding Ricky responsible."

"Maybe you should tell somebody who cares," Post said, and laughed, the kind of laugh that tells you to get lost.

"Well, I'm telling you because you keep your head so far up Ricky's ass, if I end up kicking the crap out of him you're sure to pop out."

Post took a step forward, looking down from the loading dock, and began jabbing his index finger in my direction. "Like I said, your brother's a big boy. He wants to party, he's cool. He's welcomed, if you got something more to say."

"Johnny." I interrupted. "I'm not repeating myself, my brother has any pot on him, or if he's down here smoking that shit, or whatever with you, I'm holding Ricky responsible."

"Fuck you, Alberti!"

"If you want to do more than talk, Johnny, I'm right here." I spread out my arms to show that I was unarmed.

Steve Carando jumped off the loading dock. I backed up and made fists. Steve was smaller than I remembered, or maybe I was just a whole lot bigger than the last time we met. He led with a six-inch blade in his right hand. "You turned into a tough guy, Alberti." Steve stepped forward and I backed up. "I remember when you were afraid of the dark." His voice was dry and cold.

"I remember when guys had enough balls to fight with their fists." I raised my fists, thinking, if he attacks with the knife I'm pounding his ugly face at least one good one.

"Times change," Steve said and laughed. I thought he was going to lunge at me but he turned and looked up at Post. "Should we get real crazy?"

Post feeling powerful behind Steve's defense crouched and said, "No, why waste time with him?"

I took another step back. Steve lowered his knife. "Give Ricky my message."

"Oh I will, and next time maybe we'll want to have a little fun with you."

"Any time Johnny, anytime."

Steve, his eyes hopping, big and crazy, looked at Post. "How about now," Steve asked waving his knife in the air and smiling. Post shook his head. My heart was thumping and my clothes were washed with sweat. I took several steps backwards, keeping my eyes on Steve. He put the knife in his pocket and made a gesture with his head. It was lost in the darkness, but I felt he wanted to impress his audience with more than words. I turned away and started walking out. When I was a safe distance from the warehouse my legs began shaking, and I thanked God I was in one piece.

Without thinking, I arrived at Tarzan's. Old Mike was waiting on a customer. Tarzan must have already grown tired of putting in too many hours behind the counter. From the meat-slicer Old Mike barked, "You must be a mind reader kid. Tarz was thinking of calling you." Then he turned to the customer, a woman about my mother's age in a business suit, and said, "Your mother grew up over by Freemont. Your Uncle Dimo was a hell of a guy. Hell of a guy. Boy, did we have some fun."

I walked around the deli case and Old Mike looked at me, as he wrapped up the woman's order. "You look like hell, kid."

I cleared my throat. My tongue was dry and too big for my mouth, "Yeah," was all I could manage.

Old Mike shook his head and returned his attention to the customer who ordered some fresh olives. "You tell your uncle, that Mike DeMarco from the old neighborhood says hello. I see you and it's like going back in time. You look just like your mother. She was a beautiful woman."

I felt myself breathing normal again.

Tarzan was in the backroom harassing Jose's king with his queen and a knight. I stood behind Tarzan and listened to Old Mike chatter away with the customer and felt like this was the best place in the world.

"Stand over here," Jose said, motioning to his left. "I can use some good luck."

"You need another queen," Tarzan said and moved his bishop diagonally across from Jose's king. "Check." Jose had one move, which would cost him his queen. "Danny you want to work tomorrow after school till closing?"

"Sure." I must have sounded surprised.

"My brother Leo's coming up for a few days. You remember Leo?"

I nodded. They were close in age, but Leo looked like he could be Tarzan's father. Leo had a florist shop in Falmouth, down on Cape Cod. He sold the shop a couple of years ago, when a developer made him an offer he couldn't refuse.

"It'll be good to see him," Jose said, grimacing as Tarzan took his queen.

"He's had nothing but trouble since he sold his place," Tarzan said, moving his knight in position. "Check."

"Oh," I said, absentmindedly.

"I told you last year he needed a triple bypass," Tarzan said, looking up at me for the first time. "Where the hell have you been?"

"Nowhere, why," I asked.

"I don't know," Tarzan said.

"You okay?" Jose asked.
"Yeah, I'm fine."
"You run over here?" Tarzan asked.
"Yeah."
"Maybe it's the light," Tarzan said.
The men returned their attention to the chessboard. A few minutes later Jose lowered his king in defeat.

*****

Muffled rumblings came from my brother's room. What he listened to all sounded the same, thugs on the corner. I stuck my head in the den. My mother had her nose in a book about what was wrong with America. It had become her favorite subject ever since the Iraq invasion. This one had George W. Bush on the cover, looking like he was about to sneeze all over the country. My father was reading the first chapter of his 'great project'. He looked like the *1812 Overture* was playing in his head. There was still the lingering wash of Tommy's weed caught in the curtains and rugs.

"You eat?" Mom asked, pulling me into the room.

"I got a sandwich at Tarzan's."

"Mrs. Leonetti's doing better," Mom said, lowering the book to her lap. "They're going to run some tests tomorrow."

"Oh." I remembered about Eric and sat down on the couch next to Dad.

"Good news, no heart attack," Dad said, putting his manuscript on the coffee table. "Joey was even human."

"After you straightened him out," Mom said, looking over at Dad with kindness, making me wonder if she had popped some magic pills at the hospital.

"Yeah," I said, and looked at Dad for an explanation.

Mom jumped right in. "Joey came in hooting and hollering. Wanted to know why she hadn't called him first. Why wasn't she keeping him up to date on things? Where was her doctor?" Mom giggled and raised an eyebrow at Dad. "Your father told him straight out. 'Joey', he said, 'By the time she got a hold of you she could have been dead. We're there. She's known me all my life.'" Mom smiled approvingly. "Joey began puffing up, you know the way he gets when he's about to start really ranting. 'Joey', your father said, 'your mother feels safe with us, and that means a lot to us.' Joey then starts pacing and says, he's the one responsible."

"Maybe responsible for giving her a heart attack," I said.

"That's just about what your father said. He says to Joey, you may think your helping with all this talk about Meadowbrook Village, but you're worrying her. You're stressing her out. She's old. She wants to stay in the home she's known all her life. Be around people she knows."

Dad crossed his arms and pushed back on the sofa. "This was before the doctors told us they think she's fine and they just want to run some tests to make sure. Joey was probably feeling a little guilty."

"He should," Mom said.

"He began his justification. Meadowbrook is a beautiful place. Do you know what a place like that costs? There's a waiting list up to a year. Do you know Congressman Carruthers's mother is living there?" Dad smiled and unfolded his arms. "I said, 'All I know is your mother wants to stay where she is as long as she can. And we're there to help her and you any way we can.'"

"It was more what wasn't said," Mom said, nodding. "Joey ended up thanking us. Never thought I'd say I was glad I ran into Joey Leonetti."

"I need to talk to you guys," I said, leaning forward and looking over at Mom.

"What?" she asked, still beaming from the memory of their last encounter with Joey.

"It's Eric."

"Oh," Mom whispered. Her face changed like a balloon getting pricked by a needle.

"He can't take it." I turned and looked at my father. "He's thinking of getting a room at the Y or some other dump around there." I then shot my mother a look, requesting immediate rescue. "He wants to quit school, get a GED."

"What happened?" Mom said, rubbing her hands along the side of her thighs.

"He's working as much as he can. His father wants half his pay. He's drinking all the time. Eric figures he'll never get out of there if he has to split his check with that asshole."

"Danny," Mom said sharply.

"Well, he is Mom. If he wasn't such a drunken maniac Eric would be thinking about normal stuff."

"It is what it is," Dad said.

"It is, he's going to wreck his life," I said angrily.

"What I mean is Mr. LeBlanc probably isn't going to change, and Eric has to do what's best for Eric," Dad said.

"I told him he could move in here." I waved my arm as if casting a spell on our den, which would turn into Eric's sleeping quarters if he joined us.

Dad sighed and Mom got smaller and grayer.

"I thought you guys were okay with it."

"We are," Dad said, shaking his head gently and clearing his throat. "I think we were hoping things would get better. We were okay with it, thinking maybe it wouldn't happen." I gave Dad a look that begged for an explanation. Dad put up his hands in front of his chest. "We're still okay with it. Just wish it wasn't happening."

"Then with everything here," Mom said with a shrug.

"Like what?" I was hurt, thinking she was looking for a way out.

"The tension around here," Mom said, her eyes darting out towards Tommy's bedroom. "The marijuana, God knows what else."

"Don't worry about that," I snapped.

"Don't worry," Dad said in his 'you got to be kidding' voice.

"Right, I'll take care of that."

"How?" they both asked.

"I'll talk to the people who are selling him that stuff. Don't worry about it."

"I don't want you doing no such thing!" Mom set back in her chair and her head swayed like a rowboat pushed along by the waves. "You stay away from them, and Tommy needs to do the same thing." Mom propped her head on her hand. "This place," she said it with resignation and a tinge of horror.

"It'll be okay," I said.

Dad, as if not hearing Mom, said, "Well, he's not leaving this place unless it's to go to school." It made me feel like he was really going to stay on top of Tommy.

"The sleeping arrangements," Mom pondered out loud.

"He can sleep with me or here."

"Yah," Dad said, looking around the den. "He might be more comfortable on the couch."

"I thought with all your stuff," I said, gazing over at the stacks of papers and books on and under the coffee table.

"I think I might pack it away." Mom and I both did a double take. "I think I said all that needs saying in this first chapter." Dad, almost laughing to himself, continued, "I think after so many years, so much thinking and reflection I boiled down the entire thesis into thirty pages of speculation and opinion." Dad chuckled, "Learned opinion. If I work at this rate it'll take me about fifty years to get a first draft done."

"You were writing so intensely," Mom said, not believing what she was hearing.

"Yes, but I emptied myself, thirty pages, vroom, gone. The tank is on E. It's a good thirty pages. I may try to get it published in a periodical, but I'm not the guy to turn the Art world on its head."

"Dad," I said, wanting to reach over and hug him.

"It doesn't have the same importance to me," he said, his eyes meeting Mom's. They nodded. "Eric can sleep here. Rather see him here than in some rat hole on Main Street."

"It won't be for a few days," I said, trying to sound reassuring.

Chapter Fifteen

Tarzan's laughter from along side the deli case filled the store. His brother, a couple of inches shorter, with smaller shoulders and hands, and wavy hair, more gray than anything else, was bent over red faced, screaming a silent laugh, the kind that makes your head hurt. Old Mike, sounding like a stand up comic, set a tray of freshly cleaned tripe, was telling a story about Mrs. Mezzaponti, who died like twenty years ago. What I caught was the woman, who had a raspy voice every time she saw Leo would accuse him of destroying her son Marco's life by introducing him to booze and cards behind the Italian-American Veterans Club on Fairmont. The joke was that Leo would show up for those games maybe two or three times a year, while Tarzan was there every Friday night until he went into the Army.

"That woman hated me," Leo said, through his laughter.

Old Mike, looking my way, tried to explain, "She heard DeMarco, and figured it had to be him. Then once this guy joined the Army, she didn't want to be unpatriotic blaming Anthony." He gave Tarzan a look of disbelief, as he continued, "With him over in Vietnam and all. The whole neighborhood worried about him and the other kids over there." Old Mike rolled his eyes at Tarzan. "He went from that crazy Tarz, who was certain to land in jail, to poor Anthony DeMarco."

"Mrs. Mezzaponti, years later, she'd sometimes look at me like I just clipped her wallet," Leo said, wiping his eyes.

Tarzan rubbed his chin and said, "Poor, poor Marco, he never could bluff. Always did that thing with his left eye, whenever he caught anything above a pair, it would jump, like half an inch. Boy, could he drink. He was drunk so much. He was never sober. He'd wake up drunk." Tarzan waved me over. "Leo, you remember Danny Alberti."

Leo looked up at me as we shook hands. "Jesus kid, what are they feeding you?"

Old Mike with hands on hips looked at me admiringly. "I keep telling him they must've switched the babies at the hospital. No Alberti ever reached six feet. His father's maybe five-ten, in the morning with his good shoes on, and his mother is tall, but her people aren't exactly giants. He keeps growing the Celtics will be knocking on his door. Great country, you dribble a basketball and you make more money than a heart surgeon. Then they wonder why the kids are all nuts."

"He's a better hitter. My records may go this spring," Tarzan said, approvingly.

"Going to college?" Leo asked.

I nodded.

Old Mike came right up against me, so I could see the wrinkles on his scalp. He slapped my shoulder and stuck his index finger under my nose. "If he doesn't, I'm going to kick his ass up and down Waverly."

My arrival freed Tarzan to entertain Leo without any worries about the store. After another hour of the brothers sharing childhood memories, Tarzan took Leo outside to show him the '61 Fury. Business was slow and Old Mike went home for supper. He was to return around seven and close up the place with me. Tarzan said he would be in and out with Leo, checking to make sure I was okay. Old Mike had just left; I was slicing a pound of provolone for Mrs. DiRoberto when Ricky Tarello and his two shadows, Post and Butch walked in.

Ricky stood a couple of feet behind Mrs. DiRoberto. Post, full of swagger, and Butch, trying to look tough, flanked him. Post was wearing an old, black sweatshirt that was worn at the elbows and tattered around the collar. His dungarees and hands had fresh grease stains. Butch, swimming in a grey, hooded sweatshirt and baggy jeans, jammed his hands into his pockets. Ricky, his dungarees tight, the way skinny girls like them, needed a shave. A pack of cigarettes jutted out of the breast pocket of his denim jacket. All of them wore heavy construction boots, the kind that would do serious damage if you got kicked. They looked straight ahead, each glaring as if trying to build up steam so that when Mrs. Di Roberto left they could simply blow me away with their twisted faces.

"What do you want?" I asked, as Mrs. DiRoberto put her change away.

Ricky waited a moment for Mrs. DiRoberto to take her bag and leave. "You got something to say to me? Then say it." Ricky stepped forward.

"Leave my brother alone. I don't want him smoking any of that shit, or anything else!" I stepped back behind the counter and readied myself for the worse.

"Like I told you the other day, your brother isn't my problem. If he wants to hang with us, he's welcomed."

"I'm telling you he's off limits for you guys."

"Who the hell do you think you are?" Ricky's face darkened and his eyes widened. His right arm jabbed the space in front of him. He spoke like always, calmly, but he sounded more menacing than usual. "You don't tell me or anybody around here what they do or don't do, who they hang with, who they party with. You think somebody here gives a shit what you want?"

Post moved to the counter and rested his arm on the top of the deli case. His head lurched over the counter, as if we were having a confidential chat. He gave me a look that said, 'he wanted a rematch.'

"I'm talking to you," I said, eyeing the hammer under the counter. If they pulled out a knife I'd start swinging with whatever I had. "I'm telling you the way it is with my brother. He comes home high, or I find he's got, or had pot, or any other shit I'm looking for you."

Ricky, hands on hips, said, "You're making a big mistake."

"Ricky, you're nothing, so don't come near me or my brother, because I'll destroy you."

Ricky started laughing, a phony laugh. Butch smirked. Post smiled, knowingly, as if he could hear my knees knocking.

I stepped forward. I could feel my temper about to explode. I was scared but not afraid to do what had to be done. I saw myself reaching over the counter and yanking Ricky by his scrawny neck.

Post reached for a Slim Jim, beef stick, from the carton on the deli case. I thought he was trying to grab me. I leaped back. The three morons started laughing as Post pulled out the Slim Jim. I recovered, quickly, and snapped, "You buying that?"

Post, still laughing, tossed it back on the counter.

"If you guys aren't here to buy something, I got work to do."

"You got it all wrong Danny," Ricky, in that same cool, controlled way he talked, said, "You're nothing and you don't tell me nothing."

Ricky gave me a look of superiority. I was no longer thinking. "Get the hell out of here!"

I could see Post pulling out his knife. I reached for the hammer and stepped back. Post moved in front of Ricky, his blade out, his face lit up with the action. The store's door opened. "You okay," Tarzan said, as he and Leo entered.

"Later," Ricky said, making clear with his stare this wasn't finished.

Post slipped the knife back in his pants and smiled, igniting more rage in me. "Don't like the odds now big man!" I pointed with the hammer at Ricky and yelled, "Anytime, anyplace, you and me. No knives, just you and me. We'll see whose nothing."

The trio backed up into the approaching Tarzan. "What the hell's going on here?" Tarzan stepped up nose to nose to Ricky. "I told you I don't want you coming around here causing trouble." Tarzan began poking Ricky's shoulder, pushing him with hard, fierce thrusts that hurt just watching. "Now get out of here." Butch was the first one out the door, almost knocking Leo over as he rushed for the exit. I put the hammer down and came around the counter, keeping Post in my range, ready to break his face if his hand headed for his pockets.

Ricky jumped away from Tarzan. "Fuck you." Ricky raised his arms and took a fighter's stance. Tarzan charged. His head lowered like a bull. Ricky threw a right hand that clunked painfully on Tarzan's skull. He threw his left hand catching, with little effect, the side of Tarzan's face. Tarzan seized Ricky by the shoulders and pushed him along like a snowplow moving a few inches of fluff. Ricky, unable to stem the charge, back peddled. His arms squirmed in Tarzan's grip.

Post took a step towards Tarzan and I spun him around. I slapped his wild swing away from my face and connected a big right hand squarely on his jaw. He dropped, hitting the floor hard. The knuckles on my middle and ring finger cut on his chin and a smear of blood appeared. My hand rang like after hitting a ball hard on a chilly April morning.

Ricky, getting pushed out the door, screamed how Tarzan was crazy. Post scrambling to his feet, came charging towards me. I joined my hands and raised them over my head, and with all my strength I came smashing down on Post's back with both arms. His face banged against my knees as he crumbled to the floor for a second time. "You want some more?" I snarled, victoriously.

Before Post could answer, Tarzan lifted him to his feet and holding him by the collar said, "Get the hell out of here and stay out!" Tarzan slammed an open hand into his chest, carrying a stumbling Post to the door.

I filled Tarzan and Leo in on what was going on with Ricky, Tommy, and the marijuana emporium over at the old mill. Tarzan laughed and kept telling me he was proud I had the stones to do the right thing. "It doesn't matter if it comes out right," he said, slapping me on the back. "A lot of times it won't. What's important is that when you feel it in your gut, to do the right thing, even if you take a beating, you go ahead and do it."

*****

Behind our taxi sat Joey Leonetti's black Lincoln Navigator, which stuck out like a billboard condemning our lives. I figured Joey must have brought his mother home from the hospital and would soon be parking the prized chariot back in his safe, suburban garage. Mom said how Joey has this thing about being in the neighborhood after dark. Like he thinks, once the sun goes down we all turn into serious gang bangers just waiting to carjack fat, rich boys.

That night was a first for the Alberti Family. Joey Leonetti in all his arrogant grossness was sitting at our kitchen table with Mom and Dad. Now, Joey has been in our apartment on a few occasions. These have been mainly brief cameos of him standing in the doorway either giving or getting information from my parents. His presence always made my back itch.

Mom greeted me with, "There's some spaghetti and meatballs on the counter." My eyes went immediately to a large heaping plate. "It may need to be heated up." Mom sounded worried and I knew it had nothing to do with me cleaning up tonight's supper.

"Hi, Danny," Joey said, turning towards me. I thought, 'where am I suppose to eat', with this whale taking up one side of the table. Dad seated legs stretched out and back to the wall, hands folded on his lap, giving me a tired look. Mom leaned forward towards Joey, seeming fixed on every word he blubbered.

"Hi," I said and popped my dinner into the microwave for a minute. Thankfully, Joey didn't make any clumsy remarks about me growing faster than weeds in May. The door to Tommy's room was closed and I assumed he had his music plugged into his ears.

"Go ahead, finish what you were saying," Dad said. I could feel Joey's eyes on me. Dad this time a bit more forceful said, "Its okay, we don't keep secrets from our boys."

I turned towards Joey. He looked over at my father as if needing additional reassurance and then back in my direction. "We got a pretty good scare with my mother." I nodded and pulled my plate of spaghetti out of the microwave. "She's all right, this time around."

I opened the refrigerator and took a half-gallon of apple juice out. "That's good," I said, scanning the table's seating arrangements again. No one budged to open up room for me.

"But, she's not getting any younger," Joey said and looked back at my father.

Who is? I wanted to say. "I'll eat in the den." Mom nodded. I wedged a glass under my arm, spaghetti and meatballs in my right hand, a jug of apple juice in the left.

"You see, at Meadowbrook there's nurses on duty during the day, evenings too." Joey shot this remark in my direction but I was already making for the den, which to my surprise no longer contained any traces of Dad's great project. The coffee table was cleared of all research pertaining to 19th Century musicians and Left Bank artists. The sofa's hundred odd articles had found a new home, which was nowhere to be seen from Mom's easy chair. The stacks of books on everything from Greek drama to Cubism no longer stood in the corner waiting for Dad's attention. It was over. It was really over. Dad's first reward for ten years of trying to unravel the Rubik's Cube of the Arts in Western Civilization was a visit from Joey Leonetti.

Mom's easy chair was ideal for kitchen eavesdropping. My right ear was less than a foot from the opening to the kitchen. Dad's voice if he remained staring across the table at Joey would come in loud and clear. Joey if he raised his voice slightly would sound as if he were speaking directly to me. Only my mother, who had her back to me, might pose a problem, but I was banking on Joey to get under her skin enough to raise her volume.

"Like I was saying," Joey said, hesitantly, "Mom would live like a queen there. She wouldn't have to worry about nothing. And there's a lot to be said about living with people your own age. It must be hard for her most of her friends are dead, or living somewhere else."

"I'm sure it's beautiful," Mom said, "but your mother seems to be doing alright right where she is. There are three or four old ladies that still sit in Canelli's yard in the summer. Your mother passes the days under the grapevine like always."

"For how long, I remember when there were a dozen of them all dressed in black. They'd be there every afternoon." Joey sounded strangely sentimental.

Mom said, "Right now she seems healthy enough with a little help to take care of herself." Mom paused. "Too many older people can't adjust to changes. The kind of changes you're talking about."

"That's why it needs to be gradual," said Joey, sounding edgy, "there's a waiting list, you know. It'll take probably six months. I figure she comes out to visit a few times. And, I know you guys probably think I'm crazy, but I thought if you guys talked it up, you know."

"Talked it up?" Dad said.

"Look if you do, and she goes along with it." Joey sounded a little panicky. I could sense him shrinking right there in our shoebox kitchen. "I'll leave your rent alone for a year. That's a promise."

"Have you asked yourself what does your mother want?" Mom snapped.

"Sure," Joey said, almost laughing, as if the question was ridiculous, "she wants to be thirty years younger and have a house full of kids."

"And live here," Mom said.

"I know she'd love Meadowbrook."

"What's the rush?" Dad asked.

"They have such a long waiting list."

"You need to work this out with your mother," Mom said. I could hear her disgust.

"It would make it a lot easier if you guys were with me, or at least if you stopped helping her so much."

"Do you hear what you're saying?" Mom asked. I could feel her teeth on Joey's neck.

"Then she'd realize she needs help. She misses so much. I have to yell at her if it's something important. Then, I don't now if it's safe her cooking for herself. "

The last bit of patience had left my mother. "I hope I'm half as good when I'm her age."

"Look," Dad said, I imagined him unfolding his hands and propping his head on the table. "We think of your mother as family. It has nothing to do with anything but knowing her all my life. Knowing what a wonderful mother you got, knowing, Joey, you are one lucky," Dad sighed, "guy, to have her for a mother. So, Joey, the little things we may do for your mother we have to do them. We wouldn't be able to live with ourselves if we didn't. Don't give me that face."

"What?"

"That face you make as if I'm talking Chinese and things are going to be your way, because, I guess, Joey, you're used to getting things your way."

"What are you talking about?"

"Whatever, Joey, I may be crazy, but I know our family will always be there for your mother, because, Joey, to us she's family."

"Well, it has to change. She can't keep going like this."

"Like what!" Mom roared.

"You know, everything is so hard for her. She needs a hearing aid. She can't raise her arms to get anything out of her upper cabinets."

"She's getting old," Mom yelled.

"That's why she needs a place like Meadowbrook, if not today then tomorrow."

"Well, then wait until she's ready," Dad said.

"What's the rush?" Mom said.

There was a long pause and then I heard some movement. Joey stood up. "I should be doing more," said Joey, sounding hurt. "I should be spending more time with her."

"Why don't you?" Mom asked and I think they were all standing.

"It's not easy."

"You can only do the best you can," Dad said.

"My wife, you know, she's great. A great wife, mother, but she's got this thing about me spending too much time here. It's crazy."

"Your mother is old," Mom said, "give her as much time as you can, your wife will get over it."

"Hmm, you don't know my Isabella."

"So I don't get it, Joey," Dad said.

"What?"

"How would your mother going to Meadowbrook change you seeing her more?"

"I guess I just wouldn't feel guilty. You know right now I feel like you guys are doing what me and my sisters should be doing for her. They got the excuses that they live far away. Well, an hour's drive more than once a month wouldn't kill them. But, I don't say nothing, but it eats at my wife, and she lets me know when I come here. It's always the girls should be taking care of your mother. It drives me crazy. You see if Ma was at Meadowbrook, I'd be off the hook."

"The hook," Dad said.

"You know, if I'm paying for people to look after her, then I'm off the hook. The guilt would be gone. I did my part. More than what most kids do."

"But your mother might be miserable," Mom said.

"Maybe at first, but things would be better at home," there was a pause, "for me."

"Joey, you can't pressure your mother," Dad said, "if you do and she goes down hill fast afterwards you'll never forgive yourself. You'll be thinking you killed her."

"Sam!" Mom said. Good going Dad, let this jerk know what's at stake.

"I know, I know," Joey said, sounding all choked up. "You're right, absolutely. This is not good."

"Joey, things have a way of working out." Dad sounded reassuring as he continued, "You just need to be there as much as you can. You're not in competition with us. You're her son, we're just friends."

"I know. I think maybe I'll let it go for awhile."

Dad said, confidently, "When your mother needs more help we'll let you and her know it. Believe me Joey we wouldn't want any problems for your mother if they can be avoided.

"I know," Joey said. Then he said his goodbyes and thanked my parents. I thought he was going to cry.

Chapter Sixteen

Linda swung by to get me for school. Eric was crammed into the back seat with two large, black, plastic, trash bags. Linda gave a sideways glance, as she popped out to let me slide over. Eric leaned forward, wearing a nervous smile. His face framed by an oversized Glad-bag. "It kind of made sense to get out now, you know, while everybody was sleeping."

"You didn't tell them?" I asked, maneuvering my legs against the glove box.

"I told my mother days ago," Eric said, seeming irritated. "Told her I was either going to stay with you, or get a room downtown." Eric rubbed his forehead and said, "She said, 'don't be crazy,' and walked away."

"I don't know," Linda said, shifting into drive.

"That says it all. Here I am living in an insane asylum and she says it'd be crazy if I left. There is no talking in my house, that's part of the lunacy. There's yelling and demanding, and cold stares, and above all the understanding of the Laws of the LeBlancs, which boils down to avoid Papa and don't piss off Mama." Eric gave a half-hearted hoot, and said, "If I did it when they were up it would only start World War Three. My mother will miss the cash, that's it."

"You don't believe that," I said.

"Whatever."

"Don't get pissed," I said, thinking I need to give my mother a heads up that Eric would be coming home with me. That what we talked about is happening sooner rather than later.

"I'm not. It's just I've been planning this for a while. It's like the big escape." Eric sat back in his seat. Before I could ask what or when he was going to tell his mother, he shot back his head and perched it between the two front seat head rests. "Your parents are still cool with this?"

"Yeah, I just thought it might be a few days from now."

Linda hunched over the steering wheel, giving the road her full attention. I tried to catch her eye to see if she had some misgivings that needed to come out, but she just acted like she was taxiing strangers.

"Shit, well is it okay?"

"It'll be fine. Don't worry."

"Because I can get a room," Eric said, with more fear than certainty.

"No, I'll call. It'll be fine." I grabbed Linda's pocketbook and pulled out her cell phone. Linda was the only member of our trio who had a cell phone. My dad thought it was just one more gimmick to keep average people broke. He said, 'How many times do you really have to make that call at that precise moment.' I think his use of the word precise is what gave him the edge in those arguments. Eric would have gotten one when he started working at Harpers, but he couldn't see the worth of it when that money could go to his getting his own apartment and car.

"Hey, Mom....No, everything is okay....I just wanted to let you know Eric's moving in tonight......He's got his stuff....Not much.... I'll ask....Okay."

"What she say?" Eric asked.

"She's totally cool with it. Just wanted to know if you'd be sleeping in the den, or bunking with me."

*****

My room always seemed fine to me. What I didn't realize, until Eric arrived with his two trash bags of earthly treasures, was it was a standing room only space, unless you were lying on the bed. Every corner and wall was taken. The bed occupied the lion's share of floor space. It would take creativity, or a lack of concern, to accommodate my best buddy and his belongings. My five-drawer bureau was over capacity with socks, underwear, sweaters, sweatpants, and sweatshirts. It filled the middle of the wall across from the door. In the corner a bookcase made of milk crates and plywood was overrun with books, CD's, and DVD's stacked in a precarious pyramid formation. On both sides of the bookcase were sports equipment: three baseball gloves, my current pride and joy, a Nomar Garciaparra shortstop model, a Wade Boggs model that my dad got me when I made my first Little League team, and a Johnnie Bench catcher's mitt; I inherited from Mrs. Leonetti ten years ago when she was cleaning out her closets. The gloves were mounted atop my baseball bats. Heaped around the bats were cleats, a basketball, two twenty pound dumb-bells, a tennis racket from Dad's college days, three or four tennis balls, and a skateboard that saw a lot of action the summer before I started high school. On the other side of the bed was a mahogany chest that my mother stored extra blankets, bed sheets and spreads, under which were the family's important documents, like insurance policies, and car title. Atop of the chest were my sports' trophies. Little statues with tiny figures swinging a bat or dribbling a basketball packed tight on that deck like passengers on a rush hour ferry. On both sides of the chest were pairs of well-beaten sneakers and my winter boots. My four-foot wide closet was jammed with shirts, Dad's and my winter coats, my one special occasion suit that kind of fit last year, but will make its way over to Tommy pretty soon, and a string-less guitar I picked up at a yard sale for five bucks last May. The closet's floor was covered with papers, notebooks, photo album, CD's, dress shoes to go with my suit, and a bag of Christmas lights that Linda used to decorate my room last year. Next to the window, by the head of the bed was a chair, too beat up for the kitchen, on which my dirty clothes collected, until they started falling to floor. Under the chair was my CD player. On the walls I had two posters one of Jason Varitek, rallying the Red Sox by shoving his mitt into Alex Rodriguez's face. The other was of Nomar Garciaparra, wearing his Sox number five and demonstrating his beautiful swing.

 Eric gave a ten second look-around and opted to sleep on the couch. I told him I'd make room in one of my drawers for some of his things, and the rest we figured could squeeze into the closet. He thought he could pull clothes out of the trash bags as needed, and then as they came out we would find a spot for them with my things. Given the differences in our sizes there would be little chance of us mixing up whose was whose.

 We landed in the den. Eric dropped onto the couch, feeling it out as a possible mattress. I put some Nelly on the CD-player and sat in Mom's easy chair. We started talking about what we'd do later. We thought about going to Martino's Headquarters. The election was only a week away and Eric thought it might help him to get a better job if Frank Martino could put his name and face together. Everybody we knew thought Martino was going to win big.

 "The real attraction," I said, trying to lighten things up, "are those little cuties he's got ringing doorbells."

"I don't know who's more stuck up Central's cheer leaders or the Martino air heads."

"Why, you make a move?"

"No!" Eric gave me the 'you got to be kidding look'.

"Who's that tall girl, with the golden tan? Does she go to Florida on the weekends? Nobody has a tan this time of the year."

"Nobody we know. And, nobody who wants to know us."

"Who is she?"

"Pamela something, she lives over on Pine Willow."

"Is that in the district?"

"No, not even close. Her old man is a lawyer buddy of Martino's. The more I hang around headquarters, the more I see a lot of people from all over the city, and all of them want to see Freddie Corso lose."

"You getting friendly with anybody?"

Eric shrugged and the back door opened. "Hello, hello," my mother called. "In here."

Tommy came in his jeans falling off. Atop his head was a brown paper bag. He collapsed on the couch next to Eric. On the front and back of the bag in red magic marker was 'P.O.W.'

"You moving in," He asked without looking at Eric.

"Yah, what's with the hat?" I asked.

"Prisoner of war, that's me," Tommy said, looking over to Eric. "This place is not good for your health." Eric turned towards him with a raised eyebrow. "Don't say I didn't warn you. But somehow you got the idea that my brother is cool, so you may just survive."

"Tommy, when are you going to start growing up?" I snapped.

Tommy wearing a big smile said, "Maybe we can work out a trade. The Albertis get Eric, and the LeBlancs get me, Sam and Elaine's mistake. I bet within forty-eight hours my smile returns, and Eric you'll start thinking about running away with the circus, or joining the Army. I can see it. Tommy Alberti goes on to become NASA scientist. Eric LeBlanc disappears, lost amongst the nameless homeless."

I gave Tommy my hard game face, which told me I was about to lose it.

"Eric," Mom said at the den's doorway.

"Hi, Mrs. Alberti."

"Are you staying?" Mom asked, her arms crossed and her eyes looked past Eric to Tommy, who had just grabbed his crotch and shook his package in my direction.

"If it's okay," Eric said,

"As long as it's okay with your folks," Mom said.

"They won't miss me," Eric said, and folded his hands behind his head.

"I'm sure they'll be worried if they don't know," Mom said. I could hear concern and her second-guessing the decision to let Eric stay with us.

"My mom knows."

"You like tuna casserole?"

"Sounds good, Mrs. Alberti, I plan to pay you for room and board."

"Don't be silly." Mom started to walk away and I was both surprised and proud of how easily she told Eric not to worry about the cost of things. "Tommy, that looks ridiculous," Mom said.

"Truth hurts," Tommy snarled.

"The truth is you should be grounded for life, not just a week," Mom said.

"Week," Tommy said leaping from the couch.

"That's right," Mom said, staring him down.

"A week was over yesterday," Tommy said. Mom put out her hands, as if to say, 'what do you want from me.' "Then I'm free at last." Tommy slapped the hat off and it sailed over to me, landing at my feet. "Free at last."

"Well, you can start going out after school provided your homework is finished."

"I don't have any homework." Mom looked at him skeptically. "That's why they give us studies." Tommy saddled up besides her. "And besides I'm in the general classes, teachers are happy if we show up and shut up." Mom rolled her eyes. "It's the truth."

"Well, mister, report cards are being sent home in about two weeks. If you have any F's or D's then plan B will go into effect."

"Plan B?" Tommy sounded dubious.

"Plan B, you spend at least two hours doing homework or reading a book, if as you always claim you don't have any homework."

"It's not going to matter."

"We'll see."

Tommy moved past my mother.

"Where are you going?" Mom could not hide her surprise

"Out," Tommy said, picking up speed.

"Be home for supper," she called to the slamming door.

Chapter Seventeen

The Monday before the election was the first time we were all home for supper. A big bowl of mashed potatoes was in the middle of the table. A smaller bowl of canned peas flanked the potatoes. Next to the peas were ten, over done, hamburgers and a loaf of white sliced bread. My father sat facing the back entrance. A saucer of sliced onions was next to his glass of apple juice. He loved onions and spicy mustard on his burgers. The rest of us settled for ketchup. My mother sat across from Dad, keeping her eye on the forever-miserable Tommy, who sat, a sulking heap, to her right.

Tommy, since coming off his grounding, was giving us the silent treatment most of the time. Often when he did something around Mom or Dad, like reaching for the mashed potatoes, he would hiss like an overheated radiator. Dad still picked him up after school, and to everyone's surprise Tommy was there each day. I read my parents tolerance of Tommy's after school habits as their being grateful that it had been weeks since the last call from Mr. Carmody. Tommy, upon landing home from school, devoured whatever junk food was in the house and then left saying, simply, 'I'm going out.' We all figured he was spending his late afternoons with Ricky and company. No one said anything. He was making it home most nights in time for supper. After supper Tommy either slinked off to his room or headed back outside. In his room he was entertained by rappers, who were increasingly, I gathered from my occasional skirmishes with little brother, becoming more anti-establishment, pro-violence, and in general mad at the world. He was doing, until last night, a pretty good job of keeping his curfew, which was nine o'clock on school nights and ten on the weekend. Last night he came home after nine-thirty and Mom let him have it. 'Next time you're more than a couple of minutes late you're grounded for another week.' Tommy shrugged, inserted his headphones, and made his way to his bedroom.

The few times I was home when Tommy arrived, I was struck by the smell of him. It was as if he took a bath in pot, beer, and cigarettes. Today the raunchy mix was definitely alcohol and cigarettes. My parents had to smell it, but they said nothing. I looked over at Dad, as he coated his bread with the yellow brown mustard. Mom asked Eric about our plans to hold signs for Martino tomorrow over at St. Patrick's Church. I fixed my burger and stared across at Tommy, trying to convey disgust. Tommy, a master at playing the abused victim, sat long faced shoveling his food down, avoiding all eye contact.

"We're supposed to be there from three until the polls close," Eric said.

"I'll probably vote after I drop everybody off in the morning," Dad said.

Mom, carefully scooping peas with her spoon, said, "You have to take me there after school. Why don't we vote together?"

"Yeah, maybe. I don't like the crowds." Dad put down his burger. "This election could make a difference for the city, especially Fairview. Martino is talking about putting the new high school over where the old mill is. God, would that be something if that eyesore was gone. It would change the whole neighborhood."

"Can you imagine the traffic," Mom said.

"It would change everything," Dad said.

Mom sighed and said, "The city never does anything right. They'll screw this up too."

"It's got to be better than the dump we got now." I looked over at Tommy who continued to chomp away. I thought Ricky and his morons would need a new hang out. What a nice bonus. "We won't be home for supper tomorrow," I said, remembering the party at Martino's Headquarters.

"Right," Eric jumped in, "there's supposed to be all kinds of food, soda, coffee."

"Tarzan is donating all the cold cuts, cheese, and bread," I said.

"Neighborhood has never had anyone we could believe in," Dad said, forking another hamburger.

"Not sure what kind of party it'll be," I said, wanting to reassure Mom that it wouldn't be a wild affair. "It's kind of weird, you know, having someone like Old Mike looking forward to it, Tarzan and Jose, and guys like me and Eric."

Dad nodded and looked over at Mom. "I think it's a shared joy. A community thing, that is greater than its parts."

"Sam, don't."

"What?" Dad looked at her hurt for a second. Then he giggled and said, "I was getting philosophical about something that doesn't need it."

Mom smiled in agreement.

"I do that Eric, so if ever I'm thoroughly boring you, just say, 'Mr. Alberti, I don't give a rat's tail about this,' okay."

"Well, it's just good you guys eat and talk. It's so good."

"Anything new with you," Dad said, looking my way.

"Coach Inhorn nailed me after class today."

"Nailed you?" Mom's eyes grew to the size of silver dollars.

"Yeah, about this year's team."

"It's looking like the decimated Eagles," Eric said.

I nodded and could see Mom was looking for details. "You know Riley?" Mom shook her head, "the big guy."

"Is he blond?" she asked.

"Yeah, well, he got arrested last month and is off the team."

"Arrested?" Mom was shocked.

"It was nothing," I said, wishing I had thought this through before embarking on a recap of the Central High Eagles Basketball Team prospects for the coming season.

"But, he got arrested," she pressed.

"Right, it was after a football game. Riley is an animal on defense. Him and Rosey were the line. And Lyle Woodhouse hasn't been in school for a couple of weeks." Mom looked puzzled. "Lyle he's got the sweetest outside shot in the city, maybe ever."

"Danny, what happened to Riley?" Mom pressed. She had the look, like a seagull eyeing a beach lunch.

"After the game some of the guys were drinking behind the school. Riley got caught."

"So he's off the team for that?" Dad asked, like an impartial judge who thinks there's something wrong with the evidence.

"Yeah, he's got problems," I said, wanting to change the subject, knowing there was no way I was going to tell them that Riley was caught drunk, mooning our quarterback who was hoping to get lucky with 'Little Miss Stuck-up'.

"Problems," Mom said, having stopped eating, as Riley was the only thing that mattered to her.

"They think he's an alcoholic," Eric said.

Mom's face turned into an uncomfortable snit. "No," I said, "the judge thinks he could use a residential school, that's all."

"That's all!" Mom shook her head.

"It's better than jail," Eric said. I looked at him and tried to let him know he wasn't helping.

"So without Lyle and Riley, all the pressure will be on Shawn and me. I think Coach was thinking we could make it to the finals this year."

"The important thing will be your first quarter grades," Dad said, taking a drink of his juice. I pouted a little, as I wanted to say to him, 'no, the important thing is that I show the world that Danny Alberti has the right stuff. I can compete with the big boys. I deserve a full scholarship and not to some Division III school, but to one of the powerhouses. I wanted to say that without Riley and Lyle we'll be lucky to play five hundred this year. That Shawn may not be eligible because of his grades and a sophomore long shot just got thrown out for the year for attacking a teacher. Because of all of this, instead of looking at a great season, we'll be playing for pride and I hope some scouts can see that I can be great even if our team sucks.'

"The colleges will be looking at your first quarter grades," Dad said.

"I know."

Coach gave me a pep talk after class. He said it would be up to Shawn and me to show real leadership this year. That even without Riley and Lyle we should win our share of games. There are a lot of talented kids. He called them, 'raw kids'. 'It should be a challenging season. Are you up for a challenge Danny?' I was. I imagined Rocky Balboa, pushing himself beyond what anyone imagined possible. I could do it. We could surprise everyone, including ourselves. I would dedicate myself. I'd talk to Tarzan about working a few less hours until the season was over. I felt so strong. I wanted to say to Coach, 'I'm ready. This is my year.'

"I'm going out," Tommy got up and moved away from us, not waiting for an answer.

"Be home by nine," Mom called after him.

There was a quiet that settled over us for a minute. It was uncomfortable, a little lost, like when strangers have finished making small talk and realize they have nothing else to say.

"You want me to go see if he's drinking?" I said, swapping glances with Mom and Dad.

Mom seemed a bit startled.

"No, as long as he comes home on time," Dad said, looking across at Mom for confirmation.

"We'll see how his first term grades are," Mom said, conveying they had a plan.

"I predict five F's and a D," I said. I could feel my neck and shoulders tightening.

"A, 'D'," Eric said.

"Sure, somebody will feel sorry for him and cut him a break." I was done eating and pushed my plate forward a couple of inches. "He's heading for trouble, big trouble. He smelt like a brewery."

"Oh," Mom said.

"I know he's down with those losers, Mom. Maybe I should go get him."

"No, I'll talk to him when he comes home," Dad said, looking like his onions were backfiring. I felt relieved, as if I wasn't up for another battle, yet disappointed as part of me wanted to go after Ricky Tarello.

*****

St. Patrick's Catholic Church was a block off of the Higgins Square Rotary. Where Waverly met Higgins Square was one boundary for the Fairview District. St. Patrick's was one of the neighborhood constants. You could see the bell tower from each of the many hills that ran off Waverly. Even for families like us, who were Catholic on Christmas and Easter, St. Patrick's was a special place, a silent guardian, protector of traditions, and a storehouse of memories for most of Fairview's families.

We had no idea what we would do at the polls, but we were caught up in the neighborhood buzz; finally we would have somebody in City Hall who truly represented our area. Tarzan told us, we would probably just be holding a sign and waving to cars as they zipped by on their way home. The party at Martino's Headquarters after the polls closed was unclear to Eric and me. We were afraid, since Old Mike was looking forward to it that it was going to be a big yawn, with a lot of old timers shooting the breeze and complaining about their backs and hearts. There would be some excitement if Martino won, and we were certain he would. If nothing else Eric said, we'll get a free meal and have one more opportunity for Frank Martino to know, who we were.

Election Day was as good as it got weather-wise in early November. A few friendly pillows hung on the western sky. The temperature when we got out of school was approaching sixty. Linda had to work at Blockbuster so she dropped us off at St. Patrick's. We were to relieve an old married couple. Tarzan said, 'You guys signed up for this. People are counting on you.' I nodded and wanted to say, 'have I ever let you down?' The couple we were to spell, he told us, was going to be there since the polls opened.

St. Patrick's and the Cortland Street School were the two biggest polling places of the seven precincts in the district. At Higgins Rotary there were a half dozen Martino supporters holding signs and waving to the traffic. Stuck on the rotary's grass, spaced about every ten feet, were signs for Freddie Corso. Mixed between the Corso signs were a few men holding signs for Mayor Butler. Near the Martino workers were two women waving signs for Patty Dunleavy, who was running for the school committee. Across from the Martino and Dunleavy supporters were a small group of people with Colin Cranepool signs. Cranepool was running for re-election to the school committee. The seven city council seats were each drawn from local districts. The school committee contests were six citywide races. My father said Cranepool, always the top vote getter on the school committee, was one of Inky Butler's top stooges.

"Blow the horn, go ahead blow it," I said as Linda turned off the rotary. Linda's crate was plastered with black and gold Martino stickers. Behind St. Patrick's was the church hall where the voting took place. Linda parked midway between the two buildings in the parking lot, which could easily handle a couple of hundred cars. The church was the second oldest in the city, having been built by Irish immigrants at the turn of the last century. It was also the second largest church in the city after St. John's, which was at the opposite end of town. St. Patrick's was in need of a power washing, as its formidable gray granite towers seemed gloomy even in the bright sunlight.

I gave Linda a kiss goodbye. She wished us luck and said she would see us in the morning. Eric and I walked quickly towards the church hall, a two-story tan brick building with an eight-foot tall monument of St. Patrick standing out front. About fifty feet from the hall's entry was a mob of people holding signs for a dozen different candidates. Some people had bumper stickers pasted onto straw hats they were wearing. Others had signs attached by ropes draped over their shoulders, making for a sandwich board display. There were four Martino workers there. Angela DiPisa, whose sister was Frank Martino's secretary, remembered Eric from campaign headquarters, "You coming here to vote?"

It felt good that she thought we could vote. "No, we're supposed to help out," Eric said.

I looked around and didn't see any older couple holding Martino signs. "We're to take over for a couple that's been here all day."

"Oh, Jennie and Sonny," Angela, a small woman, about forty-years-old with long flowing curly dark hair, said, "they left awhile ago. You guys need buttons." She jerked her left shoulder forward, calling attention to a pin the size of a small grapefruit. The pin was white and in red letters said, *Frank Martino for City Council*. She handed Eric her sign and trotted over to a fairly new silver Buick that had a two by three Martino sign on the roof. She was back while Eric and I were introducing ourselves to the other Martino supporters, three men who said they just got there, two having just finished work, and one who was in between dropping off and picking up his kids and wife.

"Here," Angela said, handing us buttons and me a sign. "Just smile to everyone. Don't argue with anyone." She looked over at the three Corso supporters. "I think the guy with the baseball cap is Freddie's cousin. He works at the Street Department," she said this like it was a shameful secret for Corso. "The other two, just got here." The other two were women, in there fifties who looked tired. "If you see someone you know go talk to them. After six o'clock more people will be here. You guys can probably leave then."

"We'll need a ride," Eric said.

Angela laughed. Her teeth were the whitest I had ever seen. "No problem."

There was a steady stream of voters. Between the three men from our side and Angela, somebody seemed to know everyone who came to vote. It was as if they were professional poll workers. They greeted people warmly, often shaking hands and talking about kids, health, sports, weather, and of course telling them to remember Frank Martino, or just Frank. The Corso team was quieter. People would nod at them and then start talking to one of the Martino workers. Occasionally somebody was friendly with a Corso worker, and I wanted to ask, 'what was the matter with you?' I could sense a landslide. When people from the neighborhood, or someone I knew from the store came by, at first I was hesitant, but with time I was more comfortable and spoke with them. It was a rush when somebody recognized me. Older people, like Mrs. DiRoberto, Mr. And Mrs. Gherlamo, and Mr. Guzzi, told us how nice it was that we were involved. Mr. Guzzi told me we were seeing history today, 'the city will never be the same. It's time to throw the bums out.' Then he looked over at Freddie Corso's cousin and nodded knowingly. Eric spent most of his time talking to Angela, whose son was in junior high and giving her a run for her money. Angela was probing for parenting tips and social trend updates.

As the afternoon sun faded, the flow of voters swelled. It was all good. To entertain ourselves, we began deciding as people got out of their cars if they would be more Martino or Corso friendly. Bumper stickers were running fairly close, but the edge went to Martino. Younger voters, and given the average age of those voting, I would call anyone under forty young, were going strong for Martino. Overall the Alberti-LeBlanc poll had it about eighty-twenty in Martino's favor.

It was all becoming routine but not boring. Between voters we talked about nothing of importance, Eric's job, the way the Fury looked, and the hope that Linda would look at UMASS or UCONN with an open mind. Then my stomach dropped. Mr. LeBlanc pulled into the church's parking lot. His bright red Toyota pickup truck could not be mistaken. Through all his drunken lapses and physical problems Mr. LeBlanc always kept his wheels sparkling. After 9/11 he attached small American flags to the driver and passenger side windows. An American flag bumper sticker centered perfectly under the front grill said, *These Colors Don't Run.*

A chill grabbed me as his enormous bulk began to slowly emerge from the truck. He looked bigger than ever. He looked our way for a second. He seemed angry. I knew that one day we would run into each other, but I hoped or imagined it would be after Eric had squared things away with him. Eric was with us a week and he had two phone conversations with his mother, lasting all of five minutes. The last one was Sunday night. His recap of the call was she thought things would be better after Mr. LeBlanc had his surgery, which still wasn't scheduled, because the doctor wanted him to lose more weight. Eric also promised to bring her some money after he cashed his paycheck on Friday.

Eric mumbled, "Shit."

Mr. LeBlanc walked slowly, with straight, deliberate steps. He stopped by Freddie Corso's cousin and talked for a couple of minutes. I didn't want to listen, but was compelled. Mr. LeBlanc's voice was big and deep, making it easy to hear every word. He gave a brief medical update, which brought out sympathetic moans from the campaign workers. One man cautioned him to get a second or third opinion before letting them cut into him. Mr. LeBlanc said, "I've seen so many doctors I'm starting to understand what the hell they're saying."

"He knows I'm gone for good," Eric whispered.

"So?"

"Ma said he pounded the table and said he doesn't have a son."

"I thought you said, she said it would be better after the surgery."

"She did, I just didn't mention his blowing a gasket."

"Why?"

"Didn't want to worry you, or your parents, they're so great."

Mr. LeBlanc walked past the Martino workers, giving a little nod of recognition. "Danny," he said my name as if bile had backed up his throat.

"Hi, Mr. LeBlanc," I said, shaking.

He started to pass us. Eric said, "Dad."

Mr. LeBlanc stopped and looked Eric up and down before saying, "Dad. Hmm, you walk out on your family without a word and you call me Dad."

Mr. LeBlanc turned towards the hall entrance. Eric said, "Dad, I wish I could live with you."

"Go cry somewhere else."

"I'm not crying, just saying how it is."

"Look, you were always a baby, so don't give me excuses. You'll learn someday." Mr. LeBlanc's voice rose slightly and I took a step back. I could smell the alcoholic frustration and rage that always blew off of him. A couple of oncoming voters swung around Mr. LeBlanc, who was blocking the walkway.

"I'd be there if you weren't always so," Eric's voice cracked.

"Look, Shirley, go cry somewhere else."

Eric shook his head. Mr. LeBlanc sighed in disgust and turned away from us.

"Good luck with your surgery. Tell Ma I love her."

Mr. LeBlanc waved Eric's words away and said, "Tell her yourself."

We looked at each other speechless. A rush of voters came by and they seemed like a blur. I could see tears in Eric's eyes. "You okay?" I asked.

"I hate him, but I don't want to."

"I know." I felt so bad. I wanted to hug him and tell him he did good and one day maybe his father would stop drinking, and all the crap between them would be a distant memory. But that wouldn't or couldn't happen. So I repeated several times, "I know…" My voice got softer and softer until I was whispering it to myself.

"I don't think about killing him anymore," Eric said, quietly. His eyes were drying and his hands were calm.

Voters were coming and going and we turned our backs to the parade.

"I had two fantasies, Danny, when I was little. One was that my father got killed at work. I imagined him falling off a ladder, a wall collapsing on him, or he crashed his truck into a bigger truck. I'd see horrible accidents on the news and wish the announcer would say, 'The victim was Mr. Ronald LeBlanc, a construction worker from Delmont.' I hoped for a long time.

"The other one is I'm married. I got a half a dozen kids and I load up my minivan with them, and we're off for a day at the park, the beach, anywhere. But, it's going to be great because me and my wife have six great kids. That's what it should be."

I put an arm around Eric's shoulder and said, "It'll be okay."

Eric paused, looked at me and said, "Sure." He sounded old and tired.

We heard Angela DiPisa talking to a voter near us. I took my arm off of Eric. We turned to greet people, waving our signs, and looking as we had fifteen minutes ago.

After voting, Mr. LeBlanc walked past us, as if we were strangers. His exit was as slow as his entry. Eric bit on his lip as soon as he saw his father coming our way. When Mr. LeBlanc had passed us, Eric called out, surprisingly in a calm voice, "Dad if you ever want to talk I'm at Danny's." Mr. LeBlanc kept walking, never looking back.

Chapter Eighteen

After the polls closed, Martino Headquarters was jammed with about two hundred people. Most of the workers who showed up were familiar faces, having contributed time and effort over the last two months to make Martino's election possible. That it was a landslide victory we didn't know until twenty minutes past ten, when the local radio station announced the results, 'Martino carrying all seven precincts in Ward Four. The vote total was Frank Martino 3,187 to incumbent City Councilor Freddie Corso's 1,652.

I was eating my second meatball sandwich, sitting with Eric, Old Mike, and two friends of Old Mike. Eric was complaining about working tomorrow until closing and starting at two, which meant he would cut out of school after lunch. He went back and forth between cutting and running the risk of a three-day in-house detention or showing up late for his shift. The problem with getting an in-house detention was that either Mr. or Mrs. LeBlanc would have to come to school to sign him out of the in-house room. The last thing Eric wanted was Mr. Carmody getting on the horn with his father. The way things worked at Central was one cut you got a warning from Mr. Carmody. Second cut a sterner warning was given. On your third cut you got three days of in-house detention, which meant you sat all day with a bunch of unmotivated kids in a room next to Carmody's office. Eric had already received Carmody's second warning. I was bored out of my skull, and thought after this sandwich we should try to catch a ride home. Old Mike and his buddies were arguing whether Bill Belichick was a better coach than Vince Lombardi. And then the place erupted into a prolonged scream as the vote total was announced.

Everyone was on their feet clapping and hooting. Old Mike slapped me on the back and said, "This is it Danny, this is it." A recording of *Happy Days* filled the room. Small groups of people, mostly women, started dancing. Old Mike was singing. I could hear him over the din, "Happy days are here again. The skies above are clear again."

Eric, poking me on the side, said, "Now there'll be a speech, and Martino never saw us."

"He knows what we've done," I kind of mumbled as I finished the last bite of my sandwich.

Eric nodded and looked worried.

"You okay?"

"Yeah, just don't know what I'm going to do."

"Tonight," I said.

"No, I mean. You know you're going to college. You'll probably get a scholarship. In a few years you'll probably be this mega star signing t-shirts in the mall for drooling fans. You and Linda will get hitched and have three or four little Dannys. Even if you don't become a mega star, your life is looking great."

"Yeah, right," I laughed.

"I feel like I'm one step away from prison or the state hospital."

"You know you can always stay with us."

"I'm thinking about joining the Navy. See the world."

"What happened to the physical therapist dream job?"

"That can still be."

"Don't sign up tomorrow."

"No, just thinking. I'll probably never get out of Delmont."

"There are worse places."

Eric nodded. We then heard Old Mike and his friends talking about Freddie Corso having just called Frank Martino and offered his congratulations. Old Mike said, "I don't believe it. Freddie waits until we boot him out to show a little class."

Frank Martino, surrounded by his wife, daughters, parents, brother, sisters, campaign chairman, close friends, and Tony 'Tarzan' DeMarco, gave a speech. He thanked all the people in the hall. He gave special thanks to those people who were standing around him. He thanked Tarzan for his advice, time, and the good food we were all enjoying. Martino then thanked Freddie Corso for his gracious acknowledgment of our victory. Then for about ten minutes he explained how Ward Four would no longer be the forgotten stepchild of the

Delmont City Council. If nothing else he would make sure Mayor Butler and the council knew what the district's needs were. When he stopped talking the room shook from the stomping, cheering, and clapping. Old Mike said, "He reminds me of a young Jack Kennedy." He then looked at me and said, "You guys want a ride home with me and Buzzy." I nodded and Old Mike said, "Let me go find Buzzy." Buzzy Galendo, unlike Old Mike, didn't mind driving at night. They were neighbors for more than forty years and often went together to wakes and funerals.

*****

When I got to work the next day, Old Mike was sitting in his chair eating a pepper and egg sandwich. He looked at me and I thought someone had died. He saw me come in and his first reaction was to turn away. Then as I approached without looking he said, "You're early." He sounded worse than he looked.

"You okay?" I asked coming around the counter to where he was sitting.

He shook his head as I put my books down on a shelf under the checkout counter. "This world is rotten Danny, rotten. Don't let anybody kid you. It's always been rotten, but it's getting worse."

"What happened?"

He took a bite of the sandwich and sucked a two-inch sliver of pepper into his mouth. He shook his head again and said, "What happened? Hmm."

"Tarz alright, you okay?"

"Last night everything seemed wonderful. All was right with the world. We're celebrating and some little bastard is here celebrating. That's what's killing this country, too many sick little bastards."

"What happened?" As I asked, Tarzan came out from the back room, carrying a box of honeydew melons. He was wearing a white short-sleeve shirt and his biceps swelled bigger than the melons.

Tarzan put the case on the counter and asked me, "Have you been out back yet?"

"No." He seemed disappointed, not angry like Old Mike, or upset like when something at the store that he could have prevented goes wrong.

"I want to show him the mess," Tarzan said to Old Mike, as he ripped open the cardboard flaps on the box, making it easier for Old Mike to put them in the display case.

Tarzan motioned with his head and led the way outside. "Somebody had some fun here."

"What happened?" I asked as we turned into the alley. I looked at Tarzan's pride and joy, and was struck dumb. It was like when you first see a train wreck. I automatically took a step back and felt horror. After a moment of absorbing the mess, I felt anger. Tarzan tapped me on the elbow and we walked around the mutilated Fury. There was glass everywhere. The front headlights and windshield were smashed. The side mirrors laid a dozen feet behind it. I imagined someone knocking them off with a club then kicking them like tin cans out of the way. The tires were flat to the ground. A crowbar distorted the grill into a broken tooth smile. The antenna was snapped off and hung from the gas tank like a child's fishing rod. Gouged onto the hood was, 'SWEET RIDE ASSHOLE'.

I thought Ricky Tarello, and hoped Tommy wasn't part of this.

"I'm so sorry. God, Tarz, I can't believe it." I looked at Tarzan, who stood with arms folded, looking over the damage; I guessed for the hundredth time.

"It'll be hard to prove who did it?" Tarzan said, with that same sound of disappointment.

"Who did it? Who else, but Ricky, I can see it."

"Probably, I made some calls this morning. I got in early, wanted to get a head start on making some sausage. Called a couple of detective friends, told them everything." Tarzan sighed. "I probably should have given Ricky a kick in the ass long ago. Well, I hope your brother went to school today."

"Why?"

"My friends from the PD were going to swing by the old mill around one. They said they would make one Ricky Tarello a priority. I told them he's a punk. They promised that they would jack him up enough to make him do something worth charging. Don't say nothing to your brother but keep him away from the mill."

"I know."

"If Ricky comes into the store let me know. I want to wait on him personally. Maybe he'll say something to give me a reason." Tarzan gave a little grin.

"What are you going to do about the car?"

"I got insurance. Maybe it'll pay enough to send it over to Vacca Brothers."

"I thought they were bandits."

"They are if you're paying yourself. But they're the best. So if the insurance covers it, why not the best."

CARLO MORRISSEY

*****

Things went well with the insurance appraiser. Tarzan called Jimmy Vacca and arranged for the '61 Fury to be towed over in the morning. Tarzan cleaned up the mess in the alley. The afternoon dragged. There were enough customers to keep me doing something all the time, but not enough where I had to be busting it. I would have preferred keeping it in fourth gear the whole time. My mind played a tape over and over. Whether I was slicing cold cuts, making sandwiches, stocking shelves, or cashing out customers, I had Tommy on the brain, seeing him, Ricky, Post, and Butch armed with crowbars destroying the Fury, seeing him drunk smashing the windshield, laughing a madman's laugh. Tommy and Ricky giving high-fives after one of the little morons sliced up the fat white walls. Then the scene shifted to the police sweeping through the old mill. Tommy, last man out, nailed by some young super-cop. Tommy, raging impotently, thrown up against a wall. Tommy handcuffed and escorted into a cruiser. Tommy the only one caught, showing blind loyalty to his pack of rats.

I worked with one eye on the clock. The time wasn't moving. I tried to get my mind off of Tommy. I thought about an English paper I had to write. The topic was to discuss a character from *A Farewell to Arms* who acted in ways that were surprising to you. I identified completely with Frederic Henry and racked my brains to come up with something out of character. Maybe it was the ending. He had had enough. Life finally knocked him out with the death of the person he loved. That might work. George in *Of Mice and Men* had to kill his best friend out of love. Frederic Henry falls in love and what the War couldn't destroy in him trying to live in peace does. My head kept spinning back to Tommy, Ricky, Tarzan, and the trashed Fury. Last year I would have made something up. But, last year I wouldn't have read the book. If I could get Tommy off my mind, maybe I could think straight. Frederic Henry and his World War I troubles seemed a million miles away.

Finally, the clock was at quarter to eight. Old Mike went home an hour ago. I was glad to see him go, as every customer he waited on was told how some young punks destroyed Tarzan's Fury. How Tarzan had spent countless hours buffing that baby until you would be afraid to touch it. Every time Old Mike opened his mouth I saw Tommy whacking the crap out of the Fury. Now it was near closing time, I started cleaning the meat slicer and the back counter. Jose and Tarzan were in the back room playing chess. Knowing in fifteen minutes I would be on my way home, I stopped playing the Tommy movie. I felt relieved. My back straightened and shoulders squared. No call from Mom or Dad was a good sign.

I started sweeping at the rear of the store. The door opened. I looked up and there were two Delmont police officers. I stopped sweeping and walked towards them as if in a trance. Tommy inside their cruiser flashed before me. They were young for cops. "Tarzan in?" The lead officer asked. They were both about six-foot tall, broad shouldered, and thick in the neck and chest.

"Tarz," I called. My voice was dry. I was nervous and scared.

The police officers walked around the counter as if they owned the place. Tarzan met them at the entrance to the backroom.

"Hey, Dave," Tarzan said, extending his right hand. They shook hands and the officer named Dave introduced his partner to Tarzan. I stood, at the front counter, all ears.

"Detective Lazzaro wanted us to swing by." Tarzan nodded. "That little problem you had, they nailed two kids."

"Good," Tarzan said.

"They had some ecstasy and marijuana."

"Anything about the car," Tarzan asked.

"The car," The police officer said, looking confused. "He didn't mention anything about a car."

"Maybe Lazz will get them to talk. Punks, a little pressure and they'll be sweating."

"Well, we got to get going."

"Tell Lazzaro thanks. You guys hungry?"

"We're good," Dave said, and the two officers turned around to leave.

I wanted to ask if one of the kids was Tommy Alberti. The words formed in my mouth, but nothing came out. I was paralyzed, broom in hand. Only my eyes were working, following them out of the store.

"You hear that Jose?" Tarzan hollered, returning to the game.

Two kids, when did they grab them? If it was after three, guarantee one of those kids was Tommy. I hurried sweeping, then quickly wiped down the counters, and cleaned the glass doors to the refrigerator cases. I hit the lights.

Tarzan, as if on cue, came out to walk me out and lock the door behind me. "Danny, I hope it wasn't your brother they nailed." My worries must have been showing. Tarzan patted me on the back and gave my neck a little squeeze. "How old is he?"

"Fifteen," I said.

"Good. He's a kid. They'll just give him a slap on the wrist. It might wake him up."

I shrugged.

"Let's hope this puts Ricky out of business."

I nodded and turned to leave.

"Danny, don't worry, he's a kid. They'll go easy on him."

I sprinted home. I had to see my brother. I had to know he was all right. I kept telling myself if he got busted my parents would have called me. As I turned onto our street, I tried to see if the taxi was in its normal place. It was dark and until I got about thirty feet from the house I couldn't be sure. Bang. The space was vacant. No taxi. There was Mom and Dad down at the police headquarters. Mom would be embarrassed into a coma. Dad would keep it together until he got Tommy alone. I wanted to tear Tommy's head off, yet hoped he would be in his room listening to music.

I picked up speed entering our yard. I jumped up the stairs. Our back door was unlocked. A good sign, someone was home. I caught my breath. On the kitchen table was a note in Mom's handwriting. 'Danny we went to the super market there's beef stew on the stove.' There was light coming from Tommy's room. My engine slowed. The tension that hung taut from my toes to temples vanished. I thanked God.

I went to the stove. The stew was lukewarm. I went to my room to drop off my coat and books, and get *A Farewell to Arms*. I flipped the light switch, and as if drawn to a problem like a trained inspector, my eyes zeroed in on my baseball bats. My Johnny Bench catcher's mitt was on the floor. The aluminum bat that held it was leaning too far off to the right. The other gloves were twisted slightly so the Nomar Garciaparra faced Wade Boggs rather than looking out at the doorway. I charged out, a man on a mission.

I threw open Tommy's bedroom door. He lay on the bed, listening to music through his headphones. He looked startled. His face twisted and his eyes told me to get lost. I yelled, "We need to talk!" I hovered over him. I was ready to start swinging.

Tommy reluctantly pulled the headphones off. An electronic buzz filtered out of the phones. I fought an urge to smack the Walkman out of his hands. "Were you at the mill today?"

"I don't answer to you." Tommy snarled and started to put the phones back on. I grabbed his arm and slapped it down to his side. Tommy swung his legs over and sat up on the bed. I thought he was going to attack, but he held himself back. "What the hell is your problem?"

"Your friends got busted today."

"I don't see why you should give a shit."

"They're messing with the wrong guy."

Tommy smirked.

"You think it's funny?"

Tommy stood up and took a couple of steps away from me. He moved close to the bedroom door. On the door, a hook held his hooded sweatshirt. "I think you're a riot."

I took a step forward. I wanted him to say he was sorry for being everything he was. "Those clowns wrecked Tarz's car."

"I wouldn't know about that."

I took another step closer. "Tell me you had nothing to do with it."

"Kiss my ass."

"Stay out of my room," I screamed in his face.

"Hey, asshole, have you noticed, you're the guy always barging in on me."

"Don't push it Tommy!"

Tommy smirked.

"I know you took my bats." I shook my head.

"Just stay out of my business," Tommy yelled.

"When you hurt my friends, it's my business."

"Just stay out of my business."

"You trying to impress Ricky will get you a ticket to jail."

"What the hell do you think this is?"

"You got to be kidding. You don't know how good you got it."

"Yeah, right," he said, turning his head slightly away from me and rolling his eyes.

"Yeah, right," I said, feeling myself getting hotter.

"Why don't you go screw yourself?" Tommy turned, facing me directly.

"So you gave them my bats?" I poked a finger into Tommy's shoulder.

"No, big brother, when I heard what that asshole did to Ricky, I came up with the idea. I volunteered." Tommy began laughing. "I knew you and the other turkeys would be at your party," he said, mockingly.

"What did Tarz do to you?"

"It's what he did to Ricky. But, I did it more to piss you off."

"I don't believe it."

"I felt like I was smashing your head, and Mom's and Dad's."

"You little..." I lunged for his neck. Tommy pulled a thick, six-inch blade out from his hooded sweatshirt. He swung wildly and sliced my right forearm. I could see him cutting me, but felt no pain. Blood streamed out of the long wound. Instinctively, I swung at him. He raised his knife hand to block. I tried to hold up afraid I'd get stabbed again. My hesitation emboldened Tommy. Stunned, I backed up. Tommy came forward swiping for my middle. I tried to block him with my right. The blade cut near my elbow and Tommy pressed deep. I yelled, "Oh shit!" My left hand connected with his forehead, knocking him back. Our eyes fixed for a second. His were wild. He ran out of the house.

The knife had a wide blade. The gashes in my arm were deep. Blood was everywhere and running out fast. I raised my arm over my head and grabbed one of Tommy's tee shirts off the floor. I lowered my arm and bowed my head. I felt a little dizzy. I bent my head down towards my knees. I wrapped the shirt around the wound. I was weak, but the lightheadedness was easing.

I moved into the kitchen and called Linda. A trail of blood followed me. I went to the bathroom as her phone rang. I took a towel and wrapped my arm with it, holding the portable phone on my shoulder with my chin.

"Hi," Linda answered. Her cell phone had distinctive rings for frequent callers. For our phone Judy Garland sang *Somewhere over the Rainbow*. "You stuck with your paper?" Linda asked, chuckling.

"No, listen, don't get scared. Tommy went crazy. He stabbed me. I need to get to the hospital."

"Oh, my God, he stabbed you! Are you okay? Oh my God, I don't believe this."

"I'm okay, but hurry."

"What happened?"

"I'll tell you when you get here, hurry." The blood started seeping through the towel.

I tied another towel around my upper arm, trying to slow the flow to the wounded area. I went to the kitchen sink and poured a large glass of water. I remembered reading something about replacing the body with fluids after bleeding. I debated trying to write a note, and then scribbled with my left hand: 'Mom I'm at the hospital. I'm ok, Danny'. I left the note in the middle of the kitchen table.

The November night air was cold. I managed to get my left arm in my coat sleeve. The other side of the coat hung limp behind me. The bleeding slowed. I thought of Tommy and almost cried. He hated me more than he liked or wanted acceptance from Ricky. I started thinking of when Tommy was small. I had just made the Little League All-Star Team. Tommy was about eight. He was sitting on the back stoop talking with a buddy, Andy

Charamella. The Charamellas moved out of the neighborhood the next year. I came out in my Carpi Restaurant uniform. Tommy gave me a flat stone he had found. He said it was for good luck. Tommy then explained to Andy how I was the best player on the team. Now he wanted to kill me.

Linda pulled up and unlocked the back door.

"You should have called an ambulance," she said, eyeballing the crimson tourniquet, as I eased into the backseat.

"It's not so bad. The bleeding, it's stopping, I think."

"What the hell happened?"

"Tommy wrecked Tarz's car." I shut the door, and Linda took off. "We started fighting."

"Danny!" she said, more with disappointment than alarm.

"I didn't go home wanting a fight. Which way are you going?"

"Broad to Canal."

"Okay."

"You didn't want to fight, but here you are."

"He said he smashed up the car more to piss me off than anything else." I could feel my ears burning. "He was laughing at me, called me an asshole. Everything about him was begging for beating. He's such a shit. I could kill him."

"Danny."

"What?"

"You should have walked away."

"No, I should have knocked him on his ass with the first sign of an attitude. Don't start, I've had it."

"Where were your parents?"

"Shopping. I left them a note. We get to the hospital we'll call." I was feeling better. "It hurts when I touch it."

"How bad is it?"

"I'll survive. But my hand is feeling funny, kind of numb on one side. The side with my little finger, all the way to the middle, it's cold. Numb."

"God, Danny."

"Tommy looked like a maniac with that knife."

"You should have walked away."

"Linda, this isn't my fault," I yelled.

"I know. Just would have been better."

"So, it's my fault. I don't believe it."

"That's not what I'm saying."

"He used my bats to wreck Tarz's Fury. You know what that car means to Tarz? Then he gives me an attitude, brags about what he did. No, Linda." I shuddered. "I don't know him."

"We're almost there." Linda turned off Canal Street onto Parkhurst. Delmont City Hospital was about four blocks away. "Good thing there's no traffic."

"Linda, if they ask what happened, I can't tell them."

"Well, they're going to ask. They'll probably have to file a report with the police. People getting stabbed isn't like tripping and spraining your ankle."

"I know. I'll tell them I got jumped on my way home from work."

"Jumped?"

"Yeah, by three guys, never saw them before. They were Black or Puerto Rican."

"Don't ask me to lie to the police."

"No, I called you later. Don't worry."

Linda pulled into the small side lot next to the emergency room.

Thankfully the ER wasn't too busy. I gave a nurse some information: name, address, emergency names and numbers, insurance coverage, and a brief description of what happened. When I said stabbed, she looked at me, like I had never been looked at before. I quickly added, "I got jumped by three guys." I felt it necessary to identify myself as a victim, not some crazy man, who might threaten innocent women and children. She told me to take a seat in the waiting area. We sat quietly. Linda looked worried. Her eyes followed every sound. I concentrated on the others in the waiting area. After a few minutes of waiting, I kind of figured out what brought everyone here. A little girl, about five or six years-old, was comforted by her mother. The kid was burning up with a fever. An older man with his wife had sharp pains in his stomach. A boy, about fourteen, was with his parents. It sounded like he broke his arm skateboarding. His mother looked tired and drawn, like the way my mother would look when she got here.

"I didn't mean it was your fault," Linda said, softly.

"It's okay. But, I feel like I've lost my brother." I lowered my head. "Even when I try to work things out with him it turns into a mess."

Linda began massaging my neck and shoulders. The nurse called the skateboarder. The kid winced as he stood to get into a wheelchair.

There was a storm of activity, as two EMTs rolled a man in on a stretcher. The guy was a grey-green. I thought he was dead. He disappeared through the doors that the skateboarder had just entered.

I remembered about calling my parents. Linda punched in her cell phone. No answer. She left a message, "Mr. and Mrs. Alberti, we're at the hospital's emergency room. Danny got stabbed in the arm, but."

I yelled over her, "I'm okay. Don't worry."

"He's okay." Linda shrugged and kissed my cheek.

A small, dark man came in with his wife. He had a wet towel wrapped over the top of his head and forehead. It sounded like he was working under his car and something fell, hitting him square across the forehead. The wife, with a heavy accent, explained he was trapped for a long time. There was blood on his greasy overalls. As the woman gave the nurse the vitals on her husband, my father came trotting in ahead of my mother. Dad frantically looked around and for a second I hesitated to call him over. I waved with my left arm and he hurried to me. Mom followed a few feet behind. Dad was huffing, sweaty, and pasty.

"What happened?" he asked, trying to catch his breath.

Linda got up allowing my parents room on each side of me.

"You okay?" Mom asked as she neared us. She was gray and worn, with panic leaping out her eyes. Linda stepped back, letting my mother slip between her and my father.

"What happened?" Dad asked sitting to my left. My mother took a seat and her eyes began to tear up.

"I'm okay."

"The house is full of blood," Mom said.

"I got jumped, right as I turned off Waverly. Two minutes from the house."

"By who," Dad asked, stroking my back.

"Don't know. They were Black or Puerto Rican."

"Oh this is just great," Mom said. "I can't believe this." Her voice cracked with hysteria. "Did you know them? Did you call the police? I can't believe this."

I shook my head no. I looked at her trying to say, 'calm down, you're embarrassing me.'

"Where was Tommy?" Dad asked.

"Don't know. I went in his room, used one of his tee shirts." I raised my right arm half way to show how it was used. "I thought you'd be home and take me here. So, I called Linda." Mom smiled up at Linda.

"Thank God, you're all right," Dad said. "Why did they attack you?"

I shrugged. "They had me mixed up with someone else."

"Good thing Linda was around," Dad said, and reached over to pat her hand.

A nurse, maybe my mother's age, came over with a wheelchair. "Daniel Alberti?"

I nodded. "I don't need that."

"Hospital policy," She said, smiling, and I complied. My parents and Linda followed.

Dr. Krushani greeted me with a warm smile. He was a little guy who looked and sounded Indian or Pakistani. "What have you done here?"

"I got jumped, stabbed a couple of times." I motioned with my head to my injury.

"You are very brave and very fortunate," he said, as he removed the towel. Blood was still creeping out the elbow, but the first slice was beginning to form a protective seal at one end. The doctor glided around like a dancer who had made these moves a thousand times. He helped me with my shirt then he quickly cleaned the area. He looked over at my mother and asked if I had a recent tetanus. My mother said it was at least five or six years ago. When I got caught on a cyclone fence and needed five stitches to sew up my thigh. I was ten and thought the scar was cool. I remember the next summer showing it off when I went swimming. The doctor stepped outside and in a minute was back with a syringe. He rubbed some antiseptic on my bicep and gave me a shot. Linda and my mother turned away.

It did not take Dr. Krushani long to patch up my arm. He explained to us, the elbow wound was deep. It required fourteen stitches and the numbness I was feeling was likely from nerve damage. "It may be fine in a few days, or it may take a few months. Sometimes if it does not recover you may require surgery. But you are young, and will probably recover normal use within a few weeks." Basketball season started in a few weeks, and I thought, I'll be okay. On the other cut he used some type of stitch, which he said should heal nicely. "You'll have to hunt for it. It will be like a pencil line. You are very lucky." We shook hands. My parents thanked him a dozen times and he left smiling warmly.

My mother helped me with my shirt. The relief in my parents' faces was incredible. I felt lucky and horrible. Lucky, that I had two parents who loved me. No matter how big I got, I would always be their little Danny. It was a safe and wonderful feeling. I felt horrible because if I told them the truth they would wrestle with the idea that they raised two sons; not bad kids, but kids capable of murdering each other. My mother started buttoning my shirt. Behind her stood Linda, who for the first time, since picking me up, looked disappointed and troubled. Not the worried look she had driving over here, or while we waited for the doctor. This was a look I seldom saw. It was when I acted in ways that did not measure up to her standards. It was a look that was screaming at me to come clean. Let them know what happened.

My mother finished buttoning my shirt. She looked up at me and I lowered my head so she could kiss my cheek. The nurse entered and said, "Excuse me Mr. And Mrs. Alberti, Danny, Officer Benedict wants to talk to you."

"Good," my father said.

My stomach dropped to my knees. I sat back onto the narrow bed.

"Good evening," Officer Benedict said, positioning himself so he filled the entire doorway. I glanced up at him. He was maybe forty-years-old, blond, and a little taller than my father. His upper body was rugged. I'd hate to have him on me. I kept my head down, fixing on his heavy black shoes. "Daniel, do they call you Danny?"

"Sure."

"Danny, I understand you were attacked by three guys near your home."

"Right," I said, and looked up at Officer Benedict, with pad and pencil out. He was serious like when the governor or president gets on television and gives us some news about a catastrophe, and all I ever think is thank God it's not here. But, this one was here. This one was my very own catastrophe and Officer Benedict was no Red Cross worker.

"Can you tell me what happened?"

"Not really, it happened so fast." I thought that's it, too fast, too scared to remember anything. I looked up at him, the notebook at his side.

"Well, tell me what you remember."

"I just turned onto our street."

"Whitman?"

"Yes. This guy came out of nowhere. He said, 'Remember me'. Before I knew what was happening two other guys were with him. The first guy had a knife. He came at me. It all happened fast. It's kind of a blur. It was so sudden. They came out of nowhere."

"You recognize them?"

"No."

"What did they look like?"

"I don't know. They had hooded sweatshirts on. It was dark."

"Were they White, Black?"

"Black, or maybe Puerto Rican."

"Anybody threaten you?"

"No."

"You do anything to make someone want to hurt you?"

"No."

"Is that what you were wearing?" He looked over at my coat.

I could feel my feet dancing in my shoes. My tongue turned to dry firewood. "No, I went home. Tried to stop the bleeding, didn't know how bad it was. It wouldn't stop bleeding, so I came here."

Officer Benedict asked twenty different ways about what happened and pieced together some kind of description of my attackers. He asked me about school and any problems there. He asked about gangs, about the changes in the neighborhood and if I had any beefs with the Puerto Rican kids further down Waverly. Linda sat in a corner on a metal stool, as far away as possible from Officer Benedict. She kept her head down, becoming invisible. He gave my father a card with his name and number, and told us to call if we think of anything.

It was a little after one when we left the hospital. I walked Linda to her car. My father and mother sat in the taxi maybe thirty feet away.

"You got to tell them," Linda said, unlocking her door.

"Maybe Tommy will."

"Yeah, maybe I'll be the next Miss America."

"He ran out like a maniac. The last thing he needs is a visit from Officer Benedict."

"I'm not saying tell the police, but your parents need to know."

"Why?"

"They just do."

I shook my head slightly, and thought, 'she really doesn't get it.'

"What?" Linda demanded.

"If I had kids, I'd rather think a stranger tried to kill one of them then his own brother."

Linda's little face was all eyes. She nodded understanding. I bent down and kissed her.

"Was it that bad?"

"Worse." Her face grew sympathetic and we kissed goodnight.

Chapter Nineteen

There was 'can hear your heart beat' silence for the first few minutes as my father followed Linda home. I sat in the back and replayed my encounter with Officer Benedict. I had kept it simple. It's easier to remember a simple lie. I reassured myself that by tomorrow Officer Benedict would have more pressing matters to deal with. I thought a reluctant victim and worse witness would not deserve any more of his attention. But, no matter how many times I told myself this, I was turning into scared jelly inside. I lied to the police and my parents. And how would this ever get right with Tommy. I was sick, and getting sicker.

"Kind of weird," My father said, tilting his head back in my direction. My mother looked towards him and I caught a glimpse of her face. She was exhausted. "Kind of weird," my father speaking up now, "these guys getting you mixed up with somebody in the neighborhood. I don't know anybody near us as tall as you Danny."

"I know."

There was a long silence and I prayed he would drop it.

"You know you can always tell us if there's something going on," Dad said. His voice was softer and more supportive than usual. I thought, not this, not now.

We drove on in silence until my mother almost breaking down in tears said, "We got to get out of here."

Linda parked near her three-decker. We watched her get out. My father put down his window and thanked her. Mom wished her a goodnight in a voice that never made it out of the car. We waited, watching her scurry up the stairs and into her building. My father stretched his head out the window, making sure he kept her in sight. We waited until a light went on in the McCurry's apartment. My parents agreed on what a wonderful girl Linda was. At my mother's request, she had called our home a couple of times looking for Tommy. There was no answer. My parents consoled themselves, tossing out the idea he was either sleeping or listening to music with his headphones and did not hear the telephone. They offered their explanations half-heartedly. They did not want to spend time on Tommy. They hadn't the energy or resources to deal with him now.

We got out of the taxi and my mother hugged me before we entered the yard. Tears were slipping along her cheeks and she said, "I don't know what I'd do without you."

"I'm okay, Mom."

My father led the way into our apartment. He called for Tommy and, without taking off his coat, marched over to his room. I went to my room, collapsed on the bed, and listened to my parents, fret, moan, and threaten. My father kept repeating, "This is it," and "When he gets here, that's it." I could hear my mother pacing about the kitchen. Every once in a while she would say, "I can't believe it."

I lay, staring at the dark ceiling, hoping Tommy would come home, hoping he got hit by lightning and was full of remorse.

"I'll go get him," Dad said.

"Where are you going?" Mom asked.

"Where do you think?"

I could hear a chair slam on the floor. I imagined my father lifting one of our heavy maple kitchen chairs and driving it through the floor and down into Mrs. Leonetti's apartment.

"I'll go," I said, standing in the doorway to my bedroom.

"Go to bed," Dad said, checking to see how I was managing the long day's wear and tear.

"No, I'm okay."

"You need to get some sleep," Mom said, standing between us, hands on hips.

"I know where he is, I'll go." I gingerly slipped my injured arm into the coat's sleeve.

My father stood at the back entrance as if barring my passage. "Your mother's right."

"Dad, if he's in trouble you might need help."

"Oh God!" Mom screamed. Her face contorted for a second, like when the dentist hits a nerve.

"I'm just saying it's so late. He's been out all night." I looked down at my mother and she never seemed so small.

"What could happen?" Mom latched onto my left arm.

"I don't know, but if he's with Ricky and that crew, anything is possible," I said, trying to convince my father he needed me.

"How could this be happening?" My mother released my arm and searched my father for answers. "What if those animals who attacked you," she stopped, as the thought seemed too horrible.

"We'll get him," Dad said, nodding to me.

"Please be careful, Sam."

My father took a deep breath and motioned with his head towards the door.

Mom gave me a kiss on the cheek. She looked around, tracing the trail of blood from the kitchen to Tommy's room. "Danny, be careful."

The night air felt much colder. The taxi welcomed us with warmth from our recent hospital trip. My arm was throbbing and the hand's numbness worried me. I told Dad it was fine, 'just a little numb.' My stomach did flips as we entered the mill property. I prayed we would find Tommy, sad and looking for forgiveness. I directed my father to the last building before you hit railroad tracks.

"Dad, he may not come with us."

"He'll come," Dad said as we neared the loading dock.

"You know these guys don't care."

Dad nodded. His face seemed hard and determined like I had never seen before. We were on a mission to bring Tommy back home. We would save him. He would see even after trying to kill me I was his brother. I loved him. I might kick his ass, but it was out of love.

My father put the taxi in park. "Danny, I was so scared when I saw your note."

"I'm okay."

"You boys are everything. I thank God for you both." His lips quivered. "When you have kids of your own you'll understand. We only want what's best for you guys."

I nodded. "Dad, Tommy and I have business to take care of."

"Business?"

"It's left over about his hooking up with Ricky."

"Let's get him home. Whatever business you have, let's talk it out tomorrow." I nodded. Dad seemed relieved, one less battle to deal with tonight. He started opening his door. "What if he isn't here?"

I shrugged, but had no doubt. I just hoped he was alone.

Dad yanked the warehouse's ill fitted door. The door's hinges were loose and its bottom scraped along the impenetrable cement floor. He whispered over his shoulder, "Let me do the talking." The door opened enough to let us in single file.

The room was black. I slowed adjusting to the darkness. The fireplace barrel's rim caught a stream of grey coming from the door. The barrel's fire had long gone out. A nasty mix of old ash, stale beer and marijuana filled my nose. The smells brought back memories of my pounding Johnny Post and Tommy screwing on me, leaving me to take care of myself against Ricky, Post, and Butch. A dark bundle on the floor across from us began to stir. I could make out a figure rising. My father started towards the figure.

"Tommy," Dad called.

"Get out of here!" Tommy screamed, and inched a retreat to the wall.

I felt more confident. My eyes began to pick out more of the dump, as we moved closer.

"Get out of here both of you!"

"Tommy, we need to go home," Dad said, exhausted, begging for compliance.

We were now an arm's length from him. I could see his face. His eyes glistened.

"Tommy, it's okay," I said.

"Okay!" Tommy screamed. I could see the knife in his right hand.

"Yes," I said.

"Let's go home," Dad said.

Tommy moved away. He raised his left arm, threateningly and shouted, "I can't stand this. I'm not like him, I'm not like him."

"No. It's okay," Dad said.

Tommy turned towards me. "You want more, come on, Mr. Wonderful!"

"It's okay Tommy," I said, my eyes hooked onto the knife.

"Okay," he said, mockingly. "Go to hell, Mr. Wonderful, go to hell."

"Tommy, don't." My voice cracked.

"For Christ sakes don't tell me what to do. Now screw, both of you."

"Tommy, I'm not leaving without you," Dad said, inching closer.

"What are you going to do now that I cut up your golden boy," Tommy said, tauntingly.

"What?" Dad looked shocked.

"I hate you and everything about you. God, wrecking that car I was wrecking you Danny. I hate you and all the bullshit I have to hear about how wonderful you are," Tommy screamed through tears. "All my life, why can't you be like your damn brother? Well, I'm not!"

"Tommy, don't," I said.

"Don't tell me what to do!" Tommy waved the knife in my face. "I should have given it to you good, Mr. Wonderful."

"Danny?" Dad turned towards me.

"I should have told you," I said, feeling guilt and anger.

"Leave me alone both of you, I'm warning you!"

"Put that down," Dad ordered.

"I'm staying, now get out of here!" Wildly, Tommy swung the knife close to my father's face. "I hate you! All of you."

Dad stepped forward, trying to wrap an arm around Tommy's shoulder. Tommy with his left hand shoved him. My left hand clenched. My dad's back arched and his knees bent. He stumbled backwards. Tommy raised the knife and howled through tears, "Leave me alone!" I threw my left hand, feeling I needed to knock down a wall with my fist. My punch caught Tommy on the side of the head. The force pushed him sideways several feet before he sprawled to the floor. The knife fell beside him.

Dad regained his balance and moved, hunched like a boxer trying to cut down the size of the ring, towards Tommy.

Tommy rolled to his right and picked up the knife.

"Tommy, please I'm begging you," Dad said.

Tommy puffed up, and sprang to his feet.

Dad, hands at his side, stepped forward, pleading with Tommy to come home with us.

"Leave me alone!" Tommy lunged for Dad.

I threw another left. My fist exploded on Tommy's chin. His head snapped back. Tommy's feet lifted. His shoulders and head flew parallel to the floor. There was a tremendous thud. First his head, then his shoulders smacked against the cement. His eyes glazed over and then shut. Blood squirted out his nose and mouth for a second and then stopped.

I fell to my knees. "Tommy, Tommy." I grasped his shoulders and shook gently. There was nothing. "Oh God, no," I cried.

Dad crouched on the other side of him. He tossed the knife. "Tommy," he called, softly, as if waking a sick child. He took Tommy from me and hugged him, wailing out his name.

I knew when Tommy's eyes flashed to some far away place and then closed that he was gone.

Epilogue: Three Years Later

"I'll have another Rolling Rock," I called to Gino. I like it here at Gino's, and over at Tarzan's. Most people have stopped looking at me like I'm some sideshow carnival freak. The first few months I wouldn't have noticed if they had. My mother sometimes still looks at me different. I think Tommy's death hurt her and me the most, not that Dad has had it easy. My mother took a leave of absence from school. That was three years ago. I say, 'three-years' and I fill with tears. That's part of why I like it here and at work. I cry less when I'm around people. After it happened, for a month I felt like there was an axe in my skull. My eyes hurt so much I thought there was something wrong with them. But, Mom said she felt the same way. She says she knows I was trying to help. She doesn't blame me, but I killed her son, and that's what happened, even if the evidence led the district attorney to rule it self-defense. She keeps saying she's going to take down Tommy's posters, but it's too soon. I keep playing that night over in my head. I should have stayed home, let Dad handle it. I just wish it were different. But, it's like what Tarzan tells me, "You did what you did. It didn't come out right, but you did the right thing. What would you be saying if Tommy killed your father? You acted like a man, a good man, and I'm proud you're my friend." Over the last three years he has explained to me in a thousand ways, there is no good in this, but you did the best anyone could.

Dad was a rock for the first three or four months. He held Mom and me together. At first he told the police he had killed Tommy. He changed our roles. I couldn't let him do it. The truth just exploded out of me. I was sobbing and talking. Dad, tears streaming down his face, kept telling me it would be okay. He explained to the police the true story. He told them of Tommy's stabbing me, of my covering for him, of our going to the mill to bring him home.

Dad began talking to Mom and me, about six months after Tommy died. He wasn't looking for anything. He just needed to talk. Sometimes the three of us drift into different places. I try to remember when Tommy was little, and I was his big brother. A time when he looked up to me, and I just wanted to protect him. Dad thinks it was his fault. He should have demanded I stayed home. He should have taken the lead once we met up with Tommy. He's lost some weight and he doesn't smile at beautiful sunsets like before, or talk about art. He works as many hours as he can, driving taxi and sometimes on weekends he manages the Holiday Bowling Lanes.

I'm to meet Linda and Eric for a special get together. Special because the trio, that was inseparable for most of our lives, seldom sees each other. Eric stuck it out and graduated from Central. With my killing Tommy, Eric's mother pleaded with him to come back home. She claimed to be worried sick over his safety, living as he was with the crazy Alberti Family. Eric told her, "Danny needs me. I need to be here." After graduation Frank Martino helped him get a job at the Parks' Department, cutting grass and picking up litter. For the first time in his life, Eric has a 'been to Florida tan'. Eric got an apartment soon after graduating. It's a drafty three-room, remodeled attic on Canal Street. The rent includes utilities and the always-frugal Eric was able to pay cash last year for a slightly used Ford Focus. Eric is about three-quarters done with his Associates Degree at Bunker Hill Community College.

Linda and I broke up officially when she went back to Clark University to start her sophomore year. I couldn't blame her. I was a basket case for a long time after Tommy. We still love each other, but it's more like survivors and friends than 'let's start a family'. Although Eric thinks in the end Linda and I will be pushing a baby carriage down Waverly. She got a full scholarship to Clark and her brilliance is sparkling there just as it did at good old Central High.

Killing Tommy changed everything.

I couldn't go back to school. I tried, but after six weeks I just stopped showing up. Linda, Eric, and Coach Inhorn were great, but nothing mattered after Tommy. I was reliving my killing my brother, and all the good intentions seemed empty. I know they helped, yet at the time nothing seemed to help or matter. I got my GED six months later and told myself I would try college. Tarzan gave me more hours. He told me, "When you're ready you'll get back in the swing of things." I may be getting there, as I recently applied to Framingham, and Salem State College. I've been working and saving. My hand recovered from the stabbing. I sometimes moan about the year I could have had, getting attention from big name schools. I don't have much saved, but I think I can manage the first year. Maybe I'll be able to play some ball. Linda has been screaming at me to apply for government loans after the first of the year.

I'm thinking of majoring in secondary education maybe teach English or Phys. Ed. I guess I'm getting better. I still beat myself up regularly with the, 'I should have let my father handle it', and 'I should have told Tommy that I loved him. I forgave him.' God, I wish I had. But, it no longer paralyzes me. I sometimes go the day without thinking I killed my brother. It's not that I go the day without thinking of him, I just don't always think of him that way. I like to sit on our back steps. I sit praying that Tommy's okay, and begging for forgiveness.

The End